Everyman, I will go with thee,
and be thy guide

Joyce Cary

A HOUSE OF
CHILDREN

EVERYMAN

J. M. DENT · LONDON

Critical apparatus © J M Dent 1995

Chronology and bibliography compiled by Douglas Matthews

A House of Children © J. L. A. Cary Estate 1941, 1951

First published 1941

First published in Everyman Paperbacks in 1995

J. M. Dent
Orion Publishing Group
Orion House, 5 Upper St Martin's Lane,
London WC2H 9EA
and
Charles E. Tuttle Co., Inc.
28 South Main Street,
Rutland, Vermont 05701, USA

Typeset in Sabon by CentraCet Ltd, Cambridge
Printed in Great Britain by
The Guernsey Press Co. Ltd, Guernsey, C. I.

British Library Cataloguing-in-Publication Data
is available upon request.

ISBN 0 460 87584 1

CONTENTS

NOTE ON THE AUTHOR

JOYCE CARY was born Arthur Joyce Lunel Cary in Londonderry, Northern Ireland, in 1888. He studied art in Edinburgh and Paris before going to Trinity College, Oxford. In 1912–13 he fought, and served in the Red Cross, in the Balkan War. In 1913 he joined the Nigerian political service. During the First World War he served in the Nigerian Regiment and was wounded at Mora Mountain. After the war he returned to political duty as a magistrate and executive officer and was sent to Borgu. His health never recovered from his time in active service and he was advised to retire from tropical Africa. Upon retirement he started writing. His first novel, *Aissa Saved* appeared in 1932. *Herself Surprised*, the first volume in a trilogy, was published in 1941, and was followed by *To be a Pilgrim* followed in 1942 and *The Horse's Mouth* in 1944. His other books include *An American Visitor* (1933), *Mister Johnson* (1939), *Charley is My Darling* (1940), *A House of Children* (1941), which won the James Tait Black Memorial Prize in 1942, *A Fearful Joy* (1949), the trilogy comprising *A Prisoner of Grace* (1952), *Except the Lord* (1953) and *Not Honour More* (1955), *The Captive and the Free* (1959) and *Spring Song and Other Stories* (1960). Cary also produced three volumes of verse and a number of political tracts. He died in March 1957.

CHRONOLOGY OF CARY'S LIFE

Year	Age	Life
1888		7 December, birth of Arthur Joyce Lunel Cary, in Londonderry, son of Arthur Pitt Chambers Cary and Charlotte Louisa Cary (*née* Joyce)
1892	4	28 January, birth of brother John

CHRONOLOGY OF HIS TIMES

Year	Literary Context	Historical Events
1888	Zola, *La Terre* Wilde, *The Happy Prince* Birth of T. S. Eliot	Wilhelm II succeeds as German Emperor; Jack the Ripper murders in London
1889	Jerome K. Jerome, *Three Men in a Boat* Stevenson, *The Master of Ballantrae*	Suicide of Crown Prince Rudolf at Mayerling; birth of Adolf Hitler
1890	Wilde, *The Picture of Dorian Gray* Tolstoy, *The Kreutzer Sonata*	Bismarck dismissed; first underground railway in London; Forth Bridge opens
1891	Hardy, *Tess of the d'Urbervilles* Shaw, *Quintessence of Ibsenism*	Triple Alliance renewed; Young Turk movement founded; Pan-Germany League founded
1892	Wilde, *Lady Windermere's Fan* Shaw, *Mrs Warren's Profession*	Keir Hardy first Labour MP; birth of Tito and Haile Selassie; Grover Cleveland US President
1893	Wilde, *A Woman of No Importance* Pinero, *The Second Mrs Tanqueray* Death of Maupassant	Second Irish Home Rule Bill passed; Hawaii becomes a republic; Nansen sets out for North Pole
1894	Kipling, *The First Jungle Book* Shaw, *Arms and the Man* G. & W. Grossmith, *The Diary of a Nobody*	Dreyfus arrested and convicted; Nicholas II succeeds as Tsar; births of Macmillan and Khrushchev
1895	Conrad, *Almayer's Folly* Wells, *The Time Machine* Wilde, *The Importance of Being Earnest*	Jameson raid into Transvaal; Marconi invents wireless telegraphy; Armenians massacred in Turkey
1896	Chekhov, *The Seagull* Housman, *A Shropshire Lad*	Klondike goldrush; Madagascar annexed by French; Abyssinians defeat Italians at Adowa

Year   Age   Life

1898   10   28 January, death of mother

1900   12   Father remarries (cousin Dora Stevenson); family moves to
             Chiswick, West London; Cary enters prep school
             (Hurstleigh, Tunbridge Wells)

1902   14   30 October, birth of half brother Anthony

1903   15   Begins at Clifton College

1904   16   15 January, birth of half sister Sheila; 8 May, stepmother
             dies; brother John enters Royal Naval College, Dartmouth;
             Normandy sketching holiday; confirmed into Church of
             England

1906   18   Leaves school; studies art in Paris

Year	Literary Context	Historical Events
1897	Conrad, *The Nigger of the Narcissus* Strindberg, *Inferno* Mary Kingsley, *Travels in West Africa*	Russia occupies Port Arthur; Queen Victoria's Diamond Jubilee; Zionist Congress, Basle
1898	James, *The Turn of the Screw* Wilde, *The Ballad of Reading Gaol* Birth of C. S. Lewis Death of Lewis Carroll	Battle of Omdurman; radium discovered by Curies; death of Bismarck and Gladstone
1899	Tolstoy, *Resurrection* Pinero, *Trelawney of the Wells*	Boer War begins; first Hague Peace Conference; Philippines claim independence from USA
1900	Conrad, *Lord Jim* Chekhov, *Uncle Vanya* Death of Oscar Wilde	Boxer rising in China; Umberto I of Italy assassinated; Australian Commonwealth founded
1901	Kipling, *Kim* Mann, *Buddenbrooks* Butler, *Erewhon Revisited*	Death of Queen Victoria; Boxer rising ends; first Australian PM inaugurated (Edmund Barton)
1902	Conrad, *Youth* Doyle, *The Hound of the Baskervilles* Kipling, *Just-so Stories*	Boer War ends; Balfour becomes PM; Aswan Dam opens; death of Cecil Rhodes
1903	James, *The Ambassadors* Shaw, *Man and Superman* Butler, *The Way of All Flesh* Birth of Evelyn Waugh	'Entente Cordiale' established; Britain completes conquest of Northern Nigeria; Wright brothers make first powered flight
1904	Chekhov, *The Cherry Orchard* James, *The Golden Bowl* Death of Chekhov	Russo-Japanese War begins; Theodore Roosevelt wins US Presidency; British drink licensing laws introduced
1905	Wharton, *The House of Mirth* Wilde, *De Profundis* Orczy, *The Scarlet Pimpernel*	Russo-Japanese War ends; Norway separated from Sweden; Sinn Fein founded
1906	Everyman's Library begins Galsworthy, *The Man of Property* Birth of Beckett Death of Ibsen	France and Spain given control of Morocco; Dreyfus rehabilitated; San Francisco earthquake

Year	Age	Life
1907	19	Enters Edinburgh School of Art; father marries for third time (Mary Agar); family moves to Gunnersbury, near Kew
1908	20	First published volume by 'Arthur Cary', *Verse*, privately printed, Edinburgh
1909	21	Enters Trinity College, Oxford University
1910	22	Visits Paris with John Middleton Murry
1912	24	Leaves Oxford University; lives in Store Street, London; in Antivari, Montenegro (1 November); joins Red Cross; writes 'Memoir of the Bobotes' (published 1954)
1913	25	Returns to England; awarded Oxford law degree; joins Irish Agricultural Organization (Plunkett's Co-operative Movement), but leaves; applies to Northern Nigerian Political Service
1914	26	Appointed Assistant District officer, Bauchi, Northern Nigeria
1915	27	Serves in West African Field Force; wounded in action (Mora Mountain, Cameroons)
1916	28	Home leave in England; 1 June, marries Gertrude Margaret Ogilvie; returns to Lagos

Year	Literary Context	Historical Events
1907	Conrad, *The Secret Agent* Cambridge History of English Literature (–1927) Births of Louis MacNeice and Auden	Hague Peace Conference; Lenin leaves Russia; Boy Scout movement founded; New Zealand achieves dominion status
1908	Bennett, *The Old Wives' Tale* Forster, *A Room with a View* Birth of Ian Fleming	Asquith becomes PM; Congo transferred by Leopold II to Belgium; Union of South Africa established
1909	Wells, *Tono Bungay* Maeterlinck, *L'Oiseau bleu* Birth of Spender Death of Swinburne	Girl Guides established in UK; Selfridge's store opens; Bethmann-Hollweg becomes German Chancellor
1910	Bennett, *Clayhanger* Forster, *Howard's End* Wells, *Mr Polly* Deaths of Mark Twain and Tolstoy	Mann Act passed (USA); Montenegro proclaimed kingdom; deaths of Edward VII and Florence Nightingale
1911	Beerbohm, *Zuleika Dobson* Rupert Brooke, *Poems* D. H. Lawrence, *The White Peacock* Death of W. S. Gilbert	Mexican Civil War ends; Lloyd George's National Insurance Bill; Agadir crisis; Amundsen reaches South Pole
1912	Synge, *Playboy of the Western World* E. C. Bentley, *Trent's Last Case* Death of Strindberg	Woodrow Wilson wins US Presidential election; Kuomintang founded by Sun Yat-sen; *Titanic* sinks
1913	D. H. Lawrence, *Sons and Lovers* Proust, *Du côté de chez Swann* Shaw, *Pygmalion*	Poincaré elected President of France; Balkan War; Schweitzer opens Lambaréné hospital; *New Statesman* founded
1914	Joyce, *Dubliners* Burroughs, *Tarzan of the Apes* Births of Mistral and Tennessee Williams	Northern and Southern Nigeria united; outbreak of First World War; Panama Canal opens
1915	Buchan, *The Thirty-Nine Steps* D. H. Lawrence, *The Rainbow* Maugham, *Of Human Bondage* Death of Rupert Brooke	Second Battle of Ypres; Haig becomes British C. in C.; death of Keir Hardie and W. G. Grace
1916	Joyce, *Portrait of the Artist as a Young Man* Death of Henry James	Battle of Verdun; Roger Casement executed; death of Kitchener; Lloyd George becomes PM

Year	Age	Life
1917	29	3 April, birth of first son (Arthur Lucius) Michael
1918	30	Further leave in England; tour of Borgu; 9 December, son Peter born
1919	31	Ends tour of Borgu and submits report
1920	32	Retires from Nigerian service; buys Oxford house (12 Park Road); writes for magazines as 'Thomas Joyce'
1922	34	Visit to Hungary
1924	36	Begins *Cock Jarvis* (unfinished novel; published 1974)
1925	37	14 May, birth of third son, Tristram

Year	Literary Context	Historical Events
1917	Norman Douglas, *South Wind* T. S. Eliot, *Prufrock* Alec Waugh, *The Loom of Youth*	USA declares war on Germany; Balfour Declaration on Palestine; Treaty of Brest-Litovsk; Bolshevik October Revolution
1918	Cather, *My Antonia* Hopkins, *Poems* (posth.) Joyce, *Exiles* Deaths of Wilfred Owen and Apollinaire	Armistice ends First World War; Yugoslavia formed; Russian royal family killed; Polish Republic proclaimed
1919	Maugham, *The Moon and Sixpence* Mencken, *The American Language* Lofting, first 'Dr Doolittle' story	Treaty of Versailles; German fleet scuttled; Alcock and Brown make first non-stop transatlantic flight; Civil War in Russia
1920	Colette, *Chéri* Hasek, *Good Soldier Schweik* Wharton, *The Age of Innocence*	League of Nations formed; US women given vote; Government of Ireland Act; Sacco and Vanzetti arrested
1921	A. Huxley, *Crome Yellow* D. H. Lawrence, *Women in Love* O'Neill, *Anna Christie* Pound, *Poems* Shaw, *Heartbreak House*	Northern Ireland Parliament inaugurated; Imperial Conference, London; Washington Disarmament Conference
1922	Eliot, *The Waste Land* Joyce, *Ulysses* Lawrence, *Aaron's Rod* Woolf, *Jacob's Room* PEN Club founded	Poincaré becomes French PM; Treaty of Rapallo; Mussolini forms government; Irish Free State proclaimed; Bonar Law becomes PM
1923	Svevo, *The Confessions of Zeno* Wodehouse, *The Inimitable Jeeves* Death of Katharine Mansfield	Earthquake destroys Tokyo and Yokohama; Hitler's 'Beer Hall Putsch' fails; *Radio Times* founded
1924	Forster, *A Passage to India* Mann, *The Magic Mountain*	Greece becomes republic; Hoover appointed Director of Federal Bureau of Investigation; British Empire Exhibition; deaths of Lenin and Woodrow Wilson
1925	Coward, *Hay Fever* Fitzgerald, *The Great Gatsby* *New Yorker* magazine begins	Locarno Conference; deaths of Sun Yat-sen and Lord Curzon; Reza Khan becomes Shah; Hitler publishes *Mein Kampf*, Vol. 1

Year	Age	Life
1926	38	Works as docker in General Strike at Hays Wharf, London
1927	39	12 August, birth of fourth son, George
1932	44	*Aissa Saved*, first published novel (US publication 1962)
1933	45	*An American Visitor* (US publication 1961)

Year	Literary Context	Historical Events
1926	T. E. Lawrence, *Seven Pillars of Wisdom* Faulkner, *Soldier's Pay* Kafka, *The Castle* A. A. Milne, *Winnie the Pooh*	Germany joins League of Nations; General Strike in Britain; birth of Queen Elizabeth II; Hirohito accedes to throne of Japan
1927	Cather, *Death Comes for the Archbishop* Woolf, *To the Lighthouse*	Allied military control of Germany ends; Sacco and Vanzetti executed; Lindbergh flies Atlantic solo
1928	Radclyffe Hall, *The Well of Loneliness* D. H. Lawrence, *Lady Chatterley's Lover* Waugh, *Decline and Fall* Sholokhov, *Quiet Flows the Don*	Chiang Kai-shek elected President of China; women's suffrage in Britain lowered to age 21; deaths of Haig and Asquith
1929	Hemingway, *A Farewell to Arms* R. Hughes, *A High Wind in Jamaica* R. Graves, *Goodbye to All That*	Yugoslav constitution suppressed under Alexander; Kellogg-Briand Pact; Trotsky expelled from USSR; St Valentine's Day massacre (Chicago)
1930	Coward, *Private Lives* Eliot, *Ash Wednesday* Hammett, *The Maltese Falcon* Waugh, *Vile Bodies*	Haile Selassie becomes Emperor of Ethiopia; Allied troops finally leave Rhineland; death of Balfour
1931	Faulkner, *Sanctuary* O'Neill, *Mourning Becomes Electra* Bridie, *The Anatomist* Death of Arnold Bennett	Mosley founds New Party; Alfonso XIII of Spain exiled; Invergordon mutiny; Al Capone jailed; Statute of Westminster
1932	G. Greene, *Stamboul Train* A. Huxley, *Brave New World* Morgan, *The Fountain* Deaths of Lytton Strachey and Edgar Wallace	Hindenburg elected German President; Nazis win majority in Reichstag; F. D. Roosevelt wins Presidential election
1933	Caldwell, *God's Little Acre* Orwell, *Down and Out in Paris and London* Mann, *Joseph and his Brethren* (-1943)	Hitler appointed Chancellor; Reichstag fire; Japan quits League of Nations; USA recognises USSR

Year   Age   Life

1936	48	*The African Witch* (simultaneous US publication)
1937	49	23 November, death of father
1938	50	*Castle Corner* (US publication 1963)
1939	51	*Power in Men* (US publication 1963); *Mister Johnson* (US publication 1951); joins ARP (Civil Defence) as air-raid warden (–1945)
1940	52	*Charley is my Darling* (US publication 1960)
1941	53	*A House of Children* (awarded James Tait Black Memorial Prize; US publication 1956); *The Case for African Freedom* (revised and enlarged 1944; US publication 1962); *Herself Surprised* (Part 1 of First Trilogy; US publication 1948)
1942	54	*To Be a Pilgrim* (Part 2 of First Trilogy; US publication 1949); delivers Edinburgh University lecture: 'Tolstoy on Art and Morals'
1943	55	Visits Africa to write screenplay of *Men of Two Worlds* (director Thorold Dickinson); *Process of Real Freedom*

Year	Literary Context	Historical Events
1934	Fitzgerald, *Tender is the Night* Graves, *I, Claudius* and *Claudius the God*	Dollfuss assassinated (Austria); Kirov executed (USSR); Japan renounces naval treaties; Dionne quintuplets born
1935	Compton-Burnett, *A House and Its Head* Eliot, *Murder in the Cathedral* Left Book Club founded	German Nuremberg laws against Jews; Italy invades Abyssinia; British Council founded; Beneš becomes Czech President
1936	Dylan Thomas, *Twenty-five Poems* Mitchell, *Gone with the Wind*	Death of George v; Edward viii succeeds and abdicates; Spanish Civil War begins; Roosevelt re-elected
1937	Auden/Isherwood, *The Ascent of F6* Hemingway, *To Have and Have Not* Steinbeck, *Of Mice and Men*	Moscow show trials and purges; George vi crowned; Neville Chamberlain becomes PM; US Neutrality Act; Duke of Windsor marries Mrs Simpson
1938	Greene, *Brighton Rock* Wilder, *Our Town*	Munich agreement; Germany occupies Sudetenland; *Queen Elizabeth* launched; WVS founded
1939	Joyce, *Finnegan's Wake* Llewellyn, *How Green Was My Valley* Steinbeck, *The Grapes of Wrath* Death of Yeats	Second World War begins; Spanish Civil War ends; Italy invades Albania; Britain introduces conscription
1940	Greene, *The Power and the Glory* Hemingway, *For Whom the Bell Tolls* Chandler, *Farewell My Lovely*	Fall of France; Dunkirk evacuation; Battle of Britain; Trotsky assassinated; Roosevelt elected for third term
1941	Brecht, *Mother Courage* Coward, *Blithe Spirit* Deaths of Joyce, Woolf and R. Tagore	Germans invade Russia; Japanese attack Pearl Harbor; BBC Brains Trust begins; death of Baden-Powell
1942	Camus, *L'Etranger* Anouilh, *Antigone* Douglas, *The Robe*	Battles of Alamein and Midway; Singapore falls; North African landings; Oxfam founded
1943	Balchin, *The Small Back Room* Thurber, *Men, Women and Dogs* Saroyan, *The Human Comedy*	Casablanca Conference; Battle of Stalingrad; Italy surrenders and declares war on Germany; Bengal famine

Year	Age	Life
1944	56	*The Horse's Mouth* (Part 3 of First Trilogy; US publication 1950)
1945	57	*Marching Soldier* (poem); final revision of *Men of Two Worlds* screenplay
1946	58	Indian tour with Thorold Dickinson; *The Moonlight* (US publication 1947); *Britain and West Africa*
1947	59	*The Drunken Sailor* (poem)
1948	60	Wife has operation for cancer; holidays with her in Switzerland
1949	61	*A Fearful Joy* (US publication 1950); 13 December, death of wife
1950	62	Publishes prefaces to *Herself Surprised*, *To Be a Pilgrim* and *The Horse's Mouth* in *Adam International*
1951	63	Lecture tour of USA; Prefatory Essays to *A House of Children*, *Charley is my Darling* and *The African Witch*

Year	Literary Context	Historical Events
1944	Eliot, *Four Quartets* Maugham, *The Razor's Edge* K. Winsor, *Forever Amber* Camus, *Caligula* R. Lehmann, *The Ballad and the Source*	D-Day landings in Normandy; Warsaw uprising; First V-2 rockets on Britain; July Plot on Hitler's life; Roosevelt elected for fourth term
1945	Carlo Levi, *Christ Stopped at Eboli* Orwell, *Animal Farm* Waugh, *Brideshead Revisited*	Atom bombs used against Japan; end of Second World War; Mussolini killed; death of Roosevelt; Labour government elected in Britain
1946	O'Neill, *The Iceman Cometh* E. Wilson, *Memoirs of Hecate County* Arthur Miller, *All My Sons* Death of Gertrude Stein	UN Assembly holds first session; Perón elected President of Argentina; Nuremberg trial verdicts; London Airport opens
1947	Camus, *The Plague* Anne Frank's Diary Mann, *Doktor Faustus* Mackenzie, *Whisky Galore*	British coal nationalised; Marshall Plan inaugurated; Peace treaties signed; marriage of Princess Elizabeth; Indian independence
1948	Greene, *The Heart of the Matter* Paton, *Cry, the Beloved Country* Waugh, *The Loved One* Sartre, *Les Mains sales*	State of Israel founded; Truman wins US Presidential election; Gandhi assassinated; British railways nationalised; Berlin blockade
1949	Algren, *The Man with the Golden Arm* Nancy Mitford, *Love in a Cold Climate*	Republic of Ireland proclaimed; German Federal Republic formed; apartheid established; Berlin airlift ends
1950	Hemingway, *Across the River and Into the Trees* Snow, *The Masters* Fry, *Venus Observed* Waugh, *Helena* Death of Shaw	Senator McCarthy begins persecutions; London dock strike; Alger Hiss sentenced; Korean War begins
1951	Monsarrat, *The Cruel Sea* J. Jones, *From Here to Eternity* Tennessee Williams, *The Rose Tattoo* Carson, *The Sea Around us*	Abdullah of Jordan assassinated; MacArthur relieved of Korean command; Burgess and Maclean escape to USSR; Rosenbergs sentenced to death

Year	Age	Life
1952	64	Prefatory Essays to *Aissa Saved, Mister Johnson, A Fearful Joy, Castle Corner* and *The Moonlight*; *Prisoner of Grace* (Part 1 of Second Trilogy; US publication 1952)
1953	65	8 January, death of son George; awarded honorary degree, University of Edinburgh; lecture tour of USA; *Except the Lord* (Part 2 of Second Trilogy; US publication 1953)
1954	66	Lecture tours in Italy (March), Germany (June–July), Scandinavia (Nov.–Dec.); also at British Institute, Paris (27 October); *Paris Review* 'Interview with Joyce Cary'
1955	67	Unhurt when plane crashes on take-off; lecture tour of Greece and Cyprus (Jan.–Feb.); beginnings of paralysis in leg; *Not Honour More* (Part 3 of Second Trilogy; US publication 1955)
1956	68	Clark Lectures, Cambridge, read by nephew Robert Ogilvie because of Cary's physical deterioration
1957	69	29 March, dies in his sleep; funeral and burial in Oxford
1958		*Art and Reality* (Clark lectures); *First Trilogy* (as one volume)
1959		*The Captive and the Free*
1960		*Spring Song and Other Stories*
1974		*Cock Jarvis*
1976		*Selected Essays*, ed. A. G. Bishop

Year	Literary Context	Historical Events
1952	Hemingway, *The Old Man and the Sea* Leavis, *The Common Pursuit* Doris Lessing, *Martha Quest* A. Wilson, *Hemlock and After* Beckett, *Waiting for Godot*	Death of George VI; Queen Elizabeth II succeeds; Eisenhower elected US President; Mau Mau emergency in Kenya; London trams cease service
1953	Ian Fleming, *Casino Royale* Miller, *The Crucible* Williams, *Camino Real* Deaths of Dylan Thomas, O'Neill and Belloc	Tito visits London; Korean armistice; Rosenbergs executed; death of Stalin
1954	Rattigan, *Separate Tables* Thomas, *Under Milk Wood* Sagan, *Bonjour Tristesse* Tolkien, *The Lord of the Rings* (–1955)	Nasser takes over in Egypt; Dien Bien Phu falls; Senator McCarthy censured; US rules against school segregation by colour; Independent Television Authority established in UK
1955	Waugh, *Officers and Gentlemen* Greene, *The Quiet American* Miller, *A View from the Bridge* O'Hara, *Ten North Frederick*	Eden succeeds Churchill as PM; Germany joins NATO; European Union founded; Duke of Edinburgh awards inaugurated
1956	Osborne, *Look Back in Anger* Lampedusa, *The Leopard*	Khrushchev denounces Stalin; Hungary invaded; Suez crisis and war; first Aldermaston march
1957	Shute, *On the Beach* Kerouac, *On the Road* Murdoch, *The Sandcastle* Osborne, *The Entertainer* Braine, *Room at the Top*	Macmillan succeeds Eden as PM; Bermuda Conference; Treaty of Rome; Wolfenden Report

A HOUSE OF CHILDREN

PREFACE

This book began in fact, as it begins on the page, with recollections suddenly called up by a fuchsia with its characteristic movement, stiff and springy, in a brisk wind. I was taken back to Donegal where fuchsia is a hedge plant. From an English garden, it took me not so much to memories as to the actual sensations of childhood, and I noticed, not for the first time, that these sensations are not always very clearly related to the memories.

I can recall perfectly my feeling when I sat on the boat deck of a Liverpool-Derry steamer, at about eight years old, wedged firmly between two aunts while they smoked their cigarettes and guarded themselves from flying into the Atlantic at every roll of the ship by nothing better than their shoe heels hitched against the two-inch gunwale. For we sat behind the boats where there were no rails.

I realize now that we sat there because my aunts wanted to smoke, and in those days ladies did not smoke in public. One of these aunts, indeed, a very pretty one, was later reproved by King Edward VII for that same unladylike vice. And I remember that their gossip, literally above my head, paraded before my mind aspects of known people, so strange and mysterious that they had all the excitement of Arabian tales with the added wonder of fact. I knew the people who lived these amazing lives. I can feel that wonder, that pressure, the sense of being wedged between firm thighs, and I can see the enormous dark green waves advancing obliquely against the iron sheer of the sides; I can have again the acute and continuous sense of danger; but the special feeling is something quite different; it is of a kind of elated solemn tension. No doubt this was a compound of fear, glory (at the distinction of being where no other passengers were allowed), and the interest of the talk, to which I did not so much listen as simply expose my mind.

No doubt it was because of this fear and glory that the event was fixed for ever, as pure sensation, in my cells. Another feeling that remains with me equally vivid dates from my third year when my brother, a baby in long clothes, was put into my arms.

But the feeling is almost indescribable, apart from the weight of the child and a certain anxiety, probably due to a warning to hold tight. It remains as a baffled interest, a confused excitement. And this impression is even more distinct from the picture that comes with it; the record on the senses had less relation with the visual image. I can see myself on the boat deck, and I know from this picture that we sat on the starboard side. But the feeling of tension belongs fairly closely to the memories, also direct, of the precipice, within six inches of my feet, and the huge valleys of the Atlantic opening below it.

I can see myself even more clearly with the baby in my lap, and not only myself, but the chair I sat in, even my position in the room, a double room with folding doors. I daresay the occasion was my brother's christening. And I don't think there is any doubt that the impression and the picture have the same cause, in the excitement of the moment. Because of that profound sensation, which has remained for more than fifty years, the imagination was turned upon the scene, to ask, 'What happened?' – to say, 'That was something important,' and to record every detail of it.

But as I say, the sensation that remains does not belong to the picture. It is confused and, as it were, inadequate even to itself, to my own feeling about it. A critic, a philosopher, objects that I am splitting up the world, that I must have worked on the impression as well as the picture. But I don't feel it so. I feel the impression as something that came from outside and still stands to be examined. As for splitting the world in two, in appearance it is always split. Our immediate experience is of a split between mind and body, spirit and flesh, the creative imagination and the material it works upon. Obviously this is an impossible situation, the world cannot be an accidental conjunction of incompatibles. Besides, mind and body (that is 'physical' organ-ization) are a unity and cannot exist apart. But it is the philosopher's job to explain this state of affairs, as it is a writer's, as writer, to explore and describe, as exactly as he can, the experience which the philosopher (as artist in the creation of rational wholes) can use for his raw material. And so I have only to give the fact, without comment, that even a small child records experiences from both sides of its being, in its senses and in its imagination, which can remain separate and yet react upon each other.

I am asked often if the book is autobiography. The answer is that names, places, and people are disguised, because many of the people are living. I have given myself an elder brother – why, I d not know. But I notice that this elder brother is also myself, and I suspect that I divided myself in this way because I realized by some instinct (it was certainly not by reason) that the two together as a single character would be too complex for the kind of book I needed to write; a book full of that clarity, the large skies, and wide sea views, which belong to the vision of my childhood. For what would be clear and simple to the mind even of a child, is highly complex in description; and so the book that would be 'true' to fact, would be false to the imagination.

J.C.

CHAPTER I

The other day, in an inland town, I saw through an open
window, a branch of fuschia waving stiffly up and down in the
breeze; and at once I smelt the breeze salty, and had a picture of
a bright curtain flapping inwards and, beyond the curtain,
dazzling sunlight on miles of crinkling water. I felt, too, expect-
ancy so keen that it was like a physical tightening of the nerves;
the very sense of childhood. I was waiting for a sail, probably
my first sail into the Atlantic. Somebody or something must
have fixed that moment upon my dreaming senses, so that I still
possess it. Small children are thought happy, but for most of the
time they do not even live consciously, they exist; they drift
through sensations as a pantomime fairy passes through coloured veils and changing lights. That moment was grasped out
of the flux; a piece of life, unique and eternal, and the sail also,
is still my living delight. The dinghy had a shiny new gaff, and
the mainsail was wet half-way up so that the sun behind it made
a bright half-moon on the canvas. She rose to the first swell of
the Atlantic, beyond Sandy Point, with a three-angled motion,
neither roll nor pitch. Then we were leaping from wave to wave,
squattering into rollers that had touched Greenland in their last
landfall, and the thin planks sprang and trembled under my
body, sitting down among the ballast-bags. Tens of thousands
of dark blue waves rushed towards me, rising and falling like
dolphins and spouting thick triangles of foam. The land was so
far off that the mountains and cliffs seemed like a thin lid sliding
backwards over the world to unclose its sun-gazing eye. Nobody
could see us now, I felt, even the coast-guards' telescope couldn't
pick us out. We would seem like a Mother Carey's chicken or a
hen coop dropped off a turf boat. 'Our lives are in real danger.
All depends on the steersman. A single mistake would swamp
us, down among the fish in the black valleys, and the sea trees
with their thick leaves like the beginnings of hands.'
It was Freeman, a little man whom we called Pinto, who said

to us, on that sail or another: 'I suppose the fish take us for a bird,' and at once one saw oneself with a fish's sideways glance, darting through the pale iridescent firmament, like a transparent pearl, which is a fish's sky, just as a swallow, with short wings, appeared to us in a sunset twilight, as it dived after a maybug. The boat was a bird and a boat at the same time; we sailed and flew; we were Hawkins, Drake, Hudson and a sleepy whale, combing its belly on the ribs of some iron wreck and preparing to blow us out of the water on the fountain of its spout.

CHAPTER 2

Pinto was our holiday tutor, a man who hated teaching and showed it even to us. He would sit at the head of the parlour table, with his elbows on the table, his face in both hands and an expression of despair. Then suddenly he would utter a huge groan, which often surprised himself, so that he would jump up and look fiercely at us. He was a little dark man with a pale square face and a short broken nose. His mouth was wide and mobile, the mouth of an actor or preacher. He looked like a preacher with his rather long black hair and shabby black clothes. When his own groans surprised him and he could bear us no more, he would suddenly go out of the room to the coat cupboard, where he kept a medicine bottle of whisky or potheen in his overcoat. We used to laugh at each other when he went for his drink.

But we loved him because he was bored, like us, with lessons, and because he sailed in the Atlantic, though he was strictly forbidden to take us younger ones beyond Sandy Point. We delighted to be with Pinto, because he was one of those people who could give the power of enjoyment; the sense of concrete experience.

'Sixty fathoms, down there, nasty cold death,' he said one day.

My cousin Robert, aged thirteen, not to be frightened, said: 'It's not really rough today,' but Pinto was already looking round him at the sky, the sea, the far-off land in a manner which made us, too, look keenly and know the delight of them. His remark about the nasty death had not been meant to frighten us. It had sprung out of his own passing fancy. But it still vibrated in our happiness like the bass of a tune.

Pinto did not teach us. He spent time with us and continued his own life. But that life happened to be one of the imagination. It was he and my father who seized for us, now and then, out of the passing show of things, a sharp picture, a clear experience.

Once, when my father had taken us for a deep-sea bathe, just inside Sandy Point, and we were drying in the boat, he caught me and whirled me round. His bare arm shot out past my ear: 'See, a whale.'

I gazed across miles of little jumping peaks like circumflexes. Suddenly a thin feather of brightness, like a puff of steam, appeared, all by itself, in the air. It seemed to have no connection with the water below.

'There you are – there he blows off steam – he's ocean bathing, too.'

'Is it hot?'

'Oh, yes, he's as hot as you are inside – hotter.' My father laughed, enjoying my look of astonishment.

But it was the phrase, 'he's ocean bathing, too,' which excited me. I felt the magnificence of sharing bathing-places with a whale. We both used an ocean. That whale still lives in my idea with his enormous beating heart and pumping veins, a torpedo of fiery life as big as a mountain, sliding through the small summer waves where we had bathed that morning.

CHAPTER 3

This was our first year at Dunamara, my Aunt Hersey's house by the sea lough of Mannanen, which is the biggest in Ireland. It was an old, long house with a white face and a dark, slate roof, set against the trees on the steep hill-side. It had almost no garden, for it stood on a narrow shelf between the hill and the lough; fifteen yards of rough, weedy lawn divided it from the lough which, at spring tides, flowed to the very level of the grass. There was nothing between the water's edge and the long, formal grass plot but a coping of stone, level with the grass and a foot wide. In winter storms, of course, waves broke as far as the doorstep and spray rattled on the roof like shrapnel.

The house had no beauty except the fine proportions of door, window, chimney and roof. I did not value it then for beauty, but it stands before my eye now with the dignity of a classical order which owes its forms to the shape of the real.

Aunt Hersey was a widow. Her brother Herbert lived with her, and since the three children were at school, the couple had fallen into old-maidish habits. I'm told they were so much alarmed when they heard that the four of us cousins were coming to them, that Herbert threatened to leave the house and Hersey became ill.

It was true that we had a bad name in the countryside. This was not because we were mischievous children, but because there were so many of us. Often in a summer holiday we were ten or twelve together, so that there was always some new enterprise in one of our heads, and always two or three, at least, ready to carry it out, whatever it was. They say London is so big that you can fill the Albert Hall with any nonsense, the most abstract religion or politics. Among ten children of all ages from fourteen to four, you could find enthusiasts for every plan, from tearing out bell-wires by the roots to a prayer-meeting; or to digging for gold pots under the footmark of a rainbow. New ideas sprang up among us every moment, as unexpected and rousing as partridges out of turnips.

In a tribe of that size we were so much children that grown-ups could not even be seen. I don't remember any of them above the knee before I was seven; but the faces of children surround me, and all of them, shouting, laughing, weeping, furious or affectionate, are full of impatience. We were always in a hurry for the next thing, the next game, tomorrow, our birthdays, a party, a sail, supper. The present fell out of our hands like a new toy at Christmas, before we knew what it was for.

We lived in our own tribe, among its ideas, its loves and wars; and the tribes of other children. I remember the fisherman's children about the shores and wild hordes of mountain children in their father's cut-down trousers, but not fishermen or farmers. I was always toiling up some hill with a turf in my hand to join an ambush; or running with a new-laid egg, probably stolen, to make a feast; or rushing along by some hedge pursued by a dog or a policeman. We stole boats and borrowed the saddler's pony for rides, or, on Dunvil Green, one of the grazing donkeys; which threw us against walls or into the whins.

The rides had gone, but I remember a fall, as if by the light of a lantern slide reflected from the screen. The flash of conception has this power, to photograph all surrounding memories; to fix a whole region of experience in the brain. Full of prickles and bruises, I staggered one day howling through some long lane between enormous walls as high as the Bastille. I must have been about six, for the walls could have belonged only to a lane in Dunvil, the seaside fishing village which was our market town. Perhaps they were eight foot high. The lane was full of rocks, smoothed out like scones, and there were piles of fish-boxes against the walls. Oars and masts stood against the doors. The sky overhead was full of little fat rolls of cloud; rippled like a sandbar turned upside down, except that the crooked hollows between the waves were filled with pale blue light instead of grey water. High up against this sky, strung from wall top to wall top, several ropes supported the cut-off wings and rumps of skates, which dropped brown blood on the smooth, grey rocks. There was a strong smell of bad fish, tar and salt. I was lost and despairing. As I went I howled: 'Harree – Jimmee – Deelee,' but I had no hope. My cries were curses. Suddenly I saw a dirty, ragged little girl stooping down with her eye against the bottom of a door.

I stopped crying and stared at her. I wanted to look, but etiquette, the tribal law, forbade me to use her spy-hole without an invitation. She looked up at me through the black strings of her hair and said in a hoarse, cracked voice: 'Want to look – it's old Sandy.'

I therefore stooped down and looked, supporting myself by grasping the girl round the waist. She, too, embraced me. We were now tribal allies. We gazed cheek by cheek under the hole in the door which looked as if it had been gnawed by some enormous rat, at a small yard where a large drunk man was chasing two barefoot girls and swearing at them. They were laughing at him as they dodged about in the sun; suddenly they became furious and screamed abuse; then they began laughing again. He had a murderous, stupid look.

The little girl muttered hoarsely next my ear about the language used by both parties, explaining how bad it was. She also assured me that Sandy, when he caught one of the girls, would break her neck. I could feel these hoarse remarks in the body of my friend. Her thin ribs vibrated with the rough voice. I began to turn my head round, to look at her. Several times I knocked my nose against her ear or hard cheek-bone. I felt an intense curiosity in her, not as a girl, but as a being, a person. Perhaps this was the first time that I realised another person. I studied her as I might have studied a new species, and I began to feel very fond of her. I was delighted when she, too, turned her head for a sidelong glance. Her face was wedge-shaped, thin and grey, with hollow cheeks. She urged me to go on looking under the door because Sandy might catch one of the girls any minute. We looked therefore and discussed the man, who, it seemed, was the girls' father, and the girls' chance of escape. I don't remember a word of this talk, only that it was essentially fond. Whatever we said, we were expressing a warm attachment. I remember, too, my keen sense of this other person; a sense neither sympathy nor curiosity nor wonder; but containing all three in something greater than any, an indescribable feeling of difference and community in one. It was, I suppose, as if one blade of grass should touch another and feel it and think: 'It is not me, but it is very close to me.'

But suddenly we were bored. If our boredom was not simultaneous, then one or the other almost instantly communicated it to the other. We unlaced our arms, stood up and walked off in opposite directions. Again I shouted: 'Harree – Annee – Deelee,' but without despair and merely as a routine. I did not care whether they came or not. I had so entirely forgotten my misfortune that when I was suddenly found by six or seven cousins at once who began to shout all together, to laugh, to ask questions, I could not understand why they looked at my head to find a bump, and my legs for thorns, and why Delia shook me and told me I was the bigger ass of the two. Delia, I suppose, was in charge of us that afternoon, for whoever was the eldest girl present, assumed the manner of a governess, and abused us. Delia, who, when she was not the eldest, led the mischief; in charge, was the most severe of all. She would rush at us like a fury, with her black hair blowing out behind her like a wake of rage in the air, and shake our bones out of their joints.

We were often in mischief simply because we were a crowd of children in our own world, which is as different from the grown-up world as that of dogs or cats or birds. What is enterprise, exploration in one, is mischief in the other.

Our grandparents always engaged a governess to look after us in the mornings. Aunt Hersey was glad to have the help of an unemployed tutor, and Freeman was very glad of a job. In fact, according to what he told us, he had not paid his Dunvil landlady for two months.

CHAPTER 4

Pinto enjoyed life in a concrete manner; but he took little interest in children, as children; none in me, eight that year; or my cousin Anketel at six. He was friendly with Robert, but rather as an equal than a teacher. Robert was going that winter to a public school, and he told everyone what he meant to do there. 'I shall ask my friends to tea in the study, but of course they'll have to get out when I want to work. I'm going to work rather hard so as to stop being a fag, but as I shall be doing my exercises, too, *and* extra music, I shan't have much time.'

Even his own mother, Aunt Hersey, thought Robert a little cocksure. But the boy was only asking questions. When he cried: 'I shall have my friends to tea in the study,' he was really asking: 'Shall I have any friends and will I be so happy as to entertain them?' He was a proud and rather shy boy who had not many friends. When he said: 'I shall be doing my exercises,' he was asking: 'Is it the right thing to do exercises and try to be strong?'

He thought of a public school as a place full of opportunities; where noble boys, out of the old school novels, won glory of every kind, but bad boys came to a bad end.

But when he cried his remarks at Pinto, firing them off in his most dogmatic manner, to provoke at all costs an answer, Pinto would say: 'All education is a fraud,' or 'Schools were the ruin of me.' He could not be bothered to answer Robert, so that the boy had to fall back on his mother, who knew nothing about public schools and simply told him to be good and brave and to say his prayers; and his cousin Philip. Philip was seventeen, a tall, thin, fair boy with a girlish complexion, always smiling to himself. He was not at the school of Robert's choice, but he said that he had a friend there and he told Robert various customs which new boys ought to follow; especially one by which everyone, brave enough to try, could achieve distinction. He was to go up and down a certain path, with his collar turned up, and shout a challenge to everyone to turn him off. If a prefect were to order him off the path, he must shout: 'I appeal.' He would then be given leave always to use that path, and if no other new boy had done the same thing, he would be elected President of the Fag's council. Even if another new boy had anticipated him, he would be on the council, which was a great distinction. The custom, so Philip said, dated from the time of Ethelred the Unready; for though the school was not as old as Ethelred, it had taken over the customs from one of the monk's schools which took them from Alfred.

Harry, who was then nearly ten, and even I, were suspicious of this advice, not because it seemed improbable, but because we knew Philip as a practical joker. We had both suffered from one of his tricks.

CHAPTER 5

This had happened the year before when we were staying with my grandmother Evelyn at Crowcliff, a house just outside Dunvil. Up above Dunvil, in the hills, there was an old grave-yard, surrounded by a rough wall of loosely piled stones. A church or chapel stood near this lonely place, long disused, but in the yard itself, close to the back wall, there was an ancient building, all of stone, with a stone roof. From a little distance this seemed like a chapel among its graves, in a large square of yard with a high ashlar wall round it. But as one came near, the chapel, which gave scale to the whole, diminished to less than six foot high, from the peak of its roof to the ground, the wall became a low field wall and the graveyard smaller than a cottage garden. This little stone house was said to be the tomb of a saint. By stooping low and looking through an opening about a foot square, in the thick wall, one could see thigh bones and skulls.

I had seen this place once or twice and peeped at the skulls, which gave me no fear, but only a peculiar feeling of suspense with which I always saw or heard anything reminding me of death. My mind seemed to stop for a moment like a traveller who comes suddenly upon a pool in the road and pauses because he does not know how deep it is.

One night when we children were driving home to Crowcliff from a mountain picnic, with Cousin Philip, we came near this place. Philip sat with Harry on one side of the car, facing the mountains, Cousin Katherine, Anketel's sister, and I, with Anketel between us, faced the lough. There is no more beautiful view in the world than that great lough, seventy square miles of salt water, from the mountains of Annish. We had heard my father call it beautiful, and so we enjoyed it with our minds as well as our feelings; keenly with both together. Wherever we went in Annish we were among the mountains and saw the lough or the ocean; often, from some high place, the whole Annish peninsula, between the two great loughs; and the Atlantic, high up in the sky, seeming like a mountain of water higher than the tallest of land. So that my memories are full of enormous skies, as bright as water, in which clouds sailed bigger than any others; fleets of monsters moving in one vast school up from the horizon and over my head, a million miles up, as it seemed to me, and then down again over the far-off mountains of Derry. They seemed to follow a curving surface of air concentric with the curve of the Atlantic which I could see bending down on either hand, a bow, which, even as a child of three or four, I knew to be the actual shape of the earth. Some grown-up, perhaps my father, had printed that upon my imagination, so that even while I was playing some childish game in the heather, red Indians or Eskimos, if I caught sight of the ocean with the tail of my eye, I would feel suddenly the roundness and independence of the world beneath me. I would feel it like a ship under my feet moving through the air just like a larger stiffer cloud, and this gave me an extraordinary exhilaration. It was expressed, of course, only in a shout or perhaps a quarrel; but it was a constant source of pleasure. I can remember jumping on a piece of hard ground, as one jumps on a deck, to test its spring, or simply to enjoy the feel of a buoyant ship beneath me.

In Annish we lived in a world which we realised as a floating planet, and in a beauty which we had been taught to appreciate, as greatly as small children are capable of enjoying spectacle. I at least enjoyed it by deliberate vision, for its sunrises and sunsets remain with me as pictures as well as a sense of glory and magnificence. I remember very well the aspect of the lough from the Oldcross road into Dunvil, a road over which I must have passed hundreds of times, especially in the spring or summer evenings. From above, the great lough, lying among its ring of mountains, would seem in the evening light like a long, low hill of water, following a different curve from the Atlantic beyond. This was because the sun, setting behind us, would cast its last greenish light on this side of the lough and leave the far side in a shadow, except where, if the wind was westerly, a silver line marked the surf. At this time, just before sunset, the sky would be full of a green radiance, fading gradually over the Derry mountains towards Belfast, into a dark blue-green transparency. As the car twisted in the winding road, we would come round to see the clouds behind us, like jagged coals in a grate, each surrounded by fire. But their centres, of course, were grey instead of black, and their fiery edges were as cold and lively with little sparks as phosphorescence on water.

The air itself, which was so dark, seemed made of this dark light, limpid like that coloured water which chemists show in their windows, and through it we could clearly see, when the car brought us round again, the iron piles of the Redman light, sometimes even the chimneys of Crowcliff on one side and Dunamara, a mile away to the south, against the livid sheen of the water.

At that time our legs could not reach to the footboard of an outside car. When it dipped outwards on a steep corner, our feet swung out until they seemed to hang over the gulf, and keeping tight hold of each other and Anketel and the side rails, we could see Dunvil straight beneath them, like a map cut out of black paper and stuck down upon a globe of foil. Even the separate boats in the harbour, as small as water beetles, could be seen at their moorings, or clustered round the pier like new-hatched beetles caught in the bubbles round a willow leaf.

We travelled through this enormous and magnificent scene in tranquil happiness. We were tired from running about in the heather and already growing hungry we felt the nearness of supper, and bed, with that calm faith which belongs only to children and saints devoted to the love of God and sure of the delights of communing with him. In that faith, that certainty of coming joys, we existed in a contentment so profound that it was like a lazy kind of drunkenness. I can't count how many times I enjoyed that sense, riding in a sidecar, whose swaying motion would have put me to sleep if I had not been obliged to hold on; so that while my body and head and legs were all swinging together in a half dream, my hand tightly clutched some other child's body; and the memory of bathing, shouting, tea, the blue smoke of picnic fires, was mixed with the dark evening clouds shaped like flying geese, the tall water stretching up to the top of the world, the mountains sinking into darkness like whales into the ocean and over all a sky so deep that the stars, faint green sparks, seemed lost in it and the very sense of it made the heart light and proud, like a bird.

But on this night when we were just swinging round the sharp corner over the graveyard, so that we saw the green sky between our knees instead of the water, Philip said: 'There's the bone house now – look if the ghosts are walking.'

Harry's voice, muffled like all voices from the other side of a car, said that there was no such thing as ghosts.

'How do you know?' Philip said, in his soft lazy voice. 'I wouldn't be too sure.'

There was silence for a minute or two while the car crunched down the steep hill, and then he suddenly called out: 'Hold hard, Dan – I think we'll give his old boneship a call,' and to me: 'Come along and I'll show you something – have you ever seen how a skull shines in the dark?'

Kathy, even at nine, had a sense of responsibility. She said promptly that neither she nor Anketel would stir. 'I won't have you playing your tricks on An – he's too little.'

But Harry and I were ashamed to refuse. Philip, carrying a rug and a stick, led us across the graves to the little bone house.

'Stoop down,' he said, 'and look in at this end while I go to the other. I'll light a bunch of grass and push it in and keep out the wind with the rug. Then you'll see the skull, and when the bunch goes out you'll see it shine. But mind you pick the right skull – the saint's skull – you can tell it because it's whiter – all holy men have white skulls because of their pure thought, and that's why the light comes out of them.'

Harry murmured to me: 'Look out for something – he's codding us.'

In fact, we had often had practical jokes played on us. They were common in those days, and people liked especially to frighten children. It is done even now. It is not very long ago that two cousins of mine, then a boy of seven and a girl of six, were told by their own nurse, that if they stared out of a certain window, facing the yard, about ten o'clock on a Sunday night, they would see a ghost. She placed them at the window and left them. Then suddenly an immensely tall figure in white came from behind the stables, moved across the yard, came up to their window, and beckoned to them. They saw the face of a skull, as white as snow, with open nostrils and protruding teeth; the beckoning finger was nothing but bone, probably a chicken bone.

These children, who believed that this creature was a real apparition come from the grave to summon them to die, were so struck with horror that, as they tell me, they were unable to speak or move or cry out. They were hypnotised by fear and by the sense of the creature's nearness to them; the same feeling, I suppose, that petrifies some small creatures at the sudden approach of a snake. After several minutes of this trial, the ghost glided away; and the nurse came rushing in, crying: 'The ghost – the ghost – it's after us.'

She asked the children if they had seen anything, and the children answered that they had seen the ghost.

'Did it beckon to you?'

'It lifted its finger at us.'

'And did you cross yourselves?'

'No, we forgot.'

'Oh dear, oh dear – but perhaps it was only a warning.'

According to the usual idea these children should have gone mad, or at least, been nervously damaged for life; but apparently they accepted the situation calmly and reasonably. A ghost had come to warn them of approaching death and they were going to die, possibly soon. Meanwhile life went on as before.

I daresay the calmness and resignation of the two children was disappointing to the practical jokers. Cousin Philip had more success with us. He went to the other end of the house and called out:

'Ready now, I'm just going to light the grass and put it in at the drain hole.'

We peered into the doorway, until we heard a hollow voice saying: 'Your time has come.' We jumped and saw a tall black form with fiery eyes and mouth coming towards us over the top of the house. It stooped at us. Both of us at once turned and ran. I was so terrified that I felt light-headed, as if my brain had turned into air, or at least cork. It seemed to float along with me and to have no connection at all with my rushing body and running legs. I didn't utter a sound even when I ran into the wall, as if blinded by terror, and cut a hole in my forehead. There is a piece of that wall still in my forehead. I bounced back from the wall, got up again, all in silence, climbed over it and ran on as hard as I could go. I did not look to see where Harry was, yet some instinct of fright kept us together, for every moment we bumped and even tripped each other. We fell continually over each other and over lumps in the road. We ran into bushes, gates. At one corner, after such a fall, scrambling to our knees, we clutched at each other. It was under some hedge in the narrow lanes above Dunvil. The greenish light still coming from the sky gave Harry's face, and probably mine, an olive pallor. He stared at me, with an expression not so much terrified as privately absorbed, as if he were completely preoccupied by some idea within himself.

'It's you?'

'Yes. Did you see it?'

'Was it Philip did it?'

'I expect so.'

'You've cut yourself.'

During this exchange both of us were looking round, at the hedge, the lough, and into the air. Even when Harry remarked upon my cut, he was gazing into the air above the hedge.

I followed his glance, and then, without another sound, we jumped to our feet and rushed off again towards the friendly shape of Dunvil. We knew that Philip had played a trick on us, but we felt that we were pursued; that there was some demon ready to grab us at every step.

The Crowcliff avenue winds down a hill so steep that the roots of the upper trees touch the top branches of those below. When we reached Crowcliff gates, we were so exhausted by falls and running that we missed the corner and rolled down among the trees, almost to the yard.

Philip had already arrived. He was waiting for us at the gate and began abusing us at once.

We, half stunned, after our last sudden descent, listened

stupidly till he asked: 'What on earth did you run away for, you little fools?'

'We thought it was a ghost.'

'Even if you did see a ghost, you needn't have run off like that. I thought you had more sense.'

'Did you do it with the rug?'

'I didn't do anything – I don't know what you're talking about,' he had been laughing, but now he looked at us seriously. 'Did you really see anything?'

'Of course we did.'

'That's queer – I suppose there are ghosts in that graveyard then. I'm glad they didn't come after me. But look here, not a word to Granny. She wouldn't understand. She'd think you were mad.'

We promised, of course, not to tell, and he took us into the kitchen to wash the blood off my head and to invent a lie to account for it. This was duly told and believed.

This trick did not seem, any more than that upon my cousins in County Derry, to do us any harm. It left only an odd kind of confusion in our minds. Harry and I could never decide exactly what had happened to us, and we did not even discuss it openly. We merely approached the subject and dodged away again.

'It wasn't a ghost – it was Philip.'

'Of course it was.'

'We thd run, didn't we? We were asses.'

'Well, I don't know.'

We still had the sense of running away from something; and so we felt that something had been there. A system of disintegration, a centre of anarchy was created in our minds. But among so many other inconsistent notions and confused feelings established in my brain long before, I daresay this was not the worst.

To create such a muddle, and fear, too, was, I imagine, Philip's purpose. He always liked to upset the equanimity of children. He was one of those people who feel compelled, by any spectacle of unquestioning faith or by any confident statement, to try to break it down. Words like truth and justice set up in them, by a natural reaction, an irritation, and they promptly start some ingenious lie or do some small injustice just to show their secret disgust of a world that values truth so little and has no justice at all.

Philip, I suppose, did not know why he played his tricks on

us and afterwards on Robert; he simply followed an inclination planted in him by some accident of his own life. But Pinto failed him for a different reason; because he had no idea of instructing. He had no sense of responsibility towards children. Robert, however, was perfectly satisfied with Philip as adviser. He was a simple and honest kind of boy who had had, till then, a very happy life; and he was also very good-natured. He could not conceive how anyone, especially Philip, whom he admired so much, should want to deceive him simply on account of his trustfulness, in a matter so important. So, to his natural expectation of new delights, new powers at a public school, was added the hope of a special distinction in that greater world.

CHAPTER 6

Our expectations, separating now from Robert's, were bounded by our immediate destiny. For in our wildest projects we always acknowledged, consciously or unconsciously, a practical limit. It is true we did set out once to dig up pots of gold from a circle of browned grass which, we were told, had been singed by a rainbow; but we had forks and spades; the scheme was reasonable. We could not even imagine Robert's school because it was not yet within our reach; picnics, boats, sailing with Pinto, filled our mind, and our largest anticipation was the coming of Delia from some English visit, where she had spent the first part of her school holiday. We were devoted to both the Dunamara girls, Frances and Delia. Frances, the elder, was fond of children and spoilt us with pennies and sweets. But we preferred Delia as a companion, although she was quite capable of laughing at our gravest disappointments. She was a dark strong girl, who followed her own way in life. Even when she was the dutiful daughter, she seemed to be independent in her very affections; in a certain reckless warmth of expression which seemed to say: 'This is how I feel and so this is what I do.'

We longed for Delia because we wanted to present her to our Pinto. For some reason, we were convinced that she would be charmed by Pinto, and it seemed to us that something extraordinary and delightful would arise for us, too, out of their meeting. I suppose the same hope causes that enthusiasm which with nearly everyone undertakes to promote a friendship or make a match. But it was keener in us because we had never been disappointed in the consequences.

The day when the Liverpool steamer was due happened to be rough, and we were forbidden to go out in the tender to meet Delia. But our aunt was going and we could not bear that anyone should present Pinto to Delia before us.

We therefore stole a passage in the boat. This plan was the work of the bold and ingenious Harry. While the passengers were being herded into the midship section from the old black pier, and three cows were being pushed and driven down planks into the stern, we, barefoot and dirty from the rocks, clambered in and, shielded by the cows, stowed ourselves among the heaps of baggage and the dangling legs of passengers. We squatted there in a terror so keen that it still can make a slight movement in my nerves. Roffey, who owned the boat, a huge bull of a man, was a terror to the village, and especially to small boys. We sat, therefore, Harry, my cousin Kathy and myself, in the triumph of revolution, and the paralysing terror of Roffey, among some yellow tin trunks, and whispered congratulations to each other.

Roffey's boat had always filled our imagination as something unique and formidable; something, too, more interesting than a pleasure boat, because it did real work. It acted as tender to many steamers passing Dunvil. It was the biggest open boat on the lough. The rowers, two on a sweep, like galley slaves in the pictures, put their feet into loops of rope, so that one could crawl beneath them. Under the seats I could stand upright; and the heavy gunwales, seamed and patched by a thousand crushing blows against iron plates and stone quays, were higher than Harry's head. It was nothing for Roffey's boat to carry a dozen cows as well as passengers, luggage, crew and five or six stowaways, like us three children, creeping about the bottom boards and dodging now a hoof, now an anchor.

The sea was rising and the heavy boat tumbled about with jerks which rolled us over, and made the boxes topple. The three cows in the stern staggered, and one of them, perhaps separated from her calf, kept mooing towards the shore, with a lugubrious noise which made us laugh. Their foolish round eyes gazed at us without expression, but now and then they swung down their heads as if to defend themselves from some enemy.

When the wind grew strong, Roffey put up a sail, a triangle of rust brown canvas, bound with rope like a dinghy's anchor cable, on a mast which was as thick at top as bottom. It looked like some schooner mizzen, cut off with a saw.

But even this sail, ridiculously small for our huge galley, heeled us over in the westerly half gale, and we saw the Atlantic horizon rise up before us, dark as a sailor's trousers, behind Sandy Point and the North Head. The wind sang in the thick weather shrouds with a peculiar deep note, and catching the spray, whirled it over our heads in showers like splintered moonstones mixed with hail. The squalls rushed away like black cloud shadows on fields of dark green corn; and when we clambered up the overhanging precipice of the weather side and, hooked by the chins, gazed to windward, we saw one monster charging us with little tongues of foam spurting all over it 'like wolves,' Harry said, meaning that the dark mass was like a pack of wolves hanging out their tongues as they galloped.

We shrieked together in joyful terror. We were growing drunk with expectation, which was increasing all the time. For in us children it was a pure passion and never checked itself for reason. It burned on its own fuel so that its size had no relation to its source; we were often in a fever for something so trifling that we had forgotten it before it arrived. All day one would live in the sense of something to come; it would be with one during lessons, bathing, digging, meals, until at last, getting into bed, one would notice it particularly and say: 'But what am I expecting.' Then one would discover that it had been doughnuts for tea, already eaten, but without any sense of fulfilment. The expectation had flowed over the fact as time runs over the apple flowers before one can grasp the spring. But with us, it was like an eddy on a strong tide. A specific anticipation was no more than a fresh bubble in the stream of our hope, rushing towards fulfilment. It is, after all, the natural state of children, to whom everything comes as discovery, and to whom discovery is a keen pleasure. We were not the pathetic deceived infants of the story-books, entering step by step the prison shades of grown-up disillusionment, we were confident of happiness because we had had it before. Our several expectations were sometimes not realised, but that was usually because our whole expectation

was being renewed every hour. We didn't notice the disappointments because our minds were full of something else, something
new, something interesting. For a new idea, which to our uncle,
and to old people, seemed to threaten the very mould of their
being, grown already into some ideal shape and unable to take
another, was to us delightful in its very newness. The loss of the
old home, the end of the old religion; it kills the old, but it is
nothing to children.

CHAPTER 7

At that moment Delia had become the focus of an expectation
which was simply the point of our hope, our growing. We were
drunk on her because we had the drunkenness already in us. We
were not thinking of Delia at all when we began to shout and
kick the sides of the boat, daring the crew to fall upon us. We
wanted to see what would happen. But no one took any notice
of us. Roffey himself, seated high in the stern like a Viking, did
not even look surprised or speak. Roffey had, or affected, the
moods of a tyrant and would smash a man for a whim and
overlook a real fault for another whim. He gave us one glance
and then again fixed his eyes on the steamer already turning
Sandy Point, with a great mushroom of black smoke blowing
away out of its black and red funnel.

Neither did he nor any of the crew take notice of the squall
now pressing us down. Roffey perhaps thought it beneath his
dignity to shorten sail, or take regard for the weather, for he
was often in danger and sometimes he was blown, passengers
and all, so far out of his course that he did not reach port again
till dark; or landed ten miles away. He seemed to feel, all
through his giant body, the greatness of his boat, and its clumsy
power, as a defiant and gloomy dignity. What was splintered
water-worn timber had entered into his idea of himself as a
rough mastery and commanded both his surly aloofness and his
sudden uncalled-for fist.

At last, with the fearful tilting of the boat, thrust over till the
sheet cut the waves, we slipped off the gunwale, and fell down
into the opposite side, hollow beneath us.

Black bilge water, floating dirt and oil and fish scales, had spurted through the gratings, and into this we slid. We were all startled. Harry, who detested slimy or dirty things, looked surprised and turned red; Kathy cried out in a disgusted voice: 'But I'm sitting in the water.'

This made us all laugh so much that we remained sitting in the water, leaning against the sides of the boat and stretching bare, filthy legs up the gratings, as if in an armchair. Even Kathy began to laugh and put her arms round us on both sides as if to say: 'I'm with you.'

The cows had fallen together in a heap and uttered loud moos, the boxes had tumbled; a young emigrant girl sitting above us with her new, long button boots dangling in mid-air, was speaking. But no one could hear her in the wind which was roaring and shrieking at once, the tremendous swish of the water like a thousand whips, the mooing of the cows and the clatter of the boxes. She was perhaps talking to herself, or for herself alone.

CHAPTER 8

Aunt Hersey and Robert, perched on their seat between the rowers, who were smoking short pipes, were balanced at the same acute angle. A cow just behind Aunt Hersey's shoulder was stretching out her neck and uttering moos like a cracked trumpet. We thought this scene very funny; and especially the grave faces of the two while they sat in their strange attitude and held on with both hands. We began to laugh at them and call out: 'Look at us – it's like an armchair.' We wanted to see Aunt Hersey's shocked face when she saw us reclining in the bilge.

But suddenly the enormous shadow of the steamer fell across us. We scrambled to our feet and saw it rushing upon us as if to cut us in two. A line whirled out from the forecastle head, making curls in the air like a cowboy's lasso, and fell across our bows. Roffey uttered barks like a seal challenging an enemy. The line drew a rope out of the sea, and one of the crew belayed it to the forward thwart. All this time the side of the steamer, as tall as a cliff and the colour of the cliffs at North Head, was rushing past us. Two great iron doors swung open in the side, and the motion of these doors, in contrast and harmony with the movement of the side and our own rapid passage sternward, gave us such pleasure that Harry said: 'I like those doors – I always like them,' as if he had said: 'I like cake.'

Then the rope jerked us forward so violently that we all fell in a heap among the luggage, and when we had got up again, we saw Delia already embracing her mother on the side grating. We had not expected Aunt Hersey to go up the side ladders. Aunt Hersey often surprised us by some piece of agility or enterprise, for we thought of her as a fussy old lady, whereas she was really a charming and active woman of forty-two, who had acquired, in the last few years, bad habits from the influence of her brother and the absence of her daughters.

Long before she reached the shore Delia knew all about Pinto. We saw Aunt Hersey communicating this, with all the other local gossip, into her ear as they sat huddled on their thwart in a squall of sleet. But now that this catastrophe, so long feared, had happened, we did not even notice it. We had forgotten the whole object of our passage, in its excitement, in the hope that we would be wrecked on the Iron Man or carried beyond the Heads.

CHAPTER 9

Because we had not after all presented Pinto to Delia we took no interest in their meeting. We were simply not surprised that Delia and Robert should spend all their time in Pinto's company and that Pinto was in a talkative, serious mood. Pinto had several moods. Sometimes he would tell stories, usually against himself, for instance, when he told us how he had pawned his clothes without letting his landlady know. Their charm was, of course, that of the confession; but Pinto used to mix his confessions with a cynical reflection which has remained with me only as a flavour and a look; a kind of gloomy resignation. In another mood, for instance, when we were sailing, he was like a small boy, like one of ourselves, but more dignified, jumping about and ejaculating whatever came into his head.

'Look at this one – a regular Mong Blong – the moving mountain – goodbye, friends – this is our last hour – though I can't imagine why it should always have sixty minutes,' and so on. He was rarely in the serious mood, but then he always looked angry and impatient, and talked very fast in an argumentative tone. With Delia and Robert, we noticed that he was in his angriest mood.

'He's talking about poetry, I expect,' Harry said, glancing up from the shore where we were digging out a huge bar of iron buried in mud. We had known the bar for months as a short rusty projection, but Harry had suddenly taken the idea that it must belong to a wreck, that it was of great length, and that we could make use of it.

Harry was always carried away by the project in hand. What he was doing at any time drove everything out of his head. Also it was just like him suddenly to produce and believe this theory that the iron would be valuable to us. 'You could use a bar like that for all sorts of things – there's one in the stable holding up the middle of the door.'

Only Kathy questioned now and then the use of the iron; not sceptically, but as one seeking information. She was always surprised when Harry answered her angrily: 'There's thousands of things you can do with iron – anybody knows it's the most important metal.'

At tea, exhausted and filthy, we could think only of how to get more boulders out of our way.

'We must blast them,' Harry said.

'How do you blast things?' Kathy asked.

'That's easy; the only thing is that we've got to have dynamite.'

'We could break up some cartridges.'

In this preoccupation we hardly noticed Pinto's argumentative speeches to Robert and Delia, which were about schools. We knew them already. We had heard them given to Robert; and they seemed so reasonable to us that we did not need to hear them again. Even as small children I think we could distinguish, perhaps by the man's tone, between Pinto's reasonable and unreasonable theories. When, for instance, instead of helping Robert with advice about public schools, as he might well have done, he simply abused education, and said that he himself had been ruined when they taught him to read, we all knew that this was his special kind of nonsense. In the same way he used to say that policemen were the cause of crime and that the English had ruined India by stopping the widows from being burnt alive. We used to laugh at these remarks, and Pinto would then say: 'I mean it, by God,' conveying, in the very violence of his tone, his own real indifference to any meaning.

But though sometimes he would curse all education, at other times he would say it was the only hope of a better world. Then also he would describe what schools ought to be like.

The picture that remains with me of Pinto's school is of children, all beautiful, in some kind of flowing garments, wandering among white colonnades beside fountains, and acquiring every kind of knowledge, from the conversations of tall, benevolent old men with grey beards. All this, of course, was probably from Morris or Plato, or both combined. Pinto was a Morris Socialist and often talked to Robert of the future world, where all men would be artist-craftsmen, living among beautiful things, in friendship and peace, and enjoying every moment of their long lives.

'Of course,' we thought, 'why not – that or something better. The grown-ups are seeing to it,' and we went on with our own affairs.

Aunt Hersey liked to hear Pinto talk of his Utopia. She would smile at him and say: 'I think that would be very nice, only I wonder who would do the cooking.' Her brother Herbert thought it wicked and dangerous. With him Pinto had his most violent arguments.

But it fascinated Robert, whose private school had been, without the colonnades, rather like a platonic academy. It was Harry's school and mine afterwards, and so I knew it. A plain old house, set among gardens, where the masters did in fact give their most useful teaching in the cricket field or strolling under the willows with two or three small boys hanging on their arms. The teaching, too, was little more worldly than that of a nurse, who, for her own sake, teaches the purest Christian unselfishness. It was mixed, of course, with patriotic and imperial sentiments; but all with stress upon duty and responsibility. To be an Englishman was to be born to a great destiny; as warrior and guardian of freedom and justice and peace. These doctrines became old-fashioned in the last twenty years, but Robert, and afterwards Harry and myself, breathed them as part of an atmosphere which entered into our very bones. It was an atmosphere much more truly religious than anything I have known since; for it was one of real purpose. We had our Bible lessons, of course, but the religion which actually stayed with us was something livelier, braver, keener than the Church teaching; and much more real. A lecture from a boy's parent, a sailor, about chasing slave dhows in the Gulf, went to the bottom of our feelings at one flash.

Of course we heard nothing of the other side of the old Empire: the gold grabbers; the cotton lords of India; and we had no conception, for our masters had none, of a real freedom. Our idea, like theirs, was abstract and legal, or romantic. We had no notion that poverty came into the question and was, with ignorance, the chief enemy of freedom.

For Robert, of course, much more than for Harry with his practical mind, and me, with my uncertain one, that teaching had been a gospel. He had already decided to be a missionary or a colonial officer, he could not decide which; and now through Freeman's eyes he looked forward to the time when the whole world would be remade in one united fellowship of rational and peaceful craftsmen.

CHAPTER 10

So far as we had time to think during our labours with the iron, we were glad that Delia enjoyed Pinto. For we could see that she was interested by the way she frowned at him, under her thick eyebrows, and agreed with him when he abused the Government. We felt confident that Delia would support Pinto against our Uncle Herbert, who, we knew, meant to get rid of him.

Herbert had disliked Pinto even before he arrived, because he threatened to disturb the routine of the house. Since then he had quarrelled with Pinto almost every time they met. He said every day that Pinto was useless and dangerous; he ought to be sacked. This alarmed us because Aunt Hersey, as we knew, was much under her brother's thumb. Aunt Hersey spoilt everybody who came near her. She had spoilt her husband, but luckily, since he had been a very good-natured man, spoiling only made him fat and more amiable. Uncle Herbert, on the other hand, grew still more selfish, until by turning his mind and all his interests back upon himself he had become like one of those scorpions which, they say, at any check, grow so angry that they bend back their tails and sting themselves to death. He was an unhappy man, always fretful about trifles, and so Aunt Hersey was also worried, and her own life was wasted in trifling anxieties. She had no real life at all, only a sense of strain. Yet she could still, for a moment or two, show a zest for life, in some childish game or joke, which was like the resurrection of another Hersey, gay and reckless, whose innocence had become integrity instead of the lack of information which irritated her brothers. This other Hersey I saw often even twenty years later; as a child I knew her only as the unexpected playmate who sometimes put down an order-book or forgot some pressing duty in order to play beggar my neighbour or animal grab, even more noisily than we.

Aunt Hersey defended Pinto on the grounds that he had such comical stories to tell, and his conversation was a change from local gossip, fishing and crops. But we did not rely on her because we knew she was a slave. We relied on Delia.

On the next evening, Harry asked her if she did not find him rather interesting. This was a phrase of Harry's, at that time, meaning high praise. Delia answered only: 'He does talk a lot, doesn't he?'

'He takes us sails.'

'Now I'm at home, I can take you sails.'

'But don't you like the way he tells stories?'

'What on earth was he doing in Annish – he ought to be in London, showing off his velvet breeches.'

We had never heard of velvet breeches, and I don't believe Pinto ever referred to them again. He was quite capable of catching up a new theory, often a ridiculous one, and supporting it with passionate eloquence for a whole day, and then forgetting all about it, or making fun of it, on the next.

'But don't you like him, Delia?'

'He's all right, I suppose, if he doesn't talk nonsense.'

But the next day Pinto spent all with Robert. They went off on the mail car to some concert in Derry, and Delia suddenly took her uncle's part. She said that Pinto was a bad influence, especially for Robert, and besides, he was not needed. She could look after us.

Robert, of course, defended Pinto, and the result was a violent quarrel. Both Delia and Robert had the obstinate tempers of strong and decided characters.

CHAPTER II

Delia became so furious against Pinto that she would not even go sailing with him. She borrowed from one of her numerous admirers a beautiful little mahogany dinghy with the latest fittings and a new suit of racing sails, and invited Robert, Harry and me to sail with her. Robert refused. Harry and I, who were still fascinated by Pinto, temporised.

But we sailed with Delia. We were not strong enough to refuse her anything. Therefore when Pinto arranged to take Robert and Kathy picnicking five miles across the lough, Delia sailed us two away to Shell Port, a beach beneath North Head, famous for its shells. She promised, as a treat, to let us climb into the Shell Port cave, which we were strictly forbidden to go near.

Shell Port cave fascinated us. We had then a craze for exploring caves, cellars, even quarries and holes. We had crawled into a three-foot space beneath the hay house only to sit there; and we dug two great pits in the garden with a tunnel between, for the thrill of peeping or squeezing through the tunnel.

We were exploring the world, but only with our nerves. We had no words for classifying our discoveries. We were still like feelers, antennae of some larger being, the leaves of a sensitive plant, put out to examine the world. Our senses were still like a baby's hands which wave in the air at random until they strike against some cold or hot or woolly object, which may or may not create some interest in his mind.

So we gathered sensations, smells, various excitements; only now and then consolidated into an idea by an accident of attention, some remark. Just as we enjoyed and sought the experience of sailing the Atlantic over deep water and imagined mountains, among possible whales, and the fancied smell of icebergs, we had also a peculiar delight in creeping through the middle darkness of the earth and feeling a mountain over our heads. I don't remember whether our pit in the garden showed clay or gravel, but I remember the sensation of wriggling through the tunnel, of dead weight hanging above me.

I remember Anketel, at about five, after coming out of the cave at Knock beach, pointed to the top of the cliff and said: 'There was a sheep eating grass on the top all the time.' His expression for some time afterwards showed preoccupation with this sheep, and finally he went back into the cave to know what it felt like with a sheep overhead.

But Shell Port had a far stronger attraction than the little hole at Knock. It was a sea cave whose floor was always under deep water. It had two openings: a narrow crack, below tide mark on the Shell Port side, and another, about a yard wide and twenty feet high, upon the Atlantic. Between these was the North Head, a cliff half a mile round.

The outer opening could be entered by anyone bold enough to jump from a boat upon a small tongue or bracket of rock which was exposed only at low tide. This bracket extended, as a narrow ledge two or three inches wide, into the central chamber of the cave, and there was a horizontal crack opposite, a continuation of the same fault, in which a boot sole would lodge. Thus, a climber, by straddling the rock walls, could make his way forward over the sea.

In the year before, my father, in one of his sudden unexpected visits, had taken us fishing; and when we begged to see Shell Port cave he had carried us both, first Harry and then myself, on his back, along these walls. I can still remember the feel of his short, black curling hair as I clutched it in that terrifying journey, and the calls of my aunts, his sisters, from outside: 'Are you all right? Do be careful.'

They were angry with him for taking risks with us; but we had absolute faith in his strength and his power. If he had slipped and then, after all, walked upon the air, we would not have been surprised. We should have wanted only to know how he had done it.

Yet this climb was an extraordinary feat, one of the many he performed. I did not realise then that he was little over thirty, a high-spirited young man who loved exploring and dangerous feats.

He was panting when he brought us into the central chamber. There was a tall peak of rock, an island, in the middle of this chamber. We could not reach this because to do so required a jump of five or six feet, impossible to my father with a child on his back. But he pointed to its high peak and to the dome of the roof, and said that it had fallen down perhaps a million years ago, 'and there it's been in this hole, a long time before there were any people at all, or even fish.'

These words made me see the cave as not merely ancient, but different from any other, a survival from another world. The rocks which touched my bare ankle seemed so different from common rock that they had a special chill and sliminess, horrible and strange; the dark green water, at which I gazed down past my father's shoulder, appeared strange even to the sight, a primitive water. I imagined that no fish could live in it. Above all, the light and noises in this cave seemed unique. The light was a pallid green, broken by flashes of dark silver or platinum from the waves outside the cave mouth, so that when my father set me down on the ledge, I saw the thin hook of his nose and the long line of his thin jaw, green on one side and lead on the other, as if the cave had changed him into a demon. Meanwhile, all round, as if to a great distance, there was a peculiar sucking noise, like those derisive kisses made by the village boys at street corners when couples passed in the twilight.

All of us had since looked into this cave at every opportunity, but only from the Shell Port. We would wade out at low tide and stare down the crack. I have seen Anketel thus, in all his clothes, wet to the armpits, gazing into the twilight with the absorbed concentration of those who peer through a fence at a murderer's house, after he has been hanged. He could see nothing, but his imagination was at work. I had told him, of course, that the cave was a million years old, older than the fish.

CHAPTER 12

Harry and I had promised ourselves that we would climb once more, by ourselves, into Shell Port cave, but when we got there, as Delia perhaps expected, the tide was above the ledge and we could only sail close to the entrance and peer into the darkness beyond. Delia expressed her sympathy, and cried: 'But I'll do anything you like—' During the quarrel with Robert there was a kind of vehemence in her affection for all the rest of us, even for Kathy, whom she did not like.

Harry, polite in disappointment, told her that he did not mind where we had our picnic. But suddenly Delia offered to join Pinto's party. 'That's what you really want, isn't it? Very well, we'll go. It's only fair after you've missed the shells. After all, I don't see why we should let *that man* stop us from doing what we like. He's not worth it.'

She put about and sailed directly east for Sandy Point. But as if to make up for this piece of generosity, she spent the whole time of the voyage, about an hour and a half, abusing Pinto. She called him the meanest kind of thief; robbing poor lodging-house keepers. She also hinted to us that Uncle Herbert was making inquiries about *that man*, which had already given enough evidence against him to put him in gaol.

All this alarmed us for Pinto, and Harry tried to defend him against Delia. But of course we had nothing to say against her definite charges, and the torrent of her anger was overwhelming to children. I had seen hatred before often enough, in children of my own age; the sudden furious hatred with which one small child will attack another; but I had never heard it expressed with such force.

If I had been much older I would have been struck by Delia's violence. I would have thought: 'That man, as she calls him, seems to have made an extraordinary impression on her in a very short time.' But I had no experience of the peculiar movements of feeling in girls of sixteen; and a suggestion of jealousy from Kathy made little impression on me.

We found the picnickers hard at work building a field-kitchen to cook their kettle. They included Delia's sister Frances, who had returned unexpectedly by the mail car, just after our departure; and had insisted on the party waiting for her until she could change her clothes. This was typical of Frances, who could not resist any kind of party. We found her, like Robert and Kathy, running about under Pinto's orders. We heard him even abusing her, in the roughest tone, for putting a stone in the wrong place. He was obviously in a bad temper, as usual during a piece of construction. But afterwards, also as usual, he was in extremely good humour. He stretched himself on the sand, lit his pipe and suddenly became talkative in a new way. He told one story after another, all ostensibly to Frances, to whom he had plainly taken a fancy; and all of them were about poverty-stricken people, about their misfortunes, tricks and fits of extravagance. Many of them were about himself, and whenever he described one of his own adventures, he showed himself in some ridiculous or humiliating light. For instance, he described how he had been left to take care of a friend's, an artist's, rooms in London, but without money. The friend forgot to leave any and he had none. He therefore pawned a clock in order to telegraph for funds. But the telegram did not find its addressee, and no answer came. Meanwhile, according to Pinto, he had been obliged to pawn pictures, the cutlery, and at last the chairs and tables, till suddenly while he was still hoping for funds to take everything out of pawn again, the friend himself walked in and found him sleeping on a bare floor in the empty rooms.

In another story, he had gone to help a friend out of his difficulties. He found a bailiff in charge of the house. The friend's wife and children were in tears and the friend was in despair. Here Pinto gave a description of these people and their misery which moved us strongly. He made me feel something much more than sympathy; he produced that direct effect on the nerves, which makes, as they say, the heart swell. This doesn't seem to me an adequate image for the stifling, breathless sense of helpless pity and fear with which a small child realises suffering and injustice. Pinto, of course, was an artist in description. For instance, he made vivid to us the bewilderment of the children, who couldn't understand why they were being turned into the street. After forty years, during which every kind of bewilderment has befallen the world, I still feel a pang for that family, whose name I never knew, and which perhaps never existed except in Pinto's imagination.

Pinto having brought us to this mood, and even Delia's eyes were fixed upon him with keen attention, described how he himself was nearly in tears, and promised at once to pay off the bailiff. The family greeted him as a saviour, and the wife tried to kiss his hand. So he borrowed their last half-crown to take a cab to his bank. 'But when I got to the bank and made out my cheque, the clerk took it away to the back part and the manager suddenly pounced on me from behind. He had a special pouncing door in front of the counter to catch people like me, and he asked me if I knew that I had overdrawn my account. What's more, he wouldn't believe me when I said I didn't know, and in fact, he was very rude and called me a robber, a bank robber, which of course, to a banker, is worse than a poisoner. He frightened me so much that at last I began to call him sir, and when I got out I was in such a state that I forgot all about my friend. I only wanted to hide. But when I went back to my lodgings I found that my landlady had locked me out. You see, I'd given her a cheque, too, and the bank had sent it back. She wouldn't even give me my overcoat, and it was the middle of November, and there was I, without even a coat or fourpence for a doss, a bed. So I wondered where I could go, and remembered my friend who was being sold up. Of course I was too proud to go back to him. But then it began to rain and sleet, and after about five minutes, I went back to him. But I had to walk. I didn't arrive till late in the evening. When my friend saw me, he said: 'Good God, what happened to you? We thought you had been run over. It would be just my luck—'

'"No," I said, "your luck was in this time. I nearly forgot you altogether."'

Then he stopped as if he had reached the point and expected us to laugh. But no one laughed. Frances, after a pause, said: 'How terrible for you. What did you do?'

Kathy and I wanted to ask so many questions that we could not begin. We did not dream of laughing. If Pinto himself had laughed, we might have laughed, but he told all these stories in a very serious manner, without even a smile.

Of course we were used to stories told by people against themselves. My father would tell how he had been welshed at the Derby or cheated by a trick out of a new hat, and we laughed heartily. Yet even these stories made me, as a small boy, feel uneasy. They gave me glimpses of a world full of treachery, which was something I feared. I don't know if all children fear and hate treachery; but any story of a betrayal both fascinated me and filled me with a deep alarm.

When Frances and Robert had broken the silence after Pinto's story, we all asked questions; I wanted to know if the people were saved after all from the bailiff. I imagined a bailiff as someone more dangerous and cruel than a gaoler. Kathy asked if their furniture had been sold. Pinto answered coolly that his friends had been sold up and he had never seen or heard of them since.

Suddenly Delia said something, I don't know what, and almost at once she and Pinto had an argument. Delia said that she did not consider the story amusing, and Pinto assured her that it was. He puffed his pipe, and looked at her straightly as if challenging her, and said: 'It's the funniest story I know – when I'm depressed it always cheers me up.'

'But you must be a perfect beast,' Delia said.

Frances cried out: 'Deely,' and we were shocked. But Pinto answered only in a meditative way: 'Yes, *damn* funny – one of the best chaps I ever knew, and his wife was an angel. Really an angel. And it wasn't his fault, you see. He'd lost his job at the engraving shop because of the new photographic process.'

'And you call that funny?'

'No, of course not. That's just an ordinary thing. No, the joke was that he expected me to save him – you should have seen their faces – and the wife trying to show me her gratitude. She simply couldn't express it – she was thinking of the children, of course. If you want to see gratitude, save a woman's home and children for her – but if you have no sense of humour, Miss Delia, I can't give you one.'

'I don't want your sense of humour, Mr Freeman.'

Pinto said nothing, but began to look very cheerful. He jumped up and asked Frances to make the tea. We all began to bustle. But our conversation at tea was subdued. Robert and Pinto talked together, and the rest of us hardly spoke.

When we were sailing home after tea, I asked Delia what happened to people who lost all their money. 'I suppose they go to the workhouse or starve,' she said.

She spoke angrily as if impatient of such people and their troubles. But her anger further depressed us. We sat with long faces, and Anketel began to fidget. It seemed to me that there was no sport in the world so monotonous and dull as sailing, and no prison like a small boat. My legs ached, my backside itched, my elbows were sore, I flung myself about and grumbled that we would never get home. Delia cheerfully agreed, and added with relish that her mother would have fits.

It was one of those summer evenings, common on the lough, when nearing sunset, the wind suddenly fell as if turned off. The evening became then as still as a room with no one in it, and the air had a dispersed luminosity which meant that there might soon be fog. The sky, too, which was usually a very pale blue, like skim milk, appeared to hold sunlight in solution. It was full of brightness, whereas the sun itself, as if drained, seemed like a moon, cold and dead, behind the thin banks of cloud. The sea would still be full of waves, but flattened and soft, as if melted. It had no sharp points or ridges, no white horses. Everywhere one saw rounded shapes appearing and disappearing in a slow lazy rhythm. The water seemed heavy and its lustre was greasy; the whole length appeared like cod liver oil gently agitated by some submarine disturbance.

In this glistening sea our light boat rolled about without steerage-way, so that the halliards knocked against the mast, the sail flapped, the jaws of the gaff creaked on the mast and the dipper rolled about on the gratings. These sounds seemed to me so inexpressibly dreary that I wanted to jump overboard.

Kathy suddenly began a long serious inquiry about the cost of living. She seemed to be arguing with some unseen challenger. 'You could get *quite* enough milk for three children for a shilling a day – and that's only seven shillings a week.'

This sum seemed to surprise her, for she added: '*Sixpence* a day would be enough if you got it from a farm – and potatoes are only a penny a pound and stirabout – how much is stirabout, Delia?'

'I don't know, but I shouldn't worry about Pinto's stories if I were you.'

We were silent feeling that Delia was evading the point. We didn't quite see what it was, but we felt it. Kathy said: 'And butter at eightpence a pound – salt butter. I like it salt.'

'These artists are always getting themselves into holes,' Delia said.

At this I felt much happier, and Kathy said: 'They're not practical, are they, Deely?'

'Besides, Pinto is a liar – a complete hopeless liar. I don't believe a word he says – I don't believe those people ever existed.'

'Why not, Deely?'

'Because Pinto is a liar.' She thrust out her round jaw and scratched herself furiously inside her leg. This was the sign of a reckless mood; for she never scratched herself unless she was feeling defiant and careless of everybody.

We, feeling this mood, kept on looking at her and Anketel, who had been sitting on the gratings closely examining the brass rowlock as it hung from its lanyard, suddenly got up, and, still looking back at the rowlock, threw one arm across her knees. The depression and fear were leaving us by themselves.

Delia suddenly began to hum and then to sing. She broke off suddenly to say: 'I tell you what I'd do – I'd go out in a top hat and say, "Pity the poor blind." '

'Why a top hat?' Kathy asked.

But to Anketel and me the top hat seemed very funny, and we began to laugh. Anketel said: 'I'd butter my shoes and fry on a new cap.'

This joke at once caught our fancy. Delia said: 'I'd eat the curling tongs and swallow my leader.'

Kathy gave a shriek of laughter and cried: 'But you couldn't, you couldn't.' Kathy never saw the point of a joke, but she enjoyed all jokes intensely by a kind of maternal sympathy.

'I'd toast down hill,' Delia said, 'on my new picycle and mutton to mother. Oh, venison, my bap is full of needles and pins.'

After this, we began to say any nonsense that came into our heads. We were seized with a crazy excitement; and laughed till we cried. All this excitement seemed to flow from Delia, and for some reason, we all wanted to touch her, as if to feel the source of our new confidence and happiness. Anketel put one arm round her neck; Kathy stroked her thick white arms which never browned; and I, who, having no sister, was shy of all women, and therefore apt either to be too silent or too rough with them, pulled out her pigtail and called her 'Miss Dumpy Deely.'

This name was supposed to be very annoying to Delia; but on this occasion, she paid no attention to my rudeness; she continued to smile, lazily, as if from pure enjoyment of herself. So I continued to pull at her hair and cry 'Dumpy – Dumpy – Dumpy' until my own voice had a hypnotic effect and I was using the word like a spell.

I had no idea of the meaning of Dumpy as applied to Delia. It was merely a name for her with which I expressed affection. Yet I knew quite well the meaning of the adjective dumpy. The two words existed in my brain, side by side, without connection; exactly as my own name, Evelyn, has always existed for me as a separate word with quite separate meaning from the ordinary girl's name, because mine is inherited, the name of part of my blood, and theirs is a label, put on from outside.

Dumpy could not mean for me any slight on Delia's figure; because she seemed to me beautiful. She was the most incomprehensible and dangerous of my cousins; for she could be the most delightful, the most affectionate and loyal; and also the rudest and most callous. For weeks she would pay no attention to any of us except her brother Robert. This neglect did not surprise or trouble us – we were used to this conduct in grown-ups – and especially in the half grown-ups. But Delia's sudden fits of brutality always disconcerted us.

Yet she was easily our favourite companion, above even Frances, who spoilt all children. The reason, I think now, was that she was more exciting, livelier than Frances. In my recollection, Delia seems like a being of the greatest dash, or rather of that indescribable quality which makes the possessor, of any age and both sexes, seem ten times more alive than anyone else in the neighbourhood. She was a dark brunette with eyes between violet and dark blue. Her eyebrows, black and strongly marked, were straight; or at least, they made a very gradual curve and even tilted up at the outer corners. Her skin was what is called white, that is, cream colour; but her cheeks were not colourless. There was always a little colour, brownish pink like a russet apple, high up near the eyes; and she flushed deeply, though very rarely.

Her figure was rather broad and strong; in the high-sleeved blouse of those days, her neck looked short. But it was as strong and round as a tree, and it carried her head superbly. She had magnificent shoulders and arms, rare in a young girl. She was probably mature for her age. Delia's charm, as I say, was in her quality of life. Even when she was sitting still, she had the air of intense activity within; of rapid and concentrated thought or vigorous feeling or both. At any time, when you looked at her face, you saw on it the impression of some feeling or purpose, which, in spite of the smooth forehead, the fresh dark lips, the soft full curves of cheek and chin, conveyed this idea of concentration.

Delia had been renowned for her wildness and mischief; she had ridden all the dangerous horses, climbed all the highest trees for miles around; she had smoked at fourteen, or younger, and gone out poaching, both fish and game, with a Dunvil boy called Willy Neil. She was still capable of anything, but she was now also the young lady, so that it was quite common to see her filthy and tousled in bare legs and a torn frock, covered with fish scales, asking anxiously if her new dress had come from Miss Austin's, or complaining that she had nothing fit to wear. She was either out on the tuns, fishing for brazers, or scrambling over the bogs with us children; or else she was going out to some tea-party, in a flutter because it threatened rain and there was nothing but the outside car to take her. She threw just as much feeling into an engagement to meet three or four ladies to discuss the church bazaar as into a sailing race, in half a gale of wind. Perhaps a dance caused her more excitement than either. I remember Delia, on the day before a dance, a real dance at which some of the garrison soldiers were to be present, in a condition that resembled a walking catalepsy. Her mother reproached her for not sleeping on the night before, nor eating anything on the day; and this perhaps attracted my notice. A small boy does not usually notice for himself slight alterations of look or conduct even in a much-loved cousin of sixteen. But I noticed her then with close attention, for I remember still a vision of her passing along a corridor in her underclothes, with two long pigtails of hair down her back, to have it dressed, I suppose, by Aunt Hersey's maid, and her dream-struck motions, her pallor, the fixed unseeing gaze of her eyes, her whole look of intense nervous expectation stand before me now like a transparency. She looked like a Juliet about to say the words:

Speed thy close curtain, love performing night.

Yet all this was because an ambitious distiller's wife was giving a cinderella dance and invited, in order to countenance her own daughter of sixteen, some other girls not yet officially out. But if hostesses knew what pleasure and excitement they can give to the young by the simplest arrangements, I am sure there would be more parties.

Delia came back from all her dances calm, triumphant with happiness and completely disordered; her hair down, her frock torn and holes in her stockings. She danced everything, and when she could not find a partner, she danced with herself. At one dance, I saw her dancing in the back passage with the butler. After a dance, she always complained that her partners had had nothing to say, that they were fearful bores; or fearfully stupid. Fearfully stupid meant usually that they had tried to kiss her, and according to Frances, fearful bores meant that they had not tried to kiss her. But I believed Delia's contemptuous refutation of this charge because Delia had never been a flirt, and Frances had always flirted. She could flirt even with me when we were alone together; she flirted with her mother and uncle; and I have seen her flirting with herself in a looking-glass. Like most flirts, she had a gentle temper and a most friendly spirit, but there was nothing electric about her, like Delia. It was this secret fountain of power which made us now cluster round Delia, and touch her arms, her neck, her thick black pig-tail, as round some earth mother, from whom, by mere contact, life pours exciting waves of delight and faith.

The mist had thinned and we were floating as it were in the sky; among luminous haze in which the sun was still obscured; warmer than before; but without sharp edges. It was only a centre of special radiance in the general brightness, like a concentration of it. When now and then in the air a movement, which seemed like a current of this bright haze, suddenly puffed at the sail, making the halliards slat, the shrouds crack, causing the sheet-block to rattle on the gunwale as it tripped over it, and the sheet to grate on the wood; exactly the same noises came from the unseen castle boat, somewhere in the mist, and we would hear Frances' or Pinto's voice repeat like an echo of Delia's: 'Here it comes—'

For some reason this made us laugh again. We sang out: 'Here it comes.' Then we heard again Frances' voice, small and hollow in the mist, saying: 'It's some of Deeley's nonsense.'

This made us shout with laughter, and Delia herself was seized with the infection. Every time she tried to say something, she laughed, helplessly; tearfully.

'Frankie is—' she said, and broke down; and we, thinking that we knew what she meant, that we saw something exquisitely funny in Frances' assumption of a grown-up critical tone to Delia, were seized with another fit of laughter.

The breeze suddenly stiffened; Delia, who had been steering with her bare feet on the tiller while she held Anketel, put the child down; the haze became darker, greyer; and then suddenly rolled up in front of us like a white carpet. In a moment we were flying over a gay sparkling sea in which every brisk wave was tipped with cool flames. But we were surprised to find ourselves still on the wrong side of the lough. Dunamara was below the horizon. We did not reach the creek until nine o'clock.

By then we children were so exhausted by laughter, sun and hunger, that we hardly understood common speech or knew where to put our feet. We stood dazed in the sudden enclosure of the hall under the pale face of the barometer, and still smiling, though our uncle was in a rage; and Aunt Hersey twittering in distress. Furious exchanges took place between Robert and Delia while we still grinned like foreigners at a Chinese play. Anketel, sound asleep for the last hour, and dripping salt water, had already been snatched away to bed. We staggered towards the kitchen and supper. Even there I tried to make another joke, on the lines of buttering my shoes, to revive our intoxication.

So far were we from understanding what was afoot in a normal world that we were astonished, next day, to hear that Delia was in disgrace, and that we should not again see Pinto. When we protested, we were told that we were lucky to be rid of him; he was a swindler and a rascal and so on.

It was not for a long time afterwards that I discovered the facts. Pinto, it seemed, in applying for the post of tutor, had not sent in his original references, but a copy; and from this he had left out the last paragraph saying that the writer could not guarantee the tutor's sobriety, as he had had no occasion, in this employment, to test it.

My uncle maintained that this paragraph was the key to the testimonial, for according to the necessary rules governing that kind of composition, the mention of any quality, without an express statement that it is possessed by the subject, means that it is conspicuously lacking. 'How else,' he asked, 'could testimonials be written?'

According to Pinto, he had left out the paragraph because it was unnecessary; because he could not be bothered to copy the whole thing; and also because he didn't notice it. All these may have been true. Finally it should be said that my uncle did not discover the omission by himself. He had simply, in his anger at being kept late for dinner, suddenly accused Pinto of incompetence and drunkenness and said that he was going to look into his references. Pinto then confessed that the original had this other clause in it; and at once resigned his post.

Robert was heart-broken; and Frances, to our surprise, also took Pinto's part. She said that we had committed a small-minded and stupid action, for which we ought to be punished. Aunt Hersey, moved by these words, passed some unhappy days trying to soothe her conscience and adjust a compromise between Delia, Frances and Herbert. This, of course, was impossible. Three more different kinds of people never existed in the same house. Robert had not forgiven either Delia or his mother when he went to school.

CHAPTER 13

We too missed Pinto, noticing his disappearance – not as a loss but an absence. It was only now and then in our busy life that one or other of us, wanting to tell something to somebody, noticed that Pinto was not available, and said: 'What a pity Pinto isn't here.'

After he left us, it seems to my recollection that we did nothing but wander among the rocks on the shore below Dunamara, looking for wreckage, and hunting crabs under the weeds. We were pitied for going to Dunamara that year instead of to some sandy beach with our grandmother. But already we loved Dunamara with a particular affection, so that the rocks themselves, with their great iron rings, split by rust until they showed a grain like rotten wood, old embedded crowbars, the derelict lobster pots and fish crates, the long clefts filled with anemones and fish like darning needles, charmed us. Other cousins coming to see us thought that we were a melancholy crew prowling each by himself along this broken shore, with muddy legs and rusty hands, dragging some piece of iron or old ship's timber along with us; but we would not have changed places with them on their bathing beaches. For we set a special value on our shore, as a place fit for explorers and hunters.

'It's a *wild* place,' Harry would say. 'You might find anything any day.'

When the tide was in and the water rose up the breakwater to within a foot of the lawn, we delighted in the idea, also I suspect from Pinto, that the house was an ark, floating in a stone boat, and boasted that we could fish out of our schoolroom window. This was not quite true. The lawn was too wide. But it was true, as Harry told our grandmother, that the house was full of waves. Either Pinto or my father had called Dunamara the mermaid's tavern, and shown me those waves which I had seen all my life and noticed often and never known. When the tide was up and the sun or moon shining, especially at a spring tide, the long white front of the house was in movement with reflected waves. The walls rippled with hollow curves of pigeon grey and palest yellow, a ghostly sea, which, on the tall twelve-pane windows, became so solid in colour and form, gold and blue, that one seemed to be looking through the glass at actual water. The house seemed to be full of sea; until, of course, one turned round and saw the real sea so miraculously real in its metal weight and powerful motion, its burning brightness, that it startled. One gazed at it with astonishment as if one had never before seen such an extraordinary and glorious object.

I must have turned myself hundreds of times to catch the sea in its realness. I suppose I had the same feeling about it as Anketel expressed one day, when, paddling, he stood for a long time trying to lift some water on his foot.

Kathy, who was always ready to instruct any of us, called out: 'You don't think water will stick up there, do you?'

'No,' Anketel said in a thoughtful voice, still gazing at his wet feet in the air, 'I was only feeling at it.'

I was thirty years older before I appreciated the force of the 'at'. Anketel was a small, thin little boy with very fair hair and large blue eyes, the sort of child women loved to kiss. Indeed, his sister Kathy was always mothering him, and both Delia and Frances used to pet him and spoil him. To all he submitted with the same patience, but being released, at once ran off on some urgent private affair. He was always occupied and always in a private manner upon some plan or investigation of his own. He never played with toys, but he had secret treasures hidden everywhere; pieces of stone, old bottles, rags of cloth knotted in a peculiar manner, bits of scribbled paper, loose nails, pebbles in a matchbox. All had some deep significance for him alone. He was busily engaged from morning to night selecting from the world about him materials for some private construction, and I suppose these hoarded treasures were some of them scientific specimens and some talismans or charms to invoke powers. But his ideas were too large for communication. Delia coming home one day from some visit saw Anketel running across the drive with a bottle in his hand. She rushed after him, and Anketel increased his own speed. But Delia, of course, soon caught him, lifted him up, kissed him. Anketel submitted with his usual calmness, limp as a puppy in its mother's mouth. Then Delia, impatient to get closer to him, said: 'What a nice bottle, An. What is it for?'

The bottle was full of a thin mud from the shore, mixed with tap water. Anketel said: 'It's brown-ade, and when it's dry it will be a skemeton.'

'You mean a skeleton.'

'No, because it's hollow.' Then he wriggled free, ran off, and disappeared into some corner of the stables. We laughed at Anketel and thought his remarks funny as well as original. 'He's always in the air,' we said when he did not hear, or pretended not to hear, our calls. But he was no more in the air than Harry, who having unburied two old fish boxes, was trying to build a Spanish galleon out of them; or I, when, having discovered the trick by accident, I turned round quickly to make the sea look real. We were all constructing a private and ideal world for ourselves, out of such material as came our way, Pinto's quips and cranks, my father's stories, Philip's tricks, remarks overheard in the kitchen, in the road, things even that we did not know we had heard or seen. So when I had noticed particularly the waves on the wall and felt their beauty, I looked for them and soon missed them. On a sunless day I would go, without thinking, up to a wall and touch it, hoping that some mark on the paper would move and turn into a wave.

Dunamara in my idea of it was no longer complete without its waves. It was both a richer possession to me and more likely to disappoint. But usually it had waves. Waves ran even on the inner walls of the house, reflected from window-panes and looking-glasses. They waltzed across the pages of our nursery books. If we raised our eyes to the ceiling during the day, we saw little whirlpools, like those left in water by an oar, but made of pale yellow light, revolving silently in a corner or moving slowly from one wall to another. I slept in a room with waves on the ceiling; at night, sometimes, when I opened my eyes, the whole top of the room opposite the windows was flowing with a web of pearl-white ripples and their shadowy hollows like moon-spots. This silent motion, quivering not in regular lines but in a loose net, and everywhere at once, kept the same bar time, though far quicker, like demi-semi-quavers to crochets, as the waves outside falling with a lazy cool splash on the breakwater. It was a noise at once sleepy in its monotony and fresh in its unexpected suddenness. It carried me towards sleep, but held me listening in a waking dream which was full of the sense that here I was at Dunamara. But I did not know that sense for happiness but only opportunity, so that my last thought would be 'I hope it's fine tomorrow.' It seemed to me that I couldn't afford to waste an hour or a wave.

CHAPTER 14

Though Frances had told us that Pinto would go to ruin and that his destruction would lie at our door, he got almost at once a much better job. He became tutor to the only son of some people called Maylin at their place ten miles south of Dunvil. The Maylins were rich and good-natured. They were both fat and red-faced and rheumatic. They gave very fine parties, especially at Christmas, when the little husband would push his wife, in a wheel-chair, through the lower rooms, and guests would go up to talk to her. She, however, would do all the talking, uttering cries of laughter like a parrakeet, and waving her crutch to warn you that she had still something to say, when she had finished laughing.

The Maylin Christmas party was four parties in one. It started at four with babies, went on with children till seven or eight; then the young people danced till eleven, and, finally, there was a ball till morning. But some of the young girls stayed for the first half of the ball. I've heard that the Maylins followed this plan to get all their winter hospitality into one day. They themselves did not appear except once at each party. They even dined by themselves and went to bed during the ball.

The Jubilee Christmas was the first Harry and I had spent in Ireland for some years. We went to half a dozen parties, but no vestige of any of them remains to me except a drive in the snow, when the car took the ditch because the skid would not hold the road; and the Maylin party. That, I believe, has been preserved by pure anticipation. Both Harry and I looked forward to it with such intense expectation that we could not sleep. Yet we both knew what parties were like, and though we enjoyed them, we preferred, on the whole, some expedition or hunt. We knew also what happened at parties; games and dances and that nothing else could happen at the Maylins'; but we discussed for three days what would happen there.

'I wonder what we'll do at the Maylins'?'

'I suppose there'll be games.'

Then both of us, taken aback by the small reach of our own imagination, would ponder a moment and Harry would say: 'And dances, of course.'

'Oh, yes, Roger de Coverley.'

Again we were dashed. Yet we both agreed that the Maylins' would be a wonderful party. All our expectation, that life held new delights for us round every corner, was fixed on the Maylin party.

Part of our excitement, no doubt, arose from the fact that we were going without Robert, the four of us alone in the first carriage. Robert refused to go. He said he hated parties. Robert, as we knew afterwards, had started badly at school by making a public fool of himself. He had tried to follow Cousin Philip's advice. But he told no one, not even his mother or Delia, about this catastrophe. He showed the effects only by his quietness, his sudden love of being alone, and sometimes a perplexed, absent-minded look when anyone spoke to him, as if he could not understand ordinary meanings.

Robert was out of our lives, and Harry was our senior. But this promotion could not explain Kathy's or my or Anketel's excitement.

We were asked to the first, the youngest children's party, for though Harry was already a boarder at school, as senior in charge, he was sent with me, and I was sent with Anketel. I don't know why Kathy was not put in charge of Anketel, but there was a legend even among grown-ups that Anketel preferred any other to take care of him.

We were silent in the carriage, too excited to speak. Only once Harry gave a deep sigh and said: 'They've got two hundred people coming – with grown-ups.'

Silent and oppressed we were led through a large hall into the cloak-room, and then I found myself in a small parlour full of books, with twenty or thirty other children, who stood round the walls with faces so grave and anxious that one would have thought they had all committed some crime. I have seen the same expression in criminals about to be charged, and in a very warm-hearted girl just about to be married. Nervous tension, the feeling of an important crisis, produced the same oppressed gravity in both. While we stood gazing at each other, Harry, who had waited while Kathy found a hook to button her shoes, walked slowly in, and with the same serious face, stopped for a moment, stared round at us, and then went directly to a corner of the bookshelf, from which he pulled out a dictionary. There was a copy, at Dunamara, of the same dictionary which Harry had been reading that afternoon. Harry's first term at a private school seemed to have had no special effect on him, except to give him a passion for encyclopædias and dictionaries.

He sat down on a chair in a corner and began reading the dictionary, as if he had come for no other purpose.

Harry spent almost the whole time of the party reading this dictionary. Afterwards going home in the carriage he asked me to notice the frosforescence of the lough. I asked him what frosforescence was and he said: 'It's cold and bright. It's due to little jellyfish.'

He spoke this with the voice of a mystic contemplating wonders. Harry had enjoyed himself. But when he sat down with the dictionary I was left standing against the wall, holding Anketel's hand in such painful shyness that I did not know where to look. Yet I was still overwhelmed by the thought: 'This is the Maylins' party.'

Some grown-up girls now came in and set the children to play oranges and lemons and hunt the slipper. They were experienced girls, elder sisters, and they simply pushed or carried the guests to their allotted places, dumped them on the floor or joined their senseless hands, and then propelled them through the movements of the game. In hunt the slipper four of these grown-ups, sitting like giants in the circle, had the game to themselves, three laughing and throwing the slipper to each other while a fourth chased it; and the small children, the smallest present, sat and gazed at them with awe.

One girl called to another: 'None of them are actually crying,' and another answered in the same tone of hilarious congratulation, which struck upon our ears as assumed and special to the occasion: 'Yes, we're doing rather well.'

Anketel completed my embarrassment by refusing to join any game. As soon as he was invited to hunt the slipper he flew to a chair, climbed upon it, turned himself round and sat down with the air of taking a place for the evening.

I was in terror that some grown-up would attempt to drag him into the game, in case he might fight or scream and I should be disgraced. I begged him to play, but he shook his head firmly.

'Didn't you want to come to the party?'

He nodded.

'But playing is what you do at a party.'

Two grown-up girls joined us and pleaded with him. 'You won't have to do anything – just sit on the floor and pretend you're playing.'

'They won't give *you* the slipper, will they?' I appealed to the girls, who at once promised Anketel complete freedom from responsibility.

Anketel had turned very pale, but he still shook his head. Then suddenly he got off the chair and rushed out of the room. I dutifully followed, but, finding a dance in the next room, was seized and set dancing with a girl who wanted a partner. We did not speak, and as I did not know even what the dance was, we trod on each other's toes. Suddenly Kathy rescued me and made me dance with her, teaching me how to polka. I would have resented having to dance with my cousin Kathy if it had not been at the Maylins' party. It was the fashion to resent everything Kathy did or said to us, to say that she was bossy and selfish. In fact, she was a sensible child, who was always getting us out of trouble, inventing lies for us, smuggling away wet, torn or dirty clothes when we fell out of trees or into the muddy river; or interceding for us with Uncle Herbert, who had a weakness for little girls.

Also she was affectionate and longed for affection. Her father was dead, her mother had married again and had other children. I think Kathy was unhappy at home and looked forward all the year to holidays with us. On the first day of meeting us, she would flush deeply and run up to us as if to kiss us, then check herself and take our hands. We could see that she was almost crying with delight, with relief; her mouth would shake and tears come into her lashes. She would say: '*Isn't* it lovely? Isn't it *lovely*?'

Then Harry would answer, calmly: '*What's* lovely, do you mean the weather?' or I would say carelessly: 'Hullo, Kathy.' I don't know when this fashion to snub Kathy began. She was not ugly. She had very pretty dark brown eyes and bronze hair, even thicker than Frances'. Her voice was hard, but nearly all girls of that age have hard voices. She could play all games with us and even throw a ball, quite as well as I. But because she needed our affection and sought it, we treated her always like an intruder. Perhaps like small animals, our instinct was to pursue only the female who ran away from us, and Kathy, in showing us her affection, was breaking some rule of nature, as cruel and stupid as most of her sexual arrangements.

When Kathy was pursued she could be loved. At Crowcliff the year before Cousin Tom Foley, who was nearly fourteen, had fallen in love with Kathy, and at once Harry had been furiously jealous. He had claimed Kathy, and there had been several fights in which Harry would have been defeated if Kathy herself had not taken his part. I, too, had been in love with Kathy for an hour or two, during a wet picnic, when Harry was away with measles. But since then we had both treated her with consistent brutality. It had been the idea to crush Kathy in every possible way. We even boasted of a successful snub.

At nine Kathy had already a horizontal wrinkle of perplexity between her eyebrows. She looked at us often with blank wonder, asking herself no doubt what crime she had committed, and how she could discover it and make up for it without offending us further. We, feeling her perplexity on such occasions, always looked still more calm and indifferent.

CHAPTER 15

But on this evening, at the Maylins, because I had forgotten the ideas which governed our schoolroom at Dunamara, I was delighted to see Kathy and showed it. My real feeling for Kathy, which was like a brother's, something deeper than affection, instinctive and primitive, was allowed to show itself in the frank relief and satisfaction with which I grasped her hand and cried: 'What are they doing, Kathy? It isn't anything I know, is it?'

Kathy, as usual, blushed to her eyes in pleasure of this warmth of greeting and began at once, with anxious and responsible care, to teach me the steps while I was as polite and deferential

with her as if she had been another of the strange girls who, in
puffed silk sleeves and frilled and tucked frocks, soberly danced
or conversed round me, frowning over their partner's shoulders
with looks of preoccupation and anxiety. They, too, were using
every moment of the party.

I danced with Kathy for a long time and thanked her effusively
for teaching me the steps. Afterwards we went through a lancers
together where all the girls, with shrill angry voices, cried out
instructions to their partners, and thrusting them furiously away
at the end of each figure, shouted: 'Grand chain – do think what
you're doing.'

All of us were instructors or pupils; one saw nothing but
humble-looking boys carefully performing awkward motions
and little girls beckoning at them or blushing for them. At the
end of the dance loud angry discussions broke out about who
had spoilt what figure and who had torn somebody's frock. The
loud voices and frowning faces and angry gestures were those of
a fight. Yet when someone proposed another set we clapped and
cried out in chorus: 'Please, please.' All faces were full of
eagerness, as if for a treat. We wanted it all again, anxieties,
reproaches, instruction. I suppose we felt that this was life, that
we were finding out how to do it; and that the finding out was
itself engrossing. We had not come to the party for pleasure, but
to be engrossed.

Some time during these dances I fell in love with Kathy – I
kept on looking at her and laughing with pleasure. She seemed
to me charming, kind; the nicest girl I have ever met. I began to
prance round her as I used to jump aimlessly round my father's
legs, running into him. Kathy was gravely delighted. At nine she
was far more mature than I, and I dare say her feelings were
deeper and stronger. She kept on restraining my wild leaps,
smiling in an embarrassed way, and saying: 'You must dance
the steps.' But her voice was full of apology, and when the dance
was over we walked into the passage with our arms round each
other's waists and agreed we would never love anyone else.
Kathy kept saying: 'But do you really want to marry me?' and
every time I assured her she sighed deeply and murmured: 'Oh,
dear, isn't it lovely here – isn't it a lovely party? It's the loveliest
day of my life.' We even kissed each other, and I could see that
this meant a great deal to Kathy; it was a pledge.

CHAPTER 16

After tea, of course, all our decorum, our sense of an important occasion, vanished. I had sat next Kathy at tea and we had even held hands, feeding ourselves with the other; but suddenly I jumped down and darted away from her, with a tribe of boys. Drunk with sugar cake and sweets, wearing paper caps, we flew through the rooms yelling, often revolving on our axes, pirouetting because we knew we would soon reach the end of the rooms, and be obliged to turn back.

Now again, in this riot, I came upon Anketel, being implored by two ladies to come to tea. I saw that he was nearly in tears, so I said to them hastily: 'It's no good – he never does anything you ask him – he's my brother, so I know he won't.'

I called Anketel my brother instead of my cousin to make them believe me. They did believe me and went away. I also flew away, leaving Anketel in the ante-room. At some time later when I rushed through the hall to find a partner for Roger de Coverley, I saw him sitting there, on a hard wood hall chair, in the big cold marble-paved room, completely alone. But I pretended not to see him. I had indeed already invented a lie for Frances, that Anketel had run away from me. I knew that Anketel would not contradict me, since, in his silent way, he was extremely loyal to us all. I was already at ease in my mind.

The sequel next day was unexpected. Anketel told Frances that I had been very kind to him and that he had loved the party. What's more, it seemed that he had enjoyed himself. For weeks afterwards he played at parties, by himself; a game which consisted in moving round in circles, and uttering a murmuring noise, broken now and then by sharp, loud cries.

CHAPTER 17

I myself, now free from responsibility, and, as I say, partly drunk, danced a Roger de Coverley, in which several children were battered into tears. We leaped together, stamped our feet, and when the time came to pass under the hands of the top couple, ran our heads against the behinds of the couple in front, and tried to push them down.

I was especially excited to recognise Kathy in the line of girls opposite me, two or three down. She was not drunk. She had been too busy at tea, giving me the best cakes, to eat much herself. She kept looking at me with a perplexed, mournful expression, and these looks caused me explosions of laughter, not malicious, but purely drunken. Indeed, I felt guilty towards Kathy, but my guilt, like all my other reactions, passed at once into wild leaps and shouts of laughter; into a desire for violence. Our dance grew into a war dance. Some of the girls, except the older ones like Kathy, were rougher than the boys. My partner, a fat creature with a red doll-like face, shrieked like an engine whistle, and then, uttering an insane laugh, with protruded stomach and arms held back, rushed against me and bumped into me so violently that I nearly fell. But I got the idea and I also began to bump my stomach against my neighbour's. All of us danced the whole time with our own steps. Even when I stood in the line, watching the end boy and the end girl preparing their *pas de deux* between the lines, I jumped up and down, yelled, and hopped in complete circles, turning my back on the rest. All of us were trying to make as much noise and turmoil as possible, because the noise, as we had discovered, and the wildness of our own kicks and prances, were themselves exciting.

It was during one of these stimulating performances, if not of Roger de Coverley then of some other tribal dance, that a red-cheeked boy, I think he was the brother of my former partner, the Dutch doll, suddenly said to me: 'I say, this is rather dull, isn't it? – jumping about with a lot of kids, it's silly.'

I was in the act of jumping myself round, on both feet, in fits of laughter; and the red-cheeked boy had been one of the noisiest of the party; but the moment he spoke to me in this critical and superior tone, a rapid change began to take place in my mood. It was not instantaneous, because I was never very quick to catch a new suggestion; a change of social atmosphere. I stared at him in open-mouthed surprise for some seconds. But during all this time the change, which may be described as a kind of crystallisation in the chaotic whirl of my brain, was in rapid progress. Fortunately, as it struck me afterwards, I did not say anything at once, I did not blurt out that I was enjoying myself. It was not till the crystallisation was finished, and I had a clear, sharp-edged knowledge, both feeling and idea, of the new situation, that I answered. I stopped jumping about, screwed my face in an expression similar to the red-cheeked boy's, and said: 'Yes, but it always is at the Maylins', isn't it?'

As I said, I had never been to the Maylins' party before. But the red-cheeked boy accepted my statement with respect. He put his hands in his pockets and said: 'Why do they always expect us to hop about with kids in frocks?'

'It's silly, isn't it?'

'I can't stand parties.'

'Neither can I.'

'Let's clear off and do something sensible.'

'I've been wanting to do that for a long time.'

We had already withdrawn from the laughing, jumping crowd, and now when my partner rushed up to me and began shrieking at me and trying to tell me what to do, I shook myself free and walked off with a scornful air. I felt all at once contemptuous of the games going on round me; the music; the paper caps, the yelling and romping children; I began even to feel that I had been a victim, and that I had been obliged to dance and play against my will.

'What shall we do?' the red-cheeked boy asked me. Obviously, he did not know what to do. For some time, in fact, we simply wandered about with our hands in our pockets. At last even I noticed that we were rather bored. Yet we still felt superior to the other children for amusing themselves with childish games, and kept on criticising their idea of amusement and the party. I remember standing watching some uproarious game of puss-in-the-corner, from a doorway, and feeling the most intense longing to shout advice to the corners, and even to rush in and join the game; yet I am sure my face was still fixed in a calm and aloof scorn and my voice still drawled: 'Silly, aren't they?'

'They don't even play it properly,' the other said, moved, I suppose, by my own temptation to give instructions and catch puss on his own account. We lounged there for a long time, envying and despising the happy players. It was as though some command had forbidden us to enjoy childish games, and this, I suppose, is the actual fact. For even though it operated upon me by means of an idea presented by the red-cheeked boy, that idea found in me an instant response. Something in me, unnoticed till that moment, was waiting for just such an idea to give it form and action.

CHAPTER 18

I don't mean that nature or some mysterious power ended my childhood at eight years old. I don't know when my childhood ended or if it is all ended now. The only certain distinction I can find between childhood and maturity is that children grow in experience and look forward to novelty; that old people tend to be set. This does not mean even that children enjoy life more keenly than grown-ups, they are only more eager for experience. Grown-ups live and love, they suffer and enjoy far more intensely than children; but for the most part, on a narrower front. For the average man or woman of forty, however successful, has been so battered and crippled by various accidents that he has gradually been restricted to a small compass of enterprise. Above all, he is perplexed. He has found out numerous holes and inconsistencies in his plan of life and yet he has no time to begin the vast work of making a new one. He is like a traveller who, when he has reached the most dangerous part of his journey among deep swamps and unknown savages, discovers all at once that his map is wrong, his compass broken, his ammunition damp, his rifle crooked, and his supplies running short. He must push on at high speed, blindly, or fail altogether and fail his companions. I think that is the reason for the special sadness of nearly all grown-up faces, certainly of all those which you respect; you read in their lines of repose, the sense that there is no time to begin again, to get things right. The greater a grown man's power of enjoyment, the stronger his faith, the deeper and more continuous his feeling of the waste of life, of happiness, of youth and love, of himself.

But for children life seems endless, and they do not know a grief that has no cure.

CHAPTER 19

I didn't stop being a hopeful and foolish child because the red-cheeked boy taught me suddenly that dancing with little girls in short frocks and getting drunk on sugar cakes were unworthy of my age. But I was drawn aside for a moment from the stream of childish sensation. I saw it in front of me, and felt it; but only to feel also my separation from it.

Unluckily the power which had thrust us out of the party had not given us any indication of what we should do next. It simply cut us free and left us to choose our own inventions. The red-cheeked boy began to talk to me in a grown-up superior manner. He told me that his grandpapa was eating himself to death. That's what Doctor told him, but he wouldn't stop. 'If you tell him to stop, he cries – he's a fearful old baby.'

'Really cries?' I didn't believe this.

'Yes, he cries and says he wishes he was dead.'

'Really and truly?' Again I found this hard to believe.

'Swear. And Grandmamma says she wishes he was, too – but she's quite as bad – she takes four lumps of sugar in her tea, and the doctor says she's poisoning herself, but *she* says she doesn't care.'

He told me several more stories of the same kind about his grandparents, saying that they quarrelled all the time. 'Until Rose says she wishes she was dead, too.'

'No,' I said. I contemplated these three people who wished themselves dead with amazement; as if I had never before observed grown-ups from the outside.

'Of course, everyone knows.'

'But who is it?'

'Who is what?'

'Who wants to be dead?'

'Rose is my cousin. You know Rose. She was playing the piano.'

'Rose Maylin?'

'Of course, that's her *name*.'

I was amazed to realise that he had been talking about the Maylins. However, since he had got influence over me by giving me a new and superior idea, I believed him at once and exclaimed: 'Not really.'

'Swear. I say, you don't know this house, do you?'

'Oh, of course I know it, but not all the rooms.'

'Ever been on the roof?'

'Not exactly on the roof – but I know what it looks like.'

'All right, shall we go on the roof?'

'Yes, that is a good idea.'

He promptly led me outside, into the dark, and guided me through a stable yard to a ladder. 'They've been mending the roof,' he said, 'I went up this afternoon, but they stopped me.'

I was terrified at the sight of the long ladder extending upwards into the dark shadow of the house. There was no light except from a half-moon, the windows of the kitchen and the lower story. It was not only dark, but very cold. I was in a thin shirt and silk knickers and already shivering. But the shiver of cold somehow reduced my terror to a kind of helpless obedience. I followed my leader up the ladder and, though I clung to the sides with both hands, lay flat against the rungs, so that I had to lift my knees sideways like a frog, and drew up both feet before making another step upwards, I did at last reach the top.

I found now that the house had flat leads all round the parapets, in which snow was still lying, though it had not snowed for some days. I stepped directly into this snow and soaked my pumps and stockings. But I was greatly relieved to find anything firm to stand on, and a parapet between me and the yard below. My leader now lost his calm air for a moment and said: 'I say, you weren't afraid, were you?'

'Of course not.'

'I was – I never went up a ladder before – not a loose ladder. Why, we might have been smashed to bits. Didn't you think of that?'

'No, not really.' I was going to use this advantage over the red-cheeked boy.

'Well, I did. I nearly came up through the attic window – that's the real way up.'

'Oh, but I'm glad we didn't come up that way.'

'So am I – though I don't know about going down. Are you very keen on going down by the ladder?'

'I don't mind. Of course, we have done it once. Which is the attic window?'

'Any one will do – especially if there's a light. That shows one of the girls is inside and you just knock. They always let you through. They're very decent, the girls here.'

'That would be a change, going through a window.'

'Weren't you the least bit frightened?' he appealed to me.

For some reason this appeal caused me to admit that I had been a little bit frightened.

'Only a bit?'

'Well, a good bit – really a lot in places.'

Whatever had prompted me to make this confession, I was rewarded at once by a more friendly feeling towards the red-cheeked boy. In a moment we became devoted friends. He pressed up against me, took my arm and said again: 'I say, aren't you glad you came? Isn't it simply grand? This is better than a kids' party.'

I felt that it was grand and I despised the party.

Red Cheeks, still clutching my arm, put his face close to mine so that I felt his warm breath, and exclaimed: 'It's terrific, isn't it?'

'Absolutely terrific.'

'All alone up here.'

'Nobody knows where we are.'

'We might fall off – one false step and we'd be smashed to bits.'

'It's grand.'

We were now very much excited by the sense of grandeur and went on for some time telling each other how splendid we felt. Then there was a pause, and afterwards the red-cheeked boy began to show the sights. He took me up a short ladder across the slates to show me the drift in the valley between the roofs, led me along the parapets to point out where different chimneys came up, the kitchen chimney, the dining-room chimney, and so on; and explained which of the roofs below in the yard covered the coal bin and which was the potato house.

Finally he made me look at the stars and the moon and said in the tone of a connoisseur showing off his masterpieces: 'Rather grand, aren't they?'

'Oh, yes, they're lovely.'

'So bright.'

'Oh, yes, you could almost read.'

'Can you see the mountains on the moon?'

'Yes, of course.'

'Not on the edge, you know – they're in the top corner on the flat side – that dark place.'

'Yes, volcanoes.'

'That's it – extinct volcanoes.'

He gave me a little lecture on the moon, most of which I had heard before; and in fact, even I could see that he was playing for time; that he didn't know how to use our tremendous adventure. At once I felt the same anxiety.

'It's grand,' he cried. 'Isn't it?'

'Oh, yes.'

'You're not cold, are you?'

'Not a bit – not really.'

'We don't want to go back yet, do we, to that silly party?'

'No, of course not,' and I felt sincerely that it would be an anti-climax to go back to the party.

He reflected a moment and then hung over the parapet again. 'I wonder did anyone see us.'

'They couldn't.'

'They might have – they would have been rather surprised, I should think.'

Suddenly he let out a yell and instantly took cover behind the parapet. I also took cover and asked him indignantly: 'What did you do that for?'

He made no answer, but jumped up. We looked over again. No one had heard the yell.

'You'd think they were all asleep,' he said in a disgusted tone.

'They're not noticing —'

'Let's try together,' and we yelled together. We continued yelling for several minutes, but without effect. We stared down into the yard and Red Cheeks said: 'You'd think they were dead.'

Again we reflected. Red Cheeks looked up at the stars once more as if thinking that perhaps he might yet do something with the scenery; and then at the woods. But just when I expected him to say how pretty they looked, and was making ready to enter into this plan also, his eye fell on the chimney-pots and he exclaimed: 'I tell you what – let's drop some snow down the chimney.'

My enthusiasm prepared for natural beauty at once became

enthusiastic for dropping snow down the chimney. We shovelled up the wet snow, made snowballs, carried them up a short iron ladder at the back of the chimney-stack and threw them down the chimney-pot. Then we both rushed to the parapet and gazed into the yard, waiting for cries of protest or wonder. But nothing happened.

'I know what it is,' said Red Cheeks, 'they're larking with the drivers. Grandpapa has a barrel of porter for the drivers in the back hall – I bet the kitchen girls are there, too.'

My leader's voice expressed the warmest indignation, as if the absence of the kitchen staff from the kitchen were an offence against himself. I began to feel this too when, after both of us had thrown down more snowballs, large and heavy ones, we hung over the parapet and heard nothing from below but laughter, music and the clatter of plates from the dining-room where supper was laying for the grown-up dance. We were now soaked to the skin, and in spite of our sense of triumph and glory, we noticed it. I was aching with cold, and though this hardship added to my sense of achievement, it also increased my feeling of indignation with the maids, and indeed with the whole world, which went on amusing itself and denying the least notice to our great efforts.

'Dash them all,' my leader said, 'I know they're drinking porter – I only wish Rose would catch them.'

I suggested that we hadn't thrown enough snow, but Red Cheeks said gloomily that snow was no good, it must have stuck in the bend of the chimney.

'If only we had a brick,' I said, 'or a firework.'

'It isn't Guy Fawkes' day,' he said gravely.

'Even a bucket of water.'

'We could get some water – there's a tap on the cistern, and I think there's a bucket on the landing.'

We climbed in at a maid's attic window and found a house-maid's empty bucket and some hot water cans in a closet at the top of the stairs. There was a tap in the closet, but we found that the bucket, filled, was too heavy for us. So we carried it to the roof, up the iron ladder, balanced it next the chimney-pot, a low one, and laboriously filled it with the cans. The whole operation took perhaps twenty minutes, and was carried out with the enthusiasm of crusaders preparing for a holy war. Finally, both of us together, tottering on the ladder, managed to tilt the bucket over the pot and empty it down the chimney. The result was even better than we had expected. Shrill prolonged shrieks broke out below; there were sounds of windows opening, feet running and men shouting. The music stopped, except one piano which went on the whole time, and the children's voices sank to a kind of tinkle. We even heard some child crying out for its mama. A man's bass voice from the dark yard roared out suddenly: 'I see 'em – I see 'em.'

Red Cheeks and I were already running towards the maid's window. But suddenly a figure started up in the leads right in front of us. We turned back. Red Cheeks panted something about getting into the middle. After I had run almost round the roof, I realised that he had been suggesting that we should hide in the valley between the roofs. Red Cheeks had now disappeared, I did not know where. But I was still under his influence, I at once determined to get into the valley. I made a jump at the slates, managing somehow to scramble up them and rolled down the other side into the gutter full of snow.

But now a long way in front I saw a skylight and remembered Red Cheeks' remark that if there was a light there was a girl inside and any of the girls would let you in. 'They're an awful decent lot of girls.'

I therefore made for the skylight, floundering through the half-melted snow. The skylight, much bigger than I expected, was of course closed, but it opened outwards. When, however, I began to lift it a girl's voice inside suddenly cried out. Either startled by this, or simply because I was already confused and almost frozen, I let the frame slip back from my hands, tried to catch it and prevent its making a noise, lost my footing on the slates and dived through the opening.

But in this, the first of my big falls, I was as usual lucky. I landed half on the maid and half on her bed. The girl, instead of shrieking or running away, as she might well have done, tried to catch me and actually succeeded in breaking my fall and directing my body to the bed. Then she asked me in a mild and kind voice: 'Was I hurted?'

In fact, apart from an insignificant cut on a knee and a long tear in my shirt-sleeve, I was not hurt. But I was so confused and surprised by the sudden descent that I sat stupidly on the bed until the girl, who was half-dressed, exclaimed first in wonder: 'Why, it's one of the Corner limbs,' then suddenly took me by the arm, propelled me through the door, and whispered: 'Away now – quick, the back stairs is on the left.'

As I ran off one way I heard somebody else with long steps approaching from the other, and the girl suddenly crying out in the indignant outraged voice used by a peasant girl when she makes a case for herself or a friend.

I rushed downstairs with only one idea, to find Harry or Kathy. But in the passage, by another stroke of luck, I saw Frances.

She had just arrived and was standing outside the ladies' cloakroom with a little group of girls, who were still shaking out their ribbons and patting their hair and turning outwards from each other, as if already looking for partners. Frances, with the little smile habitual to her when she felt herself well dressed, was glancing round, not towards the ballroom door, but towards the dirty, mustard-coloured walls and gloomy cupboards of the back passage, plimming her chest towards them just as if they had been a crowd of her soldier admirers. But when she saw me, she cried out: 'Darling boy, what on earth have you been up to?'

The delight of seeing Frances, in the midst of my panic, so overwhelmed me that I could not explain myself. I was almost in tears. But she took me into the ladies' room, where I spluttered my story about an accident on the roof.

Frances was our favourite stand-by in misfortune, because she always treated the case seriously, and always defended us. Delia was apt to take a severe moral view of mischief, or to say: 'Serve you right for being found out.'

CHAPTER 20

Even Frances was startled, I think, to hear in a minute or two from my pursuer, the garden boy, that I had blown up the kitchen and ruined the whole dinner and broken the roof-light and destroyed poor Bridgeen's bed; but when I partly admitted that I might have done some damage, she said suddenly: 'I know what we'll do; stay here and don't move.' She had taken off my wet shirt and knickers and wrapped me up in a coat. She left me in the chair where the new arrivals, mostly young débutante girls, coming in quickly, with gusts of cold air, in their thick scarves and coats, gazed at me with looks of haughty suspicion and disgust, as if saying: 'This is not at all what I was led to expect – dirty little boys with bloody legs in the ladies' dressing-room. What a let down.'

But now Frances came back with Rose Maylin and Pinto. The latter stood outside the door. I knew of his presence only by his voice, which said several times: 'Look here, I'm coming in,' whereupon both girls at once cried: 'No, you mustn't.'

Rose looked serious and severe. She was a little pale girl with high cheek-bones and deep hollows in her cheeks. She had big dark eyes, too big because they seemed to protrude and, catching the light, glittered with a hard look like polished agate. But her expression was not at all hard; it was more frightened and enquiring, like that of somebody who has had a great many failures and is losing confidence in herself. Rose used to look at people, even children, as if asking: 'What shall I say to him – but it's sure to be the wrong thing.' She embarrassed us by her depressed embarrassment. She spoke always rather quickly, but seldom finished a sentence. 'But, Frankie, it's really too much – the kitchen is absolutely – and Mrs Mac is scalded, and then the skylight – it takes such a fearful time for anyone to come and mend – and all just to make a sensation. I know, because Ted was in it, too – so fearfully spoilt.'

At these words I was brought to such extreme dejection that I was afraid after all that I was going to cry. It was the words 'to make a sensation 'which depressed me so greatly. They seemed to me true and caused me to feel despicable – or rather empty, as if I had suddenly lost myself altogether.

However, just at this moment, Pinto threw back the door and walked in. I was astonished to see him quite smart, in full evening dress, though with a black waistcoat; and with a red face. Also I was surprised to see how familiar he was with Rose. He spoke to her with the offhand confident tone used only by men who are on very friendly terms with a girl. 'What are you worrying about now, Rose? – come and dance – you promised to start the ball with me.'

Rose blushed and smiled a little with her lips. But the set of her face was still anxious and perplexed. 'But, Mr Freeman, I must get this other thing settled.'

'Nonsense – it is settled. Cook is settled anyhow. Is that the boy? 'He looked at me as if he'd never seen me before. 'Take him away and get him some clothes and let him dance. Dancing is the secret of life. Yes, I mean it.' His mouth twisted as if he were going to laugh. 'You do like this,' he made a step and turned slowly round in a grotesque attitude, 'and like this.'

Both the girls began to laugh at him, but Rose said again that something must be done with these wretched boys. 'It was so deliberate, and if you could see the kitchen.'

'Very well, beat them or something, but be quick – because I want to dance – I want to enjoy the poetry of motion. Well, so it is, you know, it is poetry – it goes to your head – it goes to the bottom of things – it contains the secret,' and so on, he went on talking nonsense like this for several minutes. The girls who were still coming in looked at him with haughty astonishment, and then began to laugh, too.

The cloak-room girl and Frances, who had been exchanging looks and nods, now whispered together, and the maid went out for a moment and almost at once came back. She nodded to Frances with a sudden affectionate smile, as if they had become close friends, and then at once looked very cold and aloof.

Rose looked from Frances to her and fidgeted. An expression of alarm and anger came into her big eyes and small wrinkled forehead. But Pinto now noticed me again, and said: 'Look at the villain – I say, young man, it wasn't a bad idea, was it – yes, quite an original contribution. But I suppose Ted was at the bottom of it.' Then he turned to Rose and began to reproach her. 'I suppose you'll tell Ted that he was showing off – I don't know why all of you combine to squash the only real spark in the family.'

'He was showing off,' Rose said.

'He wasn't – it's a thing he never does,' Pinto said, 'and it's wicked to tell him that he's showing off, yes, wicked, because he might believe it. That's what the bad critics say to every original genius, and I tell you why, it's because they're dead themselves and they want to kill everything else that's really alive.'

'But children do show off,' Frances said. 'A gentleman not ten thousand miles away is rather fond of it himself.'

'I don't know anything about children,' Pinto said. 'But I know Ted doesn't show off. He only likes to make a sensation.'

'Exactly,' Rose said.

'Yes, to *make* a sensation – but he doesn't think of getting anything out of it – he simply wants to *change* the situation—' and he began to talk about creating a better world and so on, making the girls laugh, and obviously amusing himself.

Rose tried to argue that Ted and I had not created a better world by causing half a ton of soot to fall on the kitchen stove and throwing the fire into the middle of the room.

Pinto paid no attention to her, but kept on practising his dance steps. Then he noticed me again and began to compliment me on my 'new contribution,' my 'stirring up the waters,' and ended by another long speech which, at first, I could not understand, about my gallant enterprise. 'Don't you let them sit on the safety valve – it'll stop your engine altogether.'

This metaphor, which seems a very bad one, was a favourite with Pinto. It always confused me, by producing a conflict of visions, like one photograph taken on top of another; and I was further confused by his next speech. Either because he never listened carefully to a story, or from perversity, he chose to imagine that I, having wrecked the roof and the kitchen, had fallen into the maid's room while trying to watch her undressing.

Frances protested against this, crying that I was too young, and that I oughtn't to hear such things; but I could not say anything because I didn't fully understand the charge, nor Pinto's arguments. His idea, of course, was the common one, among the young men of the nineties, not only the decadent, but the patriots and the supermen, that all restraint upon living natural impulse is evil, and that ugliness and unhappiness arise only from restraint; in fact, the anarchist views which now seem so old-fashioned and even childish.

I did not understand Pinto, but I saw the effect on the young ladies coming into the dressing-room. They laughed at him and blushed at his more extreme remarks; but at the same time, they took it all in. You could see them absorbing it as fresh leaves drink the rain. I was proud to see how they appreciated Pinto, whom we still called our Pinto.

Annish was then a very long way from London; at least as far as China is now, but these girls were just as ready for the new London gospel. Of course they knew already, even in Annish, that great changes were taking place in the world. They expected great changes, because it was the end of the century. Several of these girls have told me since that it was a special sensation to live in the end of a century; using the words even now as if they described something real, like a cave or a climate. Yet one of these, at least, insisted that she could feel an 'end of century feeling,' in everything, in the air, and even the frocks, and she confessed that this feeling dissolved her morals. She trembles, she says, at what might have happened to her if any man had been clever enough to see the state of her mind, which couldn't have been very difficult. 'But men are luckily such cowards with young girls.'

I was forgotten while Pinto talked in this strain; but now an arm, in a black dress sleeve, suddenly appeared through the door, holding a pair of blue knickers and some brown woollen stockings. Pinto stopped and cried: 'I am thy father's ghost.' Frances cried out sharply: 'Come in – I can't reach from yards.'

The arm was now joined by a head, peeping round the door. We recognised Mr Mackee, one of Frances' latest adorers.

CHAPTER 21

Mackee was a lawyer, over thirty, and said to be rich. He was a little man, very neatly built, with pale brown hair, already thin, and a round face. He was said to be a shrewd man of business; but in love, as we knew him, he wore always a kind of apologetic humble smile. He wore this smile now, and it seemed to irritate Frances, who said with a sharpness I had never heard her use before: 'Do come in, Mr Mackee, and don't stand there like Mrs Punch's baby.'

'I have captured the stronghold,' Pinto called out, 'it is quite safe even for our weaker sex. The garrison lies at my feet.'

However, the poor lawyer could not persuade himself to overstep the boundaries of the lady's room; and Frances had to go for the clothes. She exclaimed as she did so: 'Really, you are—' in a tone which made Mackee look so unhappy that after he had disappeared, the whole room burst out laughing.

Pinto now seized Rose by the arm and carried her away to dance. Frances undressed me, rubbed me down and put me into dry clothes. She laughed at me. 'Pinto talks awful nonsense, doesn't he?'

I was surprised at this from Pinto's special friend and admirer. But Frances went on: 'Just pure mischief, and you ought to be smacked, you know – both of you.' I agreed that it was pure mischief, and Frances said: 'Don't allow Pinto to cockle you up or you'll be really wicked.'

'Don't you like Pinto now?'

'Oh, yes.' Frances blushed as she always did when anyone referred to one of her flirtations. 'I'm sorry for him, too – he's so what you may call it – not exactly silly. But he is silly, too, quite silly. Run along now and *be good*,' with great emphasis on the last phrase.

I ran along, but I did not agree with Frances that Pinto was altogether silly. I had not understood his remarks about showing off, but I felt them. I understood that though he had not defended me personally from humiliating charges, he had defended my class, and I was grateful to him.

CHAPTER 22

Frances had many adorers. Our favourite was a long-legged soldier with a long nose, whom we called Scoop, or Sugarscoop. But we despised Mackee. We despised him entirely and completely, for his neat suits, his polite manners, his kindness and good nature, the presents with which he sought to buy our affections, the real affection which he felt for everyone related to Frances. We did not despise him merely because he was in love, because cousin Philip had fallen in love with Delia, and we did not despise him. We sympathised with him and praised him to Delia whenever we could.

Yet Harry, least spiteful of boys, and aloof even from reasonable dislikes, would imitate Mackee's anxious deprecating smile. 'Why,' he would say, 'he even sucks up to Jessy.' Jessy was the housemaid. It is true that Mackee took pains to please Jessy, but we were all fond of her, who was a charming girl.

This contempt of Mackee was active and positive. We were ready to do him any injury. We tortured him. We filled his bed with slugs and put pepper in his handkerchief; we would push him rudely aside in the room or on some picnic; going out of our way to show our dislike and to humiliate him.

This exaggerated, senseless feud against the poor man began, I think now, in a single incident. One day, when we had just bathed, Delia and Frances, instead of dressing, ran into the drawing-room and began to tell some story to their mother about one of Frances' admirers, who spik coffee on his trousers and spent the rest of the afternoon trying to hide the accident.

To us children the story seemed pointless, but the women laughed till they could not speak. They could ejaculate only: 'Oh dear, oh dear.'

We laughed, of course, because we wanted to share the joke, and Aunt Hersey's fox-terrier Spot, equally at a loss with us, wagged her tail, jumped up against Aunt Hersey's knee, and finally, distressed to be out of it, whined and made little yelping cries of appeal.

We, too, were uneasy. Between our false peals of laughter we looked at the three women on the sofa, giggling and pink. We had seen Aunt Hersey before in such a laughing fit, but we were always a little surprised to find her capable of such undignified conduct.

Aunt Hersey was very dignified. She walked upright, even leaning back from the waist, and had a very smooth step. Her features were dignified; she had a firm chin, a small, aquiline nose and well-marked, dark eyebrows, and she carried her chin high. Her dignity, however, was never stiff; she had been very well brought up in the old style which was intended to give a girl social charm. No one could be so charming as Aunt Hersey. She had a way of going towards visitors, swishing her skirts as if she urgently longed for their company, and smiling as if that one alone was specially desired. She would take a shy young man's hand and say: 'I've been wanting to ask you something,' and then she would invent some question to suit his capacity. If she knew nothing about his capacity, she would ask, anxiously and gravely, his opinion of the weather or the crops.

'You came by the point, I suppose. Now, what did you think of the potatoes – the *look* of them?' Like Delia, she emphasised words strongly, and at the same moment looked you in the eye as if giving all her thought to you.

Though her daughters seemed so different in every way, Aunt Hersey was like both of them. She had Delia's eyes, and Frances' bay-coloured hair, Delia's fine shoulders and buxomness, Frances' little fine nose. She was a little of a flirt and yet when she charmed men, she looked gravely at them and liked to talk seriously with them; not about general subjects in which she took no interest whatever, but about their affairs. I suppose half the men in the county had confessed themselves to Aunt Hersey, and many of them had fallen in love with her. It was a general complaint that so charming a woman should waste herself on the peevish, exacting Herbert. But I think that the same quality which gave Aunt Hersey her charm, laid her open to exploitation by any man. She liked people and especially men. She had a natural sympathy with men which had been increased by education and strengthened by art, so that she knew how to express it by the very turn of her neck and note of her voice. So we would see her advancing, with all that finished grace and serious coquetry which had made her a toast in her Dublin season, to charm her brother Herbert out of the sulky mood in which he always came to breakfast.

She was at the same time, like most women of her time, extremely simple in mind and taste. She had no ambition and her idea of a woman was of someone put into the world to look after a man, and a house, and children. She was therefore completely happy in this task, and kept, to old age, a certain irresponsibility. On politics she would talk like a child, only to make conversation or to provoke some response; and she was always capable, as now, of enjoying a childish joke. When Delia or Frances was frivolous, she was even more frivolous, so that they would sometimes grow tired of laughing and look at her, still giggling, with an ironical expression, as if to say: 'Do look at the silly old woman.'

But on this occasion all three were still giggling together on the sofa when Mackee arrived. He had been asked to luncheon. His smart dog-cart, always shiny with new paint, yellow and black, came rattling to the door and he rang the bell. He was the only visitor to Dunamara who rang a bell. The three women became at once serious with a special seriousness; a kind of preoccupation which appeared on their faces only when a suitor was at the door.

Aunt Hersey cried to us: 'Off with you, children – quick.' We ran upstairs, past Mackee in the hall, and reaching the school-room, began to ask each other what the joke had been.

But suddenly we heard fresh peals of laughter from below and the next moment little Mackee put his head in at the door and asked: 'Is this the schoolroom?'

We stared at him in wonder. With the same nervous, appeal-ing smile, he explained that he had been turned out of the drawing-room. 'Miss Frances said that I had better come up here till they were ready,' and then, trying to make a joke of the thing, or perhaps simply to depreciate himself and make himself seem still more foolish, as lovers do who have suffered at the hands of the beloved, he said: 'I wasn't wanted – they pushed me out.'

We perceived at once that the girls had meant to humiliate Mackee in sending him to the schoolroom, which was our nursery, and though, I suppose, they had acted only upon a sudden whim, we seized upon this idea that Mackee was despicable; a creature to be insulted in every possible way.

This, I say, was an idea and I believe, even while we spoke with disgust of the man, we knew it had no support in fact. We weren't ill-natured children, and Harry, at least, was clever and sensible beyond his years. Why did we pursue this feud with such ardour and persistence that Harry and I, in the end, nearly succeeded in drowning the poor wretch? I can only suppose that, simply because it had no support from truth or common sense, it appealed to some perverse instinct in us which made us insist that we would hate Mackee if we chose. We were in rebellion against our own sense of justice and decency. We were little anti-Christs taking a pleasure in creating an injustice, and I believe we did it in pure wantonness. People make injustice or forward a lie for all sorts of reasons, sometimes out of spite against injustice and lies, as poor children who see others better dressed deliberately tear each other's clothes; or a man who has been stuffed with party propaganda will deliberately start malicious rumours about his own party leaders.

But our spite of Mackee was purely ideal; something created out of nothing to satisfy some private lust for power; or simply for the pleasure of seeing the creature of our imagination taking its place in the real world and acting upon real people, like a knock on the head or an illness.

We all knew, of course, that we were doing wanton evil, for

we noticed with approval that Anketel took no part in it. He was fond of Dingbat, as we called him, who gave him sixpences and shillings; and he would even climb on his knee. At such moments Dingbat looked at the boy and spoke to him with such grateful and fond affection that it altered his whole face. His rather yellow dry cheeks would blush with pleasure, and he kept on smiling and raising his eyebrows as if astonished by happiness and by Anketel's good nature.

CHAPTER 23

Our great triumph over the harmless and good-natured Dingbat, when we nearly drowned him, was during a bathe at night. The family bathe had always been a family rite, an event of the same degree as a family meal, ordered by custom and civilised by rule. At Castle Corner there was even a bathing-house with a stove, so that towels should be hot and tea or coffee ready for the bathers when they left the water. In fact, at Castle Corner the ceremony, like so many human rites, attracted a meal into its office, as well as creating its chapel. At Dunamara, when I first went bathing there, I had always the sensation of guilt. I remember on some early occasion standing so long on the shore before going in, that Robert asked me what was wrong. I did not know and slowly went into the water. But I think that I was simply missing the bathing-house. I felt like a heretic.

But this year at Dunamara bathing suddenly became more important than ever before. Somebody had the idea of night bathing. I don't know who suggested it, but one reason for it was that Delia, who had left school and had decided to study music, was playing the piano all day.

Perhaps the night bathes were Delia's own suggestion; for Delia, since she had taken to music, had become impatient with everything ordinary. She was smoking again, and she smoked pipe tobacco in her cigarettes; and she liked to wear unexpected clothes, a velvet dress at breakfast and a bathing-dress for dinner. She would go out to tea in a short frock, wearing a pigtail and looking like a little girl; and to church in a picture hat of her mother's, contriving to seem like a thick-set woman of forty.

We began our night bathes from the house, but Delia was not satisfied with so tame an amusement. She wanted to go where no one would think of bathing; bare little islands or lonely rocks, far out at sea. The more unlikely the place the more it attracted her. Harry and I, too, felt this very attraction, which is supposed to be a mark of extreme sophistication or even degenerate tastes. I know that this was the peculiar attraction because we used to amuse ourselves by wild suggestions, such as putting a bucketful of sea water on Dunvil green and bathing in it at midnight; or painting ourselves in stripes with luminous paint and standing on the bollards on Dunvil pier, like statues.

So when Philip suggested that we should bathe, not from some cormorant's rock, but at the most proper and respectable bathing-place, we were enchanted by the notion. We felt at once how amusing it would be to use the huts and diving-boards, from which we ourselves, in other summers, had bathed in a conventional day-time manner, among nurses and aunts and lemonade-sellers; by night, when all would be deserted. We were attracted as by an empty house or a ruined theatre. We shouted approval and looked forward eagerly to the party.

It answered our expectations however irrational. From the moment we arrived and moored the two boats to a long foot-board over which we had often been carried, as babies, to be dipped, we all behaved like lunatics, or rebels. We shouted, splashed and ducked each other, climbed on the hut roofs, where Harry performed acrobatics and various poses plastiques. We raced along the foot-boards, jumping up and down to make them spring at the joints. We wanted to break them. There was destructive fury in our excitement, such as you see in children who break into an empty house. Delia tore the handle off a hut door in trying to get in, and then used a stone on the lock; Cousin Philip, Robert and Frances broke down a section of fencing to use it for a raft. The gentle Frances, finding that the fence resisted, brought the boat anchor to use as a lever, and fought afterwards for possession of the raft.

It was here that we ducked Mackee. For some time both Delia and Frances had been asking guests to our bathing parties. Frances asked Mackee, who came in a new suit with trousers so tight that we wondered how he could put his feet through the legs. Frances, having asked him, in a fit of conscience which often obliged her to be kind to the most troublesome or unsuitable of her young men, ignored him, and I think none of us spoke to him during the sail. At the bathing-place he placed himself on a foot-board, which joined the board walk, in front of the huts, to the diving platform, running out to sea. He had refused to bathe, perhaps because he could not swim; and he was obviously surprised by our violent doings. At any other time they would have shocked him to the soul. For a long time he stood on the foot-board watching Frances being dragged about in the water and ducked by Cousin Philip, Robert and Harry in the roughest manner; while she, with her soaking hair down, screamed and laughed like a child who defies correction, exaggerating every crudity of look and gesture. Upon all this Mackee smiled with a foolish, fond expression, not in the least like a cultivated tourist condescending to savages, but like one who, brought among people whom he admires, loyally accepts any foolish or disgusting thing they may do, as admirable. His smile annoyed us as the naïve devotion of a hero-worshipper is apt to irritate a hero who knows that he is not worthy, at that moment, of the least respect. Harry and I, finding ourselves beneath the board, and knowing it to be loose, caught hold of it and pushed. It tilted an inch or two, and Mackee slipped off into the water. This was the triumph of our evening. The whole party laughed so much that the little man might have been drowned if Delia had not set him on his feet. Frances would not go near him. All the way home we laughed at him in explosions of delight. As for Mackee, he also laughed, in an apologetic manner, as if afraid of taking a liberty. At least half a dozen times he hoped that he had not been a nuisance to us; that the accident had not spoilt our evening.

Our scorn that night of Mackee, whom we had injured, was so tremendous that it amounted to hatred. When Robert said that he wished the worm had been drowned, he was not joking, and he expressed so much of our feelings that Harry only modified the wish by saying: 'Or got his leg broken.'

The whole of this episode, our destructiveness, our attacks on Mackee, seemed to leave no trace at all on our conscience or our feelings. I think our feeling was like that of a drunk man who absolves himself from everything he has done when drunk, and even enjoys the recollection of crazy and brutal acts, saying to himself: 'I'm not so tame and there are depths in me.'

Only Frances, on reflection, having said her prayers, I suppose, and remembered her Christian principles, was ashamed, and wrote to Mackee the next day to say how she hoped his suit had not been spoilt.

Delia objected strongly to Frances' writing to Mackee, but Frances, agreeing that it was unwise, said it was a duty, and that she could not be happy unless she carried it out.

CHAPTER 24

But this riot at Cran Bay was unusual. On most of our night bathes we were all in a serious and thoughtful mood. The evening, I suppose, is the natural time for intimate conversation, and on these evenings we were not prevented from it by books or games or other substitutes. Even I, finding myself next Kathy on a rock, would attempt to express something, to explain myself and my feelings.

'It's nice here, isn't it, Kathy?'

'Rather. I say, aren't you cold? You're shivering. Come in my cloak.'

'Thanks awfully – I wonder everyone doesn't bathe at night.'

'They ought to, oughtn't they? We simply must make Aunty come.'

Kathy was in exuberant spirits. She squeezed up against me, laughing; not at all afraid of a rebuff; and because she seemed to challenge me, I did not dream of squashing her.

'Come on, swim you round the rock,' she threw off the cloak.

'All right, but not racing.' I was afraid just then of Kathy's beating me. She had a powerful breast-stroke against my side-stroke. Kathy, tactful in spite of her exuberance, answered at once: 'Oh, no, you'd beat me – just a swim.'

Then we dived in and swam abreast, enjoying each other's company.

Friendship as well as frankness seemed to belong to the time and the night air, and perhaps because of that, most of our night parties have in recollection a special kind of grandeur.

All the cousins, their faces and movements, their words, seemed to have a dignity and importance which did not belong to them by day, and it was this quality which made these nights so memorable to our childish tastes. For I think children love dignity. In all their eagerness to learn, they are seeking some glory and honour, some beauty. That was why we listened so eagerly to the long, serious talks of our older cousins and their guests on these warm evenings; not so much understanding their meaning as feeling the presence of sincerity.

Harry indeed would talk with them sometimes, but I did not venture to speak. I would suddenly grow tired of hearing, and dive into the blue shadows of the rock underneath, for the pleasure of feeling myself glide through water which I could not see. Sometimes I would swim away by myself and climb out on some point of rock, to feel cut off and alone.

On many of these summer nights, the sky, though it was free from cloud, was obscured by a special darkness. It was a very dark blue, in which the stars were almost imperceptible; an immense but opaque dome full of blue darkness which seemed to tint the air itself. A night like this, hot and oppressive and overcast, always excited us to feats of daring; but it was also apt to frighten us. A clear darkness, even without a moon, in spite of its enormous space which made us feel like insects, seemed to encourage us so that we would swim off a long way by ourselves and suddenly Frances and Kathy would call for us. But on the others we would not venture beyond the next rock and even then loneliness itself could terrify us.

On one night especially, this thick darkness threw me into a panic. The small waves which came out of it, as if from nowhere, barely raising the seaweed and splashing my feet, suddenly appeared to threaten me as if, by some will of their own, they could pull me down. I dived hastily into the sea, whose warmth I still remember, and swam as fast as I could towards the other larger rock. But I saw nothing of the party; I heard nothing; and the dark waves through which I swam appeared strange and unfamiliar; like the water in Shell Port cave. I felt their evil; their deadly quality, not aimed at me, but dangerous and treacherous in themselves. Their very warmth, of which we were accustomed to boast, when we described our night bathing, seemed horrible. I came to the rock at last and there was no one there. I had been deserted. The party had forgotten me. Or perhaps they had been drowned. I floated on my back and gazed at the sky, and wished that it were clear, that there were stars in it, and more light in the air. Then I swam along the rock, so close that I cut my knuckles on its barnacles. Suddenly I heard voices, and the sound of a banjo, very lightly touched. I looked up and saw, so close to me that I could have touched her feet, Delia in a long red cloak, a glowing purple in that light, Frances with her hair over her green dress squatting before her, holding herself by the toes. The mast of the boat rocked beyond where Cousin Philip was humming to himself some of the nigger minstrel songs which were a craze that year. I climbed up slowly, dripping, with the sensation of one returning from the grave to a family world, especially delightful. Philip for some reason usually sat in the boat and sometimes he did not speak for a long time. He was now eighteen and he was just going to a crammer to prepare for his army exams. But he had stopped growing and he was much smaller than he had expected, and he also feared to be ploughed in the exams. This made him melancholy because his whole heart was set on the army. One night he said that he would shoot himself if he didn't pass.

Delia was usually impatient with Philip, but at this time she was patient with him. 'But why?' she asked. 'There's plenty of other things you can do – I only wish I was a man to have so many.'

Philip twanged the banjo and said: 'I don't see why anyone shouldn't shoot himself if he likes. It's his own business.'

'Do you want to be ordered about all your life?'

'In the army you know where you are.'

'I'd rather have a mind of my own.'

'Well, I have – I've got a mind to go into the army.'

'Like going in the nuns,' Delia murmured.

Philip strummed and Kathy said from the boat: 'I wouldn't be a nun – I don't know how anyone can be a nun.'

'It's not a bad life,' Philip said, 'and it's a good one.'

'I shall marry a soldier,' Kathy said.

Kathy often sat with Philip in the boat. There seemed to be a strong sympathy between them.

'If you're asked,' Philip said.

But at this time Kathy would not be snubbed. She answered gaily: 'Or I'll be a nurse and go to the war like that.'

'Yes, you could do that for yourself.'

, 'Well, I will,' in a tranquil and confident tone.

'Scoop has a mind, but I don't believe he's a really good soldier,' Delia said.

'They don't grab,' Philip said. 'Not in the regiment – they aren't out for all they can get.'

'There's Florence Nightingale,' Kathy said. 'She's in London.'

There was another long silence, and then Frances said suddenly: 'I think soldiers are lucky – it's easy for them to be happy – unless there's a war, of course.'

'That is their great opportunity. Every soldier carries a field-marshal's baton in his knapsack,' Harry said, pronouncing baton, however, bayton, and holding his breath after the last word, in sudden doubt of the pronunciation.

They often discussed happiness, and Delia always maintained that it was easy to be happy, but somehow despicable. Frances objected that ugly people cannot be happy, and Philip said: 'That's a lesson for you, Kathy, not to frown and to sit up straight.'

'Yes, I wish you could stop her frowning – she's got a wrinkle already,' Frances said.

'I like my wrinkle,' Kathy said, and though I saw her a day or two later, looking at herself in the glass and passing her finger across her forehead, I don't think she was concerned about herself. She had merely noticed the wrinkle, as a curious object.

Delia always maintained against Frances that ugly girls could take to religion.

'Religious people are very happy. Nuns are always happy. Ugly people can be nuns.'

Cousin Philip would say that happiness was a matter of temperament and that even nuns could not be happy without it. He himself had not been happy and never would be.

'Neither have I,' Delia said. 'But I don't care. Nobody ought to care. You don't care, Philip, do you?'

'I used to care a lot – why shouldn't people be happy?'

'You'll be all right in the army, won't you?' Frances said.

'Yes, but I won't pass.'

'You mustn't mind it too terribly,' Frances said. 'What will be, will be.'

'If you don't want to marry Scoop, then don't,' Delia said.

'I don't want to marry anyone – I should hate it.'

'You will, though,' Cousin Philip's voice came up from below where the boat was only a black shape on the dark grey water.

'I certainly won't – I'm much too happy now.'

'You'll fall in love with someone,' Harry said.

'Frances will never fall in love with anybody,' Philip said. 'She's as hard as nails,' and he strummed a loud chord. Philip liked to say of women that they were as hard as nails; either to provoke them, or because he had some grievance against them for not falling in love with him.

All of us were interested in this question of happiness and returned to it again and again. No decision was reached, of course; happiness was never defined.

Frances, for instance, would argue that poor people could not be happy. Frances was afraid of poverty, and had a sympathy with the poor which was true and real; without condescension. She felt that they were deprived. 'If I was poor, I should be miserable all the time.'

'You could be a hermit or something like that,' Delia said. 'Indian hermits live on nothing – a farthing a day and they're tremendously happy.'

'Yes, but they believe in God,' Philip said.

'So does Frankie.'

'No, she doesn't, or she would trust Him. Nobody believes in God now – they only think they do.'

'Nonsense, Philip – you know you believe in God. You're the only one who always goes to early service.'

Philip twanged the banjo and said: 'I'd like to believe, of course – anyone would. But you can't, nobody can.'

'I couldn't live in a cave.'

'But you can be a hermit in a *room* – anywhere.'

'You need money for that.'

'Oh, everyone has enough for that – look at Mrs H. She lost all her money, she was quite ruined. But there she is at Miss Daly's and she's happy. She's exactly the kind of *hermit* I mean.'

'Her brother pays for her,' Frances said.

'*Somebody* always pays – and then you've only got to make up your mind to be a Christian about it and not worry about things that don't matter, like clothes and roast chickens, and you *are* happy at once. You can make yourself happy – it's quite easy, but it's wrong all the same.'

'I don't see why,' Cousin Philip would say, and Frances always agreed with him. 'It isn't easy to *be* happy.'

'No. It's easy if you really try – only it's simply *petty*.' Delia put extraordinary emphasis into this word, and then Cousin Philip struck a loud chord, and said: 'Hurray!'

'Of course, Deely, you're fearfully ambitious,' Frances said.

'Yes, I *am* ambitious – everybody ought to be ambitious.'

'It's not a Christian thing to be,' Frances said.

'I don't care—'

'Deely, of course you care.'

'I don't – I don't care because I know it's right. Besides, Christians are ambitious – the real manly ones. They want to make everybody Christian – they want to be terrifically good, or martyrs.'

'Do you want to be a Padarooski, Delia?'

'I don't suppose I'll ever be as good as that, but I'm going to be *very* good. I couldn't be nothing – I can't understand how anybody can be nobody – I should despise myself – I couldn't live.'

'I'm afraid you're going to be very *un*happy,' Frances said.

'I don't mind if I'm not nobody – in fact, I shall be happy then.'

These talks, passing through my ears in the pleasant sound of voices heard at night, seemed to convey ideas and images to me. But when afterwards, trying to show Harry that, though I could not take part in the conversation, I could understand it, I repeated scraps of it, I soon lost my way.

'Delia says that she isn't happy, but she is, isn't she? – of course she hates practising, but then she wants to practise, doesn't she? Though, of course, she's miserable when she can't get things right.'

Harry would listen in silence and then say: 'What *exactly* do you mean?'

'Well, isn't she happy? She needn't do music if she doesn't like.'

'That's not the point. You've missed the point. But never mind, it's rather essótteric.'

These failures discouraged me and made me feel stupid and bewildered. But I soon forgot them in some new distraction.

CHAPTER 25

The frankness during our night bathes sometimes went far. I heard much that I did not understand, even from the girls, who held strictly, except for Delia's smoking, to the standards of that day. Because it was night, another and greater world from our day, I suppose, because of the vastness and strangeness of our surroundings, we seemed to acquire other manners and notions. We children often wore no drawers and lay about naked. This was not so remarkable as the carelessness of the girls. I have seen Delia almost naked plaiting her hair on a rock, in the bright moonlight, like a mermaid, and she made no attempt to cover her breasts from Harry and me, climbing out of the water, except by a slight dip of one shoulder. She was looking at us and her eyes seemed to say: 'No, why should I mind? – it's too *petty.*'

But my feeling, too, was that there was nothing improper about our sudden carelessness of rules; I believe I would have felt it more shocking, that is, more offensive to my social idea of what was proper in the circumstances, if Delia had been prudish. For that would have been petty, as Delia herself put it, and for us children, at least, there was nothing petty about our night excursions. They had in this, too, like our riotous evening at Cran Bay and our feud against Mackee, a romantic quality. We did not know the word and I never heard our elders use it, but our sudden taste for night, for breaking the conventions, our sudden warm feelings, our talks and even Delia's boldness were romantic, revolutionary. Their good and their bad, the warm friendliness, the feeling, which even I shared, that we had been brought closer together than ever before, in a fonder, more sympathetic relation; and their fits of irresponsible violence, even the discussions about happiness, love and so on, which seemed so important and original, all belonged to a form as old as mankind. Savages, too, in their harvest feasts, stay up all night, form suddenly tender warm friendships, so that you see the pagan warriors walking about hand in hand under the moon, and murmuring together over the fire all night; or suddenly they take a fancy to go and burn somebody's house.

We were so disinclined to be ordinary and conventional that

even when we went home we never went to the dining-room, but always to the kitchen. There, still in bathing cloaks, we would make ourselves buttered toast and tea, and chatter over the kitchen fire for another hour.

Delia would sit on the cook's knee, Mrs Fee, who was an immensely tall, thin woman, with a long sad face and hollow eyes, and say: 'This is my knee where I've always sat, isn't it, Noody?'

Mrs Fee would smile and say: 'It's what you say it, Miss Deely.'

'Why, Miss, Noody – aren't I your Deely any more?'

Mrs Fee would blush and laugh. She blushed in dark patches high up on her bony cheeks. She was very shy with three or four, but talked easily with any one of us, in a soft, rather monotonous voice which went strangely with her formidable looks. Her talk fascinated us because of her view of the world. She was a hell-fire Protestant who did really believe in the old Semitic god and a flaming hell, so that her conversation, full of a wise sympathy and patience, floated, as it were, over the everlasting furnace, and was shot with gleams of its fire. 'Will I go to hell, Mrs Fee?' I would ask her after some crime, and she would say: 'I hope not, my duck, but it's for God to say. Only He knows—'

'God wouldn't be so cruel.'

'Hsh, dearie, you don't know what you're saying. God could never do a bad thing. It's we that are the wicked ones – black-hearted sliders all of us, there's Roe forgot my wood again. The poor man – it puts my heart across to see him so down.'

'Shall I run and tell him about your wood?'

'No, sweetheart, you bide here by the fire and keep your wee feet dry – we don't want you coughing again.'

Mrs Fee never permitted anyone to help her, or, indeed, to do anything for her. She worked from five or six in the morning till such time at night as the rest of the family chose to go to bed. For she could allow no one else to bar the doors and shutters and draw the fires. She loved work and she was jealous of anyone who polished or cleaned or waited on any member of the family; even of the housemaid and Roe's daughter who came in by the day to sew and to maid Aunt Hersey. But I don't think Mrs Fee had any possessive sense. She was not like those old family servants who feel that the house belongs to them; and tyrannise over the family. She simply loved cleanliness and felt a kind of tender sympathy towards chairs and tables, baths and carpets, as well as people. I remember Mrs Fee, in Dunvil market, looking at a broken fender lying under an old clothes booth, and saying: 'It's done, and all it needed was a rivet. But they wouldn't take the trouble with it – the poor thing.' Then she would shake her head, and as I jumped round her, waiting for the moment when she would buy me some alphabet lozenges, she would murmur that there was too much wickedness in the world. God's judgment could not be far off.

Just as people, under bombardment, show the same character as before, but a little intensified; the selfish a little more cunning in getting their own ends while seeming to be full of self-sacrifice and virtue; the affectionate more anxious; the detached more remote; and all pursue their private purposes with the same eagerness or languor; so Mrs Fee, under the daily fear of the end of the world, and possible hell-fire for herself, continued to plan meals and bargain over every penny of Aunt Hersey's money, and to love people and chairs and tables and fenders, only with a little more intensity. But her grim look and grenadier's carriage frightened most people away from her. We, like Delia, used to sit in her lap, but we never dared to chaff her or call her Noody; or romp with her as we did with Jessy, the housemaid.

Jessy was as different from Mrs Fee as possible. She was a little plump girl with a big nose and a lovely complexion of cream and rose. Her eyes, too, were lovely; not big, but of a beautiful shape and colour; dark blue-grey. She was a gay, dreamy girl, slap-dash at her work, but so fresh, clean and neat, so sweet-natured that even Uncle Herbert used to smile involuntarily when he spoke to her. A stranger coming in at the door always looked twice at Jessy's plain features. Gaiety shone from her like beauty.

She was a Catholic, but Mrs Fee was devoted to her and treated her like a daughter; mending her clothes and sewing her linen.

Jessy had many followers, especially a tall police sergeant, one of the handsomest men I ever saw; who was very much in love. But she laughed at them all and said of the sergeant: 'Peelers and tinkers – they're all the same but the soap. He med be in Connaught this day week and Belfast the day after.'

She was a close, independent person; and very unsentimental.

I don't think she cared deeply for anyone, or even valued greatly
the affection which all gave her. She enjoyed life too much, like
us, with whom she was always ready to romp. She would play
tig, hide-and-seek and even wrestle, getting her aprons torn and
her hair pulled down; and she would always back us up in a
scrape. When one day I pushed her backwards through a
window, she cheerfully took responsibility for the broken glass.
'It was my elbow, mam.'

CHAPTER 26

We always loved the kitchen at Dunamara for its different air
from the house. It was a complete change to go under its smoky
ceiling hung with clothes-racks and feel the stone floor under
one's feet, to see the work going forward and to know the
presence of Mrs Fee, Jessy, Roe the gardener, and their various
relations or dependants, of whom two or three, of any age from
two to ninety, were usually sitting about the walls. In this world
all the talk was exciting to us. Mrs Fee's hell-fire, Jessy's love
affairs with their frank talk of what this boy was worth if his
father died soon before he had drunk the horse; the endless talk
of hard births, hard lives, and hard deaths which was the daily
news out there on the stone floors; sprang new sensations in our
brains, which floated into clouds of a new shape; the clouds
which in children are the first stuff of notions. I seemed to feel
them, as one feels the shape and colour of something at which
one does not directly look, as larger, darker, more rich in shape
and colour than those which passed through the clear sky of the
schoolroom, visions of sails, and bathes, and explorations, and
picnics. These were like spring clouds, scarcely thicker than air,
volatiles of hope; but in the kitchen, all was darkness and fire;
the crimson light of sunrise and sunset, hell fires which cooked
our goose, and the kitchen fire which cooked our meals, the
shadow of some poor woman's pain, two days in labour, or
some young man's dying, 'a year in bed till you could see
through his chest, and he that was the only son, a dear lovely
boy. He cries for his mammy still when the fear of death comes
on him, but she's dead herself this seven weeks.'

'But he won't go to hell, Mrs Fee?'
'Ah, who could say – who could know what God knows?'

CHAPTER 27

'Am I wetting your knee, Noody,' Delia would say, 'with my cloak? That will give you your rheumatism.'

She spoke as if she enjoyed the idea of giving Mrs Fee rheumatism. There was something in Mrs Fee's infinite patience and good temper which prompted Delia to try her, just as Roe's claim that the new plank he had put into the garden seat would bear a ton caused us to go and jump upon it till we broke it.

'I'm too heavy for you, Noody – I'm killing you after you've been running up and down all day long.'

'Oh, no, Miss Deely, you always sat light.'

'So poor old Manly's dead?'

'Aye, this evening at seven minutes past four.'

'Poor old man, all alone out there on the bog,' Frances would say, and they would wonder how the old man had managed to cook and bake for himself, living alone in his miserable hut for the last forty years.

Captain Scoop would sit on the table with his long knees drawn up to his nose and a piece of clean drawer paper under him to keep his smart trousers from stain. He was the perfect type of a military dandy, though he stooped from the shoulders and liked to talk about Greek philosophy. It was from his lips I first discovered that Plato was not a dog's name, like Juno or Grouse, but that of a great man. For a long time it still seemed to me trivial and ridiculous for a philosopher; and even now I can't be reconciled to it.

Frances would always sit beside her darling Captain, unless another Captain, whom we called Moonlight, a little dapper man with a red moustache, were present. Moonlight had a cynical eye and little sentiment. Though he was a serious suitor and had proposed to Frances, he was quite capable of criticising her and making jokes at her expense. He seemed to think of her as a young, unsteady creature, like a filly of charm and quality, but requiring to be trained and developed. Frances did not care to flirt with Scoop in the presence of Moonlight.

Moonlight talked horses, or, if he had been recently in London, musical comedy, actresses; but he would also discuss philosophy with Scoop. They were friends and had a common taste for philosophy which they read in little pamphlets and digests, or out of the encyclopædia. I can remember Moonlight saying that old Plato had hit the right nail on the head when he said that every man ought to stick to his own job. Scoop, who knew some mathematics, was more interested in the forms and used to puzzle us by talking about the beauty of the number three, which would never stand any nonsense. 'That's why we put a maxim on a tripod – a platonic maxim is a steady friend.'

During these evenings when the Captains were there, or even one of them, Philip would disappear into a corner, or into the scullery. He was always shy and gloomy in the presence of officers as if from envy or perhaps merely a feeling of inferiority; like a novice in the presence of a priest.

Often he used to stand against the scullery wall out of sight, and talk to Jessy in a low voice. He and Jessy had an old friendship and I think Philip had been in love with the girl. If so, she kept him in his place. But they used to talk together with a thoughtful, brooding look, which was strange in Jessy's lively features, and made her seem haggard. They talked, too, of the strangest matters; of Jessy's lovers; of the difficulty of establishing oneself in life; sometimes even of religion.

He would say: 'And what did little Muldoon talk about last week?'

'About old Mrs Laughlin that died, and about charity and not thinking too badly of people, for we're not fit, he says, to judge them.'

'That's true enough – about not being fit, but someone has to keep up the standards.'

Sometimes we would call for Philip's banjo, but if the soldiers were there, he would not play. He would make some excuse and stay behind the scullery door muttering with Jessy.

Aunt Hersey, scandalised by the lateness of the hours we kept, would threaten every night to stop our night bathing. But she could not make up her mind to this severity; and therefore she only continued to worry.

CHAPTER 28

Suddenly the night bathes came to an end. I can't remember any reason for this. Perhaps it rained for two or three nights running. W children said often for a week or two: 'We must go and bathe to-night,' and the girls said vaguely: 'Yes, we must.' But we did not go and something delightful, unique, suddenly came to an end. Neither after a few days did anyone but Harry seem to regret it or even to remember it. For a long time he continued to urge a night bathe, but the rest of us sat contented after supper as if we had never heard of such a pleasure; and if Delia had looked up from her book to tell us something about her feelings or her secret ambitions, we would have wondered at her.

Delia used to read a book, whether it was Mrs Humphry Ward or a life of Beethoven, with her elbows on the table and a frown of concentration. She was too much absorbed in her music and reading, in whatever she did, to look back on a past enjoyment; Frances, naturally rather lazy, would curl herself up in a chair, visibly delighting in its softness; Cousin Philip, if he were there, would smoke and strum and meditate gloomily with one leg hooked over the arm of a chair; and we children, once more properly dressed for the evening with ties and collars, would doze over our books or some quiet game in a quiet corner.

Once more we were deep in the Dunamara routine; and enjoyed the sense of its regularity. Especially it was delightful to come to the drawing-room after supper, tired after playing all day; full fed; and to drowse in a peace of mind and body so deep that it, too, could be enjoyed by itself. Dunamara under its hill was a sleepy place. The noise of the waves was hypnotic in its slow repetition of soft long notes; the falling cadence of the break, the tinkle of the thrown spray, the sigh of the flow upwards across the shingle; and the hollow murmur of the ebb sinking back into the roots of the next wave. We nodded to it over our Ballantyne or Henty, draughts or chess; and fell upstairs to bed in its echo, muffled like an orchestra heard through two walls. But when we were in our room and Aunt Hersey had heard our prayers, tucked us up, said goodnight, and opened the windows, it burst upon us again with an immense noise, not overwhelming, but soft and enveloping, like the orchestra heard from a stage box. Its music seized us and carried us away with it into a sea dream; a sleep which had no clear division between a dream-like delight in the sea sounds, the wave-marked walls of Dunamara to which we fell asleep, and the sound of falling waves, the sight of waves of light, all about us on walls and ceiling, to which we gradually awoke.

But these sounds, these drowsy evenings, were still like parts of a dream, vivid at the time, fading gradually from memory and experience, preserved only by snatches. My memory of them is the residue of hundreds of nights, mixed together. I lived in them like an ant in the grass or some small busy creature under a hedge, scarcely yet aware of myself or of my happiness. So I did not enjoy it then and thank God for that sweet life as I have enjoyed it since. The little animal of mine was but half alive, half formed; his senses, keen and sharp, had few forms of precision and wasted themselves in vague confusion, in perplexity, in mere existing. For often when I was busily engaged on some task, digging waterworks on the shore or prowling the rocks with a bucket and landing-net, I was unconscious of any purpose. I was not bored, because all my muscles were active and happy. But I myself was dozing or dreaming in terms so vague that I dare say Spot, who often wandered after me, wagging her stump hopefully whenever I stopped at a pool, had clearer visions in her imagination.

CHAPTER 29

Frances, having apparently committed herself to Captain Scoop, suddenly accepted Dingbat and married him within six weeks. In June she was running races with us and arguing with Harry, like an equal; in August, she was mistress of a big house, a fortune and Dingbat. This startling change, the first in our experience among the cousins, impressed us, not by its suddenness, which seemed to us nothing abnormal, but its greatness. Not that we showed such a feeling. I don't remember that Harry and I took any interest in the engagement or in all the excitement of shopping and dress-making, present receiving and letter-writing that went on in the house for six weeks before the wedding. Harry even expressed impatience with it as women's folly, and I felt with him that it was absurd for three women to be in such agitation about the fit of a dress, that we were all twice deprived of a picnic, because the only available horse was galloping to town with a dress box. But though we were disgusted and Philip used to say of women that they spent their whole lives thinking of petticoats and ribbons, we knew very well that marriage was an important event for Frances. In those times it was accepted that a woman's marriage was the most important event in her life. At least half the conversation we heard as children, among grown-ups, was about engagements or hoped-for engagements, marriages and births. We heard girls pitied because they had not got husbands, though, as Aunt Hersey said: 'They were really thoroughly good nice girls,' and men debated as possible husbands. The question whether soldiers made good husbands was a common one, and another was, whether it was better for a girl to marry young some local man, and stay in Annish all her life, or go abroad first and see something of the world.

All this talk was no more to us than the natural state of things like that religious or universal idea which later we soaked up at our prep. school as if from the air. The difference between men and women was so obvious to us that we did not even think of it or reflect upon it.

We were much more interested in a new development in our affairs. Because Mackee's house, Blackhall, was far down the lough on the opposite side, it was often convenient to sail there, and for this we were allowed, since no other was available, to use the Dunamara boat. We considered it our boat, and though we were not allowed to sail in it alone, we were often allowed, in a light wind, to steer. Therefore, we were delighted when the cry went up that something had been forgotten at Blackhall, or that there was a message for Mackee.

'What a nuisance – Dingbat was to come to dinner if we let him know and no one has let him know. Must we have him?' Frances would cry.

'Of course,' Delia said in a severe tone.

'But he's such a fearful nuisance, especially now when we're so busy.'

Delia would look severely at Frances and say that if there was a message, the boys would be delighted to take it in the boat.

We noticed Frances' attitude to Dingbat with surprise. But we supposed it was the thing for a girl, about to be married, to call her betrothed a nuisance, a bore; and to say that he looked perfectly idiotic in a frock-coat.

I think now that Frances was really asking us to praise Dingbat, or to settle some confusion in her own mind. One day Delia said to her: 'If you think he's a stick and a bore, I don't know why you're marrying him.'

'Oh, goodness, neither do I,' said Frances, laughing and blushing. 'I suppose one has to marry somebody.'

'I thought you were going to marry poor Scoop.'

'Oh, that daddy-long-legs – but he's so stupid and his ears are too big. He has the most enormous ears – do be careful with that satin ribbon, darling. It would be a *complete* and *utter* disaster if it got creased. There's no more to be had that width nearer than Paris.'

Young girls getting married are supposed to take this careless frivolous tone, to cover a shyness, a reluctance, which is natural to the sex. The hen partridge shows the same indifference or coolness when the cock is strutting round her. But I think in Frances it covered also a real confusion of mind; that she really did not know why she had accepted Dingbat and what was happening to her. She was a girl who did not like the trouble of making up her mind about anything; who was always content with her present. She had refused three or four proposals, merely from dislike of any change in her peaceful happy existence at home. But suddenly, on account of something which she could not explain to herself, perhaps some trivial remark about the fate of old maids, or even a passing sensation, half-feeling, half-imagination, of the passage of time, she had accepted Mackee. I daresay he came upon her at the only moment of her life when she would have accepted anybody.

But now she was obviously very happy. She was happy as she had always been, in her temperament, in that fatalism which she had expressed by saying: 'What will be, will be.' She trusted herself to life and events just as we did when we felt growing up could not fail to be pleasant and exciting.

But Delia did not approve of this attitude towards life; and especially towards marriage. She found fault even with her mother for laughing when Frances abused Mackee. The two would laugh together on the sofa, surrounded by piles of silks and fine linens, their laps buried in underclothes, so that they looked like mermaids of dress, half-submerged in their proper element; while Delia frowned at them and said: 'I wish Ding could see you.'

'Oh dear, oh dear!' Aunt Hersey would cry, rosy with laughter, and looking far younger and prettier than Frances, 'but it's quite true – he does look as if he'd swallowed the thermometer.'

'I shall really have to do something about his hair,' Frances would say, suddenly grave, as if on this point at least she had a clear opinion. 'I was looking yesterday and it's like Patsy Nielie's oats – one here and one there.'

'It's a pity,' Delia said, 'that people like you can't order husbands from the shop and keep them in the bedroom cupboard till you want them, out of the way, like pigs in summer.' A pig was a stone hot-water bottle.

'Indeed it is,' Frances cried, 'for then I'd get a brass one for Christmas – they're warmer.' But her mother suddenly disapproved and said mildly: 'That's not a good way to talk, darlings. A joke's a joke, but we'll leave out the pigs.'

This difference between Frances and Delia became after Frances' marriage a quarrel that divided the sisters for a long time and involved us all.

CHAPTER 30

But meanwhile we passed gladly from the rooms full of dress boxes, with needles and pins stuck in the chairs, to the open air and the creek, where we spent all day scraping and painting the boat which, since it had been handed over to us, had become full of merits.

The Dunamara boat was a huge clumsy tub, built for the roughest work; for fishing along the rocky coast, and conveying stores. It was moored in the Dunamara creek, and its heavy mast was always stepped so that one saw its tip from the yard, jerking to and fro in the short backwash. Land birds used it for a perch, and it was always covered with droppings. It had a sprit-sail, which, wrapped round the sprit, stood usually in the potato house, with hoes, potato spades, coal shovels, lawn-mowers and baskets of bulbs. It was a domesticated boat. Grass grew among its bottom boards, and hens pecked in the gratings for dropped grains of maize which always stuck there together with rotten potatoes, decayed apples, cabbage leaves and lumps of coal. The yard cats kittened in its locker. We called it the scow.

The scow was regarded as part of the house; a kind of floating annexe. It was used as an extra nursery, a wash-house, a drying-ground, and as a safe pen for very small children. As babies, Harry and I had been tethered there, by ropes to the gratings, and left to play with our bricks and wooden horses.

The carpenter would lay a plank across the thwarts when he wanted a saw bench; and the maids, in spring, would spread the carpets from gunwale to gunwale and beat them with the tiller.

It was nominally in charge of old Roe, who was gardener, coachman, pumpman and sailor to the house. Roe was a melancholy stooping old man who looked like the wandering Jew, with a long thick drooping nose and little black eyes. But he was pure Donegal and had no Jewish blood. He had been a man-of warsman under sail and he might have been expected to care for the boat. But he cared for nothing except his pipe and his evenings. Every fine night he would stroll in the road above the house smoking a short clay pipe, and stopping now and then to look at the sea or the sky. On wet nights he would sit in the stable and smoke there, in silence and alone. This was the great pleasure for which he lived. Sometimes in the winter he came into the kitchen, but even then he did not speak unless someone spoke to him. One of us children, always curious about foreign parts, would ask him: 'Have you been in Japan?'

'Aye.'

'What was it like?'

'Full of a lot of Japanese heathen – no good for nothing.'

Once after we had pestered him too long he pulled out his pipe and said in a severe tone: 'None of those people's any good – and we're not much better ourselves.'

He and Mrs Fee had the same idea of people's fundamental worthlessness; but they had nothing else in common and were not good friends. Roe was detached from the world and from people; an exile and wanderer. He loved things only; and only a few of them: his pipe, the piece of road above Dunamara, the views, his cottage. Mrs Fee had sympathy with all people and all things.

Old Roe's one fear was that he would become unfit for work and would have to go to the workhouse, where he would not get his pipe or his evenings, as he called them. He was already a shaky rheumatic old man, but he had all sorts of tricks for hiding his stiffness and his lame knees. It was no good telling him that Aunt Hersey would always give him house room in the cottage, and pension enough to live on; because he was convinced that she herself would soon be ruined. 'The gentry are done,' he would say. 'They won't last this hundred,' meaning that they would end with the century in a year or two. 'It's only the old queen keeps them up now. When she goes, that's the end of them and England, too.'

Old Roe had a nephew, Oweny, to help him in the garden. We used to see the two of them, the old man bent like a davit, and young Oweny, with his large head and long thin arms, tugging the scow down tide to fetch turf or coal. Old Roe had a navy stroke, he put in the oar and threw himself back with a jerk. Oweny rowed with a long swing. Neither seemed to affect the course of the scow, drifting sideways down the lough on the ebb, or back again on the flow.

Sometimes we had gone to row with them, and as we could not alone manage the long sweeps, we sat on the same thwarts, Harry with Roe, and I with Oweny, tugging and pushing. But we found these trips slow, for the old man never spoke; and Oweny would only grin and spit over the side between his broken teeth. At sixteen Oweny's teeth were already broken and black. His hair, too, seemed to be coming out. But he wore a perpetual grin as if he found the world a very comical sight. He grinned at his old uncle's deep sighs; he grinned at us equally when we struggled to swing the oars and when we gave up and began to look over our shoulders to see how far we had still to go.

Oweny had been in prison twice for stoning the police, and breaking windows, but this gave him, for us, a peculiar attraction which it is hard to describe. We had with Oweny a sense of adventure and enlargement; but also I at least felt that he had solved the problem of life in a way not beyond my own powers, by doing nothing about it.

I was not often seized with a feeling of insecurity, but it was acute. Some tale like Pinto's, of a ruined family, or of children losing both parents at once, would give me a shock of uneasiness. A dog or cat has the same feeling at any threatened change in its world. Spot barked and whined herself almost into hysterics when the furniture was taken out of the lower rooms in order that the floors might be reboarded.

Small children, I suspect, have this sharp and deep fear much oftener than we or they know. It makes them suddenly quiet, or rough or affectionate. It brought up before me at that time the vision of Oweny, and even of an old lunatic tramp called Doily who seemed to say: 'We know nothing and do nothing, yet see how we manage to eat and to live.'

I was always curious about Oweny. I used to ask him: 'Did you have a good breakfast, Oweny?'

'Oh, aye, a drink of butter milk and a sup of good air.'

'Why are your teeth so black, Oweny?'

'Ah, who wants teeth? – they're only in your way.'

'Why did you break the windows, Oweny?'

To this question Oweny would grin a little more widely, look slyly out of the corners of his pale blue eyes and say: 'Ah, it didn't do those ones any harm.'

When we were given use of the old scow and allowed to call her our own, and began to paint her and scrape her, old Roe said only that it was a waste of time. 'She's not worth a kick.' But Oweny helped us so well that he, in the end, did all the dirty work. For this he received nothing but abuse from old Roe, who threatened to turn him away if he caught him wasting his time and the mistress' kitchen basins on 'that fool's work.'

But Oweny only grinned at him, and on the first chance slipped back to the scow. I think Oweny was the kind of lad who would work only at what took his fancy; and his fancy was always for something that did not pay. Aunt Hersey said that she had once found Oweny weeding the lawn and offered him sixpence an hour to finish the work. But Oweny had quietly disappeared and had never weeded again. He had lost his taste for weeding as soon as it became a mercenary job.

Oweny was not Aunt Hersey's servant, but old Roe's. Aunt Hersey would tip him sometimes, and Frances gave him clothes;

he was paid, too, for carting turf or cutting wood; but, for a
regular income, he depended on his uncle. I daresay he received
a shilling a week, in odd pennies.

CHAPTER 31

When we went to see Frances after her return from the honeymoon even Delia had a look of curious expectation. She, like us,
on first meeting Frances, stared at her as if great events must
have printed themselves on her face. But Frances, though a trifle
fatter, seemed completely unchanged. She welcomed us with
cries of delight, and then at once made us see the house and all
that she intended doing to it. She had already bought two new
chairs which she told us were early Georgian. 'Ding doesn't like
them because they stick into his back, but I tell him that he
needn't sit on them.'

Nearly all the other furniture, inherited by Mackee from his
parents, she condemned as rubbish. But she said, too, that it
was good, and she turned one armchair over to show us that the
upholstery was nailed with solid brass. We gazed at these brass
nails, which were like little portcullises, with a sense of embarrassment. No one knew what to say about them, and Delia
relieved us all when she turned away and threw up her head and
looked round the room as if for some larger object of admiration. But she found nothing.

We now all felt our disappointment, or rather we felt Delia's
disapproval. But Frances, delighted with her new house, continued to chatter, to point out the view from the windows, and
even Delia's tone in which she said: 'Yes, not a bad *view*,' or
'Quite a nice *fender*,' did not seem to strike her as ironical.

Finally Dingbat came in, smiling and humble, obviously
nervous of us, even of Harry and Kathy and myself, and at once
Frances began to order him about like a slave. She also made
jokes at his expense and told us all his faults. He was a bad
traveller and terrified of the sea. 'You couldn't believe what a
coward he is – he has a night-light in case of ghosts – and when
it thundered the other night, he clutched me so hard that I was
black and blue.'

Meanwhile Mackee, with the same humble expression, smiled at us and her as if to say: 'Isn't she wonderful?'

When we went away at last Frances begged us to come again soon. She had been longing to see us, she said. We must come at least three times a week. But Delia answered that perhaps Dingbat was not so anxious for our company.

'Good gracious,' Frances said, laughing, 'Ding wants what I want.'

'Then he shouldn't,' Delia answered. 'It's disgusting.'

Frances looked astounded at this, became sad and tearful. She wrote to her mother bitter complaints against Delia. But though the quarrel was patched up and we were sent, by order, to visit Frances, we supported Delia, treated Frances coldly, and went out of our way to be polite to Mackee. An idea is not easily removed or disturbed. We never ceased to condescend with Dingbat all our lives, even when he became an important and distinguished person. But we were polite to him before Frances as a reproach to her.

In the upshot we did pay many visits to Frances, partly for the chocolate eclairs with which she fed us and which even Delia loved, and partly because on these visits we could go by our own boat. This had proved to leak under sail, and old Roe told our aunt that it would open under us like a basket. But Delia, who also enjoyed sailing the scow, proposed a treaty with her mother under which we were to visit Frances, provided we went in the scow.

Aunt Hersey, after suffering sleepless nights of indecision, at last agreed to let us risk our lives for Frances' sake. I suppose the newly-married Frances was then especially dear to her and it was true that Frances suffered a great deal by our coldness. She was an affectionate girl and apparently she could never understand why we had suddenly taken a dislike to her, or why Delia treated her with such contempt. None of us of course, ever explained the cause to her. We children could not explain it; we merely felt disgusted with Frances, and Delia herself either did not think fit to explain or found it equally difficult to put her feeling into words. But possibly for this very reason, because our notion of Frances' crime was vague and foggy, we exaggerated our disgust. It became soon an amusement as well as a moral act. As in those national feuds which occupy off-moments of holiday time in millions of minds, there was an element of pastime in our denunciation. We played at it. This indeed was our only excuse for so much cruelty to a girl who had always been good to us and who was too good-natured, even now, to take up the quarrel.

Just as it had been enjoyable to invent new insults for Dingbat, now even Harry obviously enjoyed discovering new reasons for attacking Frances, and especially new phrases in which to express it. 'Frank and her old chairs,' he would cry, and 'Frank and her new toys,' was one which we both repeated often. The proper response to this, expressed with passionate indignation, was 'But where does Dingbat come in?'

Yet I would call this out while actually full of excitement, perhaps because of the excitement, while the scow was bucketing through the heavy seas off Culdee point. Any cry will do to express happiness, and I'm sure many of our cries against Frances were simply cries of joy, moved by the noise of the wind and the glimpse of black squalls on the open lough beyond. The scow was unmanageable in a light wind; but before a strong wind or better, half a gale, it left everything behind. Its huge sprit, which seemed to us as big as that of a Thames barge, when thrust up to the furthest stretch of the sail peak, caught the wind like a modern Bermuda rig and drove us along with a power which seemed different even in kind, from the push of the light Castle sails, with gaff and boom. The Castle Corner boat, which Pinto had used, galloped and leaped over the fields and banks of water like a race-horse; the scow surged and butted through the water, tearing a huge furrow through the green and leaving a wake like a steamer. It did not spring over the waves, but crashed down upon them and broke them into great spouts of foam which curled back in glittering arcs on each side of us like the fin-waves of a dolphin. But there was nothing of the dolphin in its movements. It was an enemy of the sea, fighting it, crushing it, with a brutal force. It had neither grace nor finesse. All its attitudes were stiff and ugly. Its mast did not swing; it jerked, changing one rigid point for another. Its thick timbers did not spring and quiver like the delicate skin of the Castle boat, as sensitive as muscle fibres; they merely shook under the weight of their own clumsy bows. A sail in the scow, especially in high winds and rough weather, was like a battle, a series of battles; a campaign carried on with the greatest possible violence and noise. The very memory of these roaring days deafens my ears; the continuous howling, like a distant angry crowd, of the wind in our thick shrouds; the groans and shrieks of the sprit against the thick mast, in proportions resembling a carrot; and the bumping of the mast itself in its iron ring, which was much too big for it, the loud creaks of the timbers which seemed ready not to fly but to rip themselves apart, the clangs and thumps of the anchor tumbling about in the bows among two or three empty buckets; and above all, the ceaseless crashing, tearing, boiling, whistling, spitting, sobbing of the broken water through which we smashed our way, makes for the mind a sort of sea tunnel or hollow in the past when one stoops into a long green darkness of excitement and noise. I suppose the sense of darkness, of the tunnel, comes from some childish feeling of the stormy pressure of the air, the brown sail leaning overhead, the arching spray, the swag-bellied clouds rolling down upon us.

CHAPTER 32

We triumphed in our scow, and every time it smashed through a sea I felt a personal victory. Harry would often call out for admiration: 'I say, she took that one well, didn't she?'

'You could sail her to America.'

'Look how she stands up to the wind – I should think it must be a gale now.'

'A gale – it's a hurricane. Isn't this a hurricane, Deely?'

'Getting that way – as far as a strong breeze – and why does she always bully Ding, just because we're there?'

'Perhaps she always does it.'

'It's so disgusting – it's really so horrible that I can't be bothered with Ding any more. He's not a man – he's a tame calf.'

All these remarks after the first week had a settled form; as in a game.

Yet the vendetta was not quite senseless, like our old attack on Dingbat himself. I think it had a real basis. Delia, for all her romantic love of the unconventional, had strong feelings about conduct, especially married conduct. She was a severe critic of all the bad wives in the county, and even of bad housekeepers. She would say of some visitor after her departure: 'Yes, she gets her dresses from Paris, but her wretched husband has to eat Dooley's bacon.'

We agreed with Delia because we felt, in the same way, that Frances had failed in her duty, and that this duty was important. Like most children, in any question affecting marriage or the home, or the different responsibilities of men and women, we were conservatives so strong and convinced that we never examined our judgments. As soon as we understood from Delia that Frances was treating marriage in a frivolous, trifling spirit, and behaving badly to her husband, we felt a real indignation against her, a natural anger. For our conservative feelings were that of nature itself, so deep that they cannot be changed by an idea, but only distorted. To us the family was the structure of society, the only one we knew. We felt it sacred as a savage feels the sacredness of earth and water, simply and without thought.

Delia, and therefore we, were specially indignant because Frances ran down her former lovers. 'But they all do it,' Delia would say. 'Maisie was the same when she married that fool in Dublin.'

The truth was, I suppose, that Frances was still trying to be sure that she had made the best choice of a husband, and like a man who has bought one picture out of three or four shown by the artist, at once began to depreciate the others. But that occurred to none of us.

CHAPTER 33

Since we chose the strong winds for our visits to Blackhall, in order to show off the wonderful qualities of our boat, we had some of the most exciting sails I can remember. Her motion in a following sea, such as usually drove behind us when we ran home with the tide, was especially awkward and surly. As each wave came up behind her, she yawed, and hung upon the crest of what my father called a three-cornered angle, referring to a table with one short leg. She clung to the wave as long as she could, then with a tremendous crack of the sprit and thump of the mast, fell suddenly down the back of it into the trough, where all Delia's strength was needed to prevent her from broaching to. But just when the following wave was curling over her and about to swamp her, she would take the wind again and swoop forward, bow down and stern up, driving her blunt nose so deep that she seemed ready to sail to the bottom. So she would rush and batter forward with short, sudden rolls, which threw us out of our seats, until the wave slowly gained upon her, lifted her tail first, shipped half a sea over her counter, and once more sent her yawing like a swing at a fair.

Delia loved to wrestle with the scow on such a day. With two hands on the tiller and her bare foot braced against the leeward stern seat, she struggled with it like a bullock wrestler in a rodeo. Her hair, usually clubbed, though she had begun to put it up, was blown over the top of her head like a black cock's comb, and as she showed her teeth and grinned as if in rage with the boat, she was smiling with pleasure at the same time.

'But it's so unnecessary,' she would cry. 'Why, why does she go on at him? Oh, I despise us. I wonder why anyone marries a woman?'

'But people have to marry,' Harry said shocked.

'I won't, it's too petty altogether. Or yes, I'll marry a rich old man – I don't care what he's like or how old he is – I'll marry him tomorrow,' and she went on for the rest of the journey, telling us that nothing in the world mattered but money. To be rich, to do what you liked, to be anything you chose, to travel, to have the whole world at your disposal; that was the grand life. The only life.

Delia often talked thus of the delights of being rich, and we didn't hear that kind of talk from grown-ups. They were all careful to depreciate money to us, for they assumed that we would be poor. But Delia did not make us feel: 'We must get money at all costs.' She did not disturb in the least that deeper impression, perhaps too deep, which we had gathered from my father and his sisters, from all the Corners, that money did not matter; she made us feel only: 'What a grand life is waiting for us when we're grown up and leave school.' For to us, of course, even Delia seemed well off. She could go to town whenever she liked and she always had money in her pocket.

When she shouted at us through the noise of the wind and the sea: 'I shall be rich, rich, and buy a concert grand of my own, and a six-ton cruiser with mahogany doors in the cabin,' we used to laugh like children at a party who suddenly catch sight of the birthday cake. We had a rich feeling which belonged to our other feelings in the scow, of possession, of power. Several times, in our eagerness to test her strength, we were caught in real storms. Then Aunt Hersey, warned by the Dunvil fishermen of our danger, forbade us to sail again. But of course she soon gave way, for all our peace.

In one of these storms we missed our handfall at Dunamara, and, unable to make the scow stand up to the wind and tide together, were carried beyond Dunvil and wrecked on the sandspit just outside Crowcliff house. That is, we were driven ashore, broadside on, and rolled over by the waves; the sprit fell out, the mast was sprung; and all of us children were tumbled into the surf and rolled about until Delia, a fisherman, and the village idiot, Dan Doilie, as usual at storm time mooning among the rocks, came and pulled us out, full of water and bruises. Harry had a black eye, Kathy a broken finger, I had a cut over the eye which bled down my cheek into my mouth. But I did not know anything about this wound until Delia began to howl over me and Doilie told me that I wasn't dead yet. Delia herself was unhurt and complained only of the loss of her shoes and stockings.

It was now past ten. Our wearing and tacking in the hopeless attempt to make Dunamara had wasted three hours. We did not get home till past eleven. But we entered in triumph. In all our families of cousins, a disaster of this kind was treated as a glorious event, to be saluted with shouts. I suppose this was because all our grandparents and aunts, who looked after us in the holidays, were inclined to spoil children; and to be anxious about us.

Aunt Hersey was specially anxious when we sailed the scow and so we competed to be first with the bad news. All of us, even Delia, wet and dirty and bloodstained, pressed forward round her, laughing and telling the story together, while she, distressed by hours of anxiety and angered by the wreck of the boat, kept saying: 'Do be quiet, children – it's not a joke. Do you mean that the boat is lost? You ought to thank God you weren't all drowned, as I know some day you will be. I'm very disappointed in you, Delia,' and so on.

Her distress gave us pleasure, both by magnifying our exploit

and assuring us of her affection. We plagued her for both
reasons.

Kathy's broken finger was not discovered till an hour later
when she remarked mildly that it hurt her. It looked then like a
sausage. It was crushed as well as broken and Kathy was blamed
for not demanding treatment at once. But she said modestly that
she thought Harry and I were worse. Kathy was heroic so
conscientiously that she never received any credit for it.

CHAPTER 34

The weather must have been bad that August, for apart from
the wreck, and from a very rough passage to meet Robert
coming back from school, I remember that we were often shut
up in the house behind streaming windows. We did not mind
this, because I, like Harry, was beginning to enjoy books, and
on wet days we could read as much as we liked without being
accused, by Delia and Kathys of stuffing in the house.

We bathed from the house, complaining that we supposed we
must bathe. We would stumble among the rocks, hunching our
shoulders against the driving rain and putting our hands into
our armpits, just as my father did on such a day; and imitating
him, purse up our lips as if tasting something sharp and strong.

My father enjoyed everything in the open air; all scenes; the
east winds and brilliant skies of spring with their exciting sense
of expectation and change; a warm summer day was luxury to
him; and cold winter gales stimulation. With him we had
enjoyed every kind of weather, and Harry, hobbling and crying
out: 'Brrr,' when the rain struck him, or grinning at us and
saying: 'This is what they call summer,' was copying even his
voice and movements. These cries of pain and disgust amused
us and made us laugh at ourselves just as my father laughed at
his own chattering teeth.

When the rain was warm, we called out: 'I say, it's quite hot,'
asking each other to enjoy the feel of the warm drops falling on
our bare skins, and when we rushed into the sea, daring the
waves to hurl us down, we shouted: 'It's freezing – I'm frozen,'
and because we shouted, and, as they say, made a song about it,

it too became a pleasure. But when the rain was cold, stinging us, we exclaimed: 'It's freezing – it's too cruel – it's real sleet – it's taking my skin off,' and fought through it, feeling extremely brave; and then taking cover in the sea, we cried in astonishment: 'I say, the sea's quite warm – I could stay in for hours.'

Although Delia was practising the piano five or six hours a day, she nearly always bathed with us because, as she said, her music master had ordered her to keep fit. Delia always spoke of this master, a little shabby old man, who came sometimes to tea, as a tyrant. She would say: 'Mr Dolling says I must go to bed early – I've got to be quite fresh for my practising. It seems rather absurd, but I suppose it's necessary.'

She was preoccupied even while she bathed, and after one dip she would fly back to the house, and when we returned, blue and shivering since she had not been there to drive us out of the water, we would find her already at the piano in the schoolroom, frowning into the air and playing some difficult scale or practising a piece over and over again.

Robert was usually lying in a corner, doing nothing. Robert had come back late because he had stayed with his English godmother on the way. He was so unhappy that he would not even bathe. He lounged about all day with his hands in his pockets, stooping and hollow-eyed like an old man, and picked quarrels with his mother and Delia. He would follow his mother from room to room, saying in a spiteful, furious voice: 'It's no good discussing anything with you – you don't want to find out the truth. You only want not to be worried.'

But when our poor aunt tried to please him by carrying on the argument, he accused her of shifting her ground. ' Just now you said that the Bible wasn't true – now you say it is.'

Many of these quarrels were about religion. Robert had suddenly begun to attack religion, though it was easy to see he did not really care what anybody believed. In fact, it was he who shifted his ground, if anyone said a word against religion to him; for instance, when we complained against going to church, he would attack us and show us that our objections were merely selfish.

He picked quarrels with Delia about her music, and even her manners. He would say to her: 'Your petticoat's falling off – I suppose that's because you're a genius,' or 'The female Paddy-rooski wears her hair like a haystack – more Paddy than rooski.'

In fact Delia, who had been tidy in her room, and when she chose, neat in her dress, had become untidy and careless. She wandered about upstairs in bedroom slippers, without a blouse. Aunt Hersey protested, but Delia said that she had no time to dress. She was too busy. It was Robert who accused her of affecting the genius, putting the idea into our heads that Delia was affected. Evcn my father, who was very fond of Delia, got this idea and chaffed her on the holes in her stockings. Her only defender was Pinto who, calling one day about the dramatic society, heard Uncle Herbert abuse Delia for affectation, and suddenly lost his temper.

He astonished us all by his furious indignation. 'That's the meanest thing you can say about anybody who's trying to study an art,' and he argued, as when he had defended us at the Maylins', that criticism might spoil Delia's confidence.

'When I was in Paris,' Herbert said, 'you could be sure that the chaps who dressed up in big ties and velvet caps were either lawyer's clerks or rotten painters.'

We had heard this very often from Uncle Herbert. He used it against anybody who dressed for a part, even sportsmen in leggings. For he himself always went about in neat suits, as if dressed for an informal party. Pinto then argued that many great artists had dressed their parts; that Wagner, for instance, had worn the most extravagant clothes.

'Oh, Wagner,' Herbert said. 'That mountebank.'

Uncle Herbert never lost his temper. He had very good manners, like his sister, and though his face would get red with anger so that his white moustache and his bald head seemed whiter, he always kept his dignity and self-possession. He had therefore a great advantage over Pinto, who now began to say that it was no good talking about anything that really mattered to spiteful vegetables. This was his name for anyone whom he disliked; and when Delia came in to take a chocolate from her mother's Wednesday box, he shouted at her: 'Don't you let them turn you into another cabbage stalk.'

Aunt Hersey, laughing, said that Delia would never be a cabbage stalk, and Delia went out as if she had understood nothing. Afterwards she said coolly that Pinto had been a failure himself and that was why he was always talking about the blowflies who wrecked a man's faith. 'But I don't believe a real artist ever fails – genius is always recognised, that is, of course, if he does a reasonable amount of work. Pinto didn't work, that's why he failed – and he never sticks to anything either.'

Robert, of course, picked this up and said: 'So you do think you're a genius.' But Delia, who never lost her temper with Robert, answered calmly, no, she didn't think so, but Mr Dolling thought she might be good enough for a London début, and then she could be a professional.

She spoke the word professional with a kind of respect and impatience, as if to say: 'And I really haven't time to explain what professional standards are.'

On these wet days Delia would play all the morning while Harry and I, coming in from our first bathes, ate our buns and drank our milk, and then read magazines. Aunt Hersey had borrowed from Castle Corner, which was full of every kind of old paper, a pile of old magazines, *Wide World* and *Strands*, to amuse us on the wet days, and we gorged them.

What a delight it was after the heroic bathe, often with new cuts on our ankles and new bruises on our feet, to sit in the schoolroom window-seat, slowly eating buns and reading true stories of adventure, amidst a storm of Beethoven from one side and of rain from the other; I would look up between stories to enjoy the wet and the wind outside from which I was safe; and to admire the storm. In an easterly wind, the lough would first grow as dark as a rain-washed plum; but soon the whole landscape would be so closely covered with whitecaps, from those not yet large but very long, tumbling on the stones just below, to the minute flecks of white in the distance, catching the watery sun's rays, that it took the grey-blue colour of a plum on a tree in its fresh bloom. The clouds which were rusty like a collier's sails, bulged down close over this flat, rushing sea, as if they were just going to fall on it and let all their water out in one flood. But in fact they were holding up strongly; they had burst only here and there; so that one saw half a dozen rain streams pouring down, each blackening its own piece of sea and flattening the breakers. These storms seemed to trail over the water; one would have thought a group of gigantic nuns, very fat for their size, were moving across the sea, with the smooth motion of the religious, trailing their long black skirts behind them, and dragging along the breakers like cherry petals, fallen on a dark cinder path.

Whenever the clouds broke into rain, the sunlight shone down through their rags, which became as blue as pigeons, floating in a yellow, diffused brightness, so pale and luminous that it seemed to be a pure white light, and to have no colour at all, except in contrast with the pale intense blues, and the glittering foam. Between this thick, confused sky and the charging seas which looked as regular as household cavalry, the far shore of the lough, five miles off, in bright sunshine, came so near that the raindrops, just fallen on the bright leaves, seemed to be sparkling under your eye. But the drops were probably white cottages, or rushing streams, the leaves were whole woods and the trees separate mountain-sides.

As each nun advanced upon us, the rain beat upon the windows in sudden gusts, making a noise like a basket full of pebbles dashed against a new-mortared cottage wall. They did not rattle, but each drop made a quick, loud slap. Then they poured down so fast that they ran over each other; the top ones, sliding in water, beat the bottom ones on the pane. The window would be three or four streams thick, and each stream added to the pleasure of our warmth and dryness.

There was a fascinating contrast between the grand, silent approach of the black squall in its long streamers and the sudden angry noise of its attack. It was as if a very dignified person had suddenly lost his temper. The movement of the nuns, with this sudden collapse of temper, was itself fascinating like the rhythm of Delia's music; it carried one into a sleepy, hypnotised state. While still half-enchanted by the last story, I would pass into this lazy fascination; knowing all the time that there was another story, and another enchantment waiting under my hand.

CHAPTER 35

Delia's music was part of our enjoyment; even scales can sometimes please me now by taking me back to that upper room with its streaming windows; Robert, lounging in his corner, ostentatiously doing nothing and refusing to do anything, did not trouble us. We avoided him, but we did not take particular notice of him. We knew that he was very unhappy at school; but for us he was almost a grown-up; we hardly expected or tried to enter into his feelings. Besides, I think that children rarely get a clear idea even of another child's unhappiness, unless it is made plain to them. One of us was often unhappy without the others noticing it; or rather, the others saw only the details and not the fact. Harry passed one whole Easter holiday in dejection, because of some crime he had committed which Uncle Herbert reported to my father. But we did not give him any consideration. We were too busy to remember that he was suffering except when we actually noticed his face or found him listless. Then we murmured: 'Poor Harry,' or politely refrained from pestering him. In the same way we did not notice Robert's despair and we had no idea of it as a permanent condition until we saw it through Delia's eyes.

This happened one wet morning when Harry and I, caught by the rain, had come in wet, with wet towels. We kilted ourselves with the towels and came for our buns. Delia was already at the piano with a towel round her shoulders. Her legs were bare and her slippers had fallen off, so that she had her bare feet on the pedals. Her hair had got wet and it hung down over the towel; I remember the wet points made short stiff curls like briar thorns. She was playing a new piece and stumbling over one quick passage. Robert was in his usual place at the far end of the long room, but we did not notice him.

We drank our milk at once and began to gobble our buns, meaning to go and dry ourselves in the kitchen and dress, when Harry noticed his magazine lying open on the table and picked it up. Then at once, as if shot down, he sank into the window-seat. I, unwilling to be separated from Harry, took up another magazine and also at once forgot my wet and shivering state.

It was the truth of the *Wide World* stories which carried me away. I was arguing all the time: 'This is the real world – this is what really happens in it.' Harry was in the middle of a story, but I was starting a new magazine, which was even more exciting. I sat down on a chair and also began to read and shiver. Delia, without looking round, said: 'You two idiots are not going to start reading like that – you'll catch pneumonia.'

Neither of us answered. We seldom noticed interruptions when we were reading. We heard, but we did not attend. Harry had actually stopped in the middle of a bite and was holding the bun in his mouth as he turned a page. He, who felt the cold, had cheeks so blue that even I noticed it, and said: 'You ought to dress, Harry.'

For answer, without lifting his eyes from the book, he took the wet towel from his waist and put it round his head. Then he pushed the rest of the bun into his mouth. I pulled off the table-cloth and wrapped it round myself. At once I felt warm, and also I enjoyed the sense of using the table-cloth for what it was not meant for. I felt the enjoyment of a wet day at Dunamara, with a new magazine; and a fresh delight in this special wet day because of the table-cloth, Harry's absurd towel, and a sense of lawless peace.

Suddenly Delia jumped up from the piano and went to Robert and said something to him in a conversational tone. Robert did not answer; and Delia asked him if he had made up his mind. She was referring to some private matter between them, and several times we had heard and seen her urging Robert in some course.

What this was, as we knew afterwards, was a plan for Robert to go away with her to his godmother in London. This Foley godmother, an aunt, was devoted to them both and very troubled about Robert's unhappiness. She agreed with Delia that he ought to be taken away from school. Whether she was actually privy to Delia's scheme for running away from home, I don't know, but Delia was quite capable of carrying it through. Her idea was that Robert should go to an army tutor near by, and complete his education there; while she could continue her music. She was sure that this was the only way to bring Robert's misery to an end. For Aunt Hersey could never make up her mind about anything, and changed it every day about Robert's future.

When Robert made no answer, Delia began to reason with him, urging him to leave the school. Robert answered: 'Thanks very much, but I don't want to leave. I like my school.'

'You know you hate it,' Delia said. 'It's killing you – right through. How can you fight a whole house full of boys, Robbie; besides, it isn't fighting them – just going on bearing them. It's really letting them beat you – because they are killing you – they're turning you into somebody else, into somebody like them – somebody ordinary – somebody afraid to be the least bit different from the stupid brutes they are – the reason why you must leave school is just because you don't want to be beaten. If you don't want to do anything different, that *is* letting them beat you. It's letting them have a perfect triumph over you, and not only that, but they're making you into somebody else. They're filling you up with hatred until you even *look* different.'

Robert did not move or even show that he was listening. Delia had gradually slipped down so that she was kneeling beside him and trying to pull him into her arms. But he kept squeezing himself back against the window-frame so that she couldn't get her arms quite round him. She waited for a moment and then smiled and said: 'Robbie, why do you hate us all – why do you hate me – it isn't really necessary, is it? It doesn't *add* to your happiness – we aren't really your enemies.' Then suddenly she frowned and spoke in a reasoning tone: 'Oh, I know that nothing is more annoying than to have people worrying about you when they don't even understand what's wrong – people who love you can be perfectly maddening – yes, nothing is more hateful than to be loved by someone who simply pesters you with worrying about you and never does anything. But, darling, I *am* suggesting something – and I *know* it would make the most terrific difference. It's the only sensible thing to do. It would change your whole life and you would be able simply to laugh at them – silly filthy schoolboys being badgered by masters, while you were free and doing just what you liked. And it won't waste your time because you'll learn more, too – it's a place for teaching stupid young men how to pass into the army, so you'll simply ramp along.'

'I wish you'd leave me alone,' Robert said, 'really, I'd rather be at school.'

Delia smiled at him as if humouring him. But when she began to speak, her voice shook and it was obvious that she was nearly in tears. She told him again that he mustn't be beaten, that he could never be beaten as long as he did not allow those boys to have any real effect on him. 'You mustn't think you're a failure, Robbie – you aren't – you simply aren't a failure. You got an exhibition – and you're high up in the school already – you're streets cleverer than any of those brutes, and you're far braver, too. I bet they couldn't have stood what you've stood – not for a day. They'd go howling to their mamas at once. You've done simply marvellously. Only you mustn't let them change you now – I'm so afraid you will get quite full of hatred so that there'll be nothing left – you mustn't let hatred take hold of you, because that *will* cut you off from everyone.'

'Why not,' Robert said. 'That would have its advantages.'

'Yes, you are changing – they are changing you,' Delia was crying, and obviously she began to speak without thinking; wildly. Her passionate love for Robert and her fear for him overcame her cautious tact. 'You're different already – sometimes I couldn't believe it was you at all – you don't even look the same or think in the same way – everything you say and do is full of spite, but why, why must you hate the only ones who can do anything for you—?'

'Oh, go away and let me alone,' Robert said loudly.

'If I go away I won't come back. I can't, can I – I can't say anything more.'

'I hope not.'

'Darling Robbie, I'm not trying to pester you – I don't care if you do hate me, I'm only asking you to do something – to make some decision. Or leave it to me if you like – I'll do everything. You needn't even say. Say nothing and I'll know – I have the money for the tickets—'

Robert tried to push her away and there was a miserable kind of struggle. Delia begged him: 'But listen, Robbie. Robbie, just one minute, please—'

I suppose Delia loved Robert as much as it is possible for one human being to love another, and with a sister's love, which, when it is strong, is the deepest of all. I don't mean that most sisters have a very intense love for their brothers; it is more enduring and familiar. It is loyal and faithful, but not often passionate. Delia was passionately fond of Robert. Like a loving wife or husband, she was a different person when Robert was not at home or near her; not always more gay and lively, or as now, more unhappy, but gay or unhappy in a different way which took account of Robert's presence. It was as if, when Robert was there, she reflected some light from him, which gave a colour, bright or dark, to her own nature. She was also, like an affectionate wife, extraordinarily quick to detect the smallest change in Robert's mind; and she had even the power, much rarer, of knowing the cause of such changes. I suppose at that time Robert was as wretched as anyone can be. He was not only miserable, but he did not know how to escape from his misery. A boy of fifteen in Robert's position, who has found every action a mistake leading to fresh misery, who has failed to manage his own life or even to understand how life should be conducted; who has found all his ideas wrong, all his instruction false or useless; loses faith so utterly that he cannot believe in any way of escape; any resolution. He distrusts every action; and becomes empty of purpose. His will turns back on itself and tortures him with self-contempt. He hates, as Delia saw, with such bitter hatred, just those who love him most devotedly, because their love is another burden laid upon his aching tortured spirit, which finds even the weight of self-love too heavy for it. He hates himself for existing as his own disease, his own burden, and Robert hated Delia for reminding him, by her love, that he was still somebody, still a living creature for whom decisions must be made and actions performed.

They struggled for a moment, and then Robert shouted: 'It's you are the worst.'

'I don't mind what you say to me, Robbie, if you'll only act.'

'Act – act – but what can I do – don't you see there's nothing.' Robert suddenly burst into loud sobs and then struggled to get free of Delia. He actually dragged her away from the seat before he could get clear. Then he rushed out of the room. Delia remained where she was for a long time, kneeling on the floor and apparently reflecting on the late scene. Then she went back to the piano and began to play scales. We were still sitting over our magazines. I had been astonished by the conversation, which, like so many overheard grown-up conversations, had opened new windows for me almost at every sentence. I don't mean that I saw clearly, at that time, the misery of Robert's position, and the fact that such a position can ruin a child's whole nature in a short time; change him from the brave, confident and enterprising boy that Robert had been a year before into a spiteful useless kind of being, dangerous to himself and everybody else. Neither did I form a clear notion of Delia's love, and her desperation while she tried to make some break in Robert's misery. But I felt these things as one feels suddenly the presence of unexpected large spaces in the dark; I knew that stretches of unfamiliar strange experience were opened to me, but I did not know what I ought to think of them. I looked several times at Harry, to see how he was taking them, but he, with the towel partly twisted on his head like a turban, partly hanging over one ear like a hood, was still reading. His eyes darted over the lines, and though he was still blue and his teeth chattered from time to time, he was obviously quite unaware of being chilled.

I did not know what to think therefore. My sudden and violent changes of feeling did not produce any ideas on the subject of Robert's unhappiness and Delia's attempts to extricate him from it.

I thought Delia had forgotten our presence. So I was again surprised when, after two or three minutes' playing, she stopped, hands in air, and said, without turning round: 'Get me a hanky, Evelyn, there's a dear. Harry, if you don't go and dress this minute I'll really be cross with you.'

I brought her a handkerchief and saw that she was still weeping silently. Her whole face was wet. But she blew her nose with a perfect composure and commanded me not to tell Robert that she had been crying. 'He's upset about that beastly school. But it's private – you understand.'

She herself showed no embarrassment. Delia, like some great ladies with their servants, seemed indifferent to what we smaller children knew of her private affairs and feelings.

We knew therefore in the next few weeks that she was very unhappy. She used to sit about idle, which was very unusual for Delia; and though the scow was now salvaged and repaired, with a long binding of rope round the split mast, she would not go sailing. 'No, I haven't the time,' she would say as if reminded by the very suggestion that life was a serious matter, and she would go back to the piano with a determined, angry frown.

CHAPTER 36

Harry, after all, had heard or absorbed the conversation between Robert and Delia, for when we went to dress, he looked up from the magazine which he was still reading and said: 'You heard her.'

'Yes, do you think that Robert will leave school?'

'I hope not. Philip says that a chap never gets over that, and I shouldn't think so either.' Harry spoke with the authority of his year at prep. school. 'It was Philip's fault, you know, he codded

Robbie again,' and he told me that Robert, for the second time, had taken Philip's advice and made a fool of himself. I think Philip had persuaded him to get up at a house concert and recite some long pathetic poem.

Harry gave me this news in an impatient careless manner. It produced in me, as always when Robert's misery was forced on my notice, a sense of dismay and confusion. I felt suddenly very small and ignorant; above all, I felt that I was surrounded by the most dangerous problems to which I ought to find an answer at once. I was myself going to boarding-school that winter for the first time. How could I avoid Robert's mistakes. It was no good asking questions. Even of Harry, a good and affectionate brother, I dared not ask: 'How shall I avoid disaster at school.' I knew even at nine that the question was too vague, that it would make Harry raise his dark eyebrows and ask impatiently: 'What do you mean – what *exactly* do you mean?'

Harry demanded always precision.

Harry, too, was full of confidence and energy. He was enjoying success at his own school. He was in the top form and had been bowling for the first eleven. He did not care even to discuss Robert's troubles which obviously perplexed him.

I was troubled also by Robert's relations with Philip. He went to see Philip almost as soon as he came home and obviously he admired him more than ever. How, I would ask myself, could Robert still like Philip; forgetting that we, who had also suffered from Philip's tricks, also admired and respected him. It seemed to me that telling lies to children was an accepted thing; and I felt, if the brave and wise Robert had come to disaster at school, what would happen to me. I used to have fits of panic which made me jump out of a chair, or if I was attacked on the beach run off somewhere else, as if chased by a wasp.

It was about this time that Aunt Hersey suddenly accused me of being dirty and acquiring bad habits.

'It's because of Oweny,' my uncle said. 'He's always with Oweny. I wish you'd get rid of that blackguard.'

'He only comes here with the turf, dear, and to help Roe sometimes.'

My uncle answered that Oweny was always about and that he would set the house on fire one day. Aunt Hersey looked troubled and said gently that Oweny never came into the house.

'If there was a flea, it was one of the children caught it from the poor boy; but I think it was just a harvest flea.'

As usual, Oweny stayed. Aunt Hersey, for all her submission to her brother, never changed an old-established routine. She had great powers of resistance to nagging, like those metals, at once ductile and precious, which are proof against acids and rust.

I was surprised to hear that I spent much time with Oweny and that I caught fleas from him. I remember only a few incidents in which Oweny and I were together; when we went to the bog, up in the mountains, on the ass cart, and Oweny told me about his brother who was in the American police. 'That's the good life – if anyone says boo to him he'd split their skull open with his club.'

I asked Oweny if he would like to be a policeman and he answered: 'Ah, no, why would I want to change. I'm well enough.'

For a time I practised spitting, like Oweny. This habit disgusted my aunt, and one of my Corner Aunts, Rose, was disgusted with me because I attended while Oweny killed some chickens, cutting their necks through a piece of newspaper. I was thought to be turning bloodthirsty. In fact, as always, when I was troubled or felt insecure in my own world, either because of mischief or some private alarm, I sought the kitchen's or Oweny's. I was accused then of trying to escape trouble, but I think really I was seeking reassurance. My spitting was probably an attempt to be like Oweny, based on the unconscious argument: 'If I am like Oweny, I shall have his power of getting along with life. Even if I fail at school like Robert, fail at everything, I shall still have a pleasant alternative.'

CHAPTER 37

I can remember very well the sharp uneasiness I suffered at Robert's failure. Yet this must have been in the same summer when I was enjoying intensely the new kind of sailing in the scow, the magazines and half a dozen other new discoveries in experience.

The truth was that like most small children I had great powers of putting away and ignoring fears or even actual sufferings. Savages have the same power. I saw, later on, in Africa, during a famine and in a big outbreak of smallpox, the strange resignation of the people. I did not know what patience meant until I saw old men dying by the roadside, with dying children in their arms; or the smallpox camps where whole families sat all day, with their enormously swollen faces, waiting upon fate with a submission so complete that I had to have some of them spoon-fed. They had lost all confidence in remedy and even in food. I daresay they felt that the familiar corn might poison them. They were some of those millions who have died every year, in peacetime, for countless thousands of years, in misery which no war could exaggerate, and they accepted their fortune in such patience that they did not even resent it. They did not dream of blaming anyone for it. They were prefectly good-natured and ready to be cheerful. They laughed at a joke, especially if they thought they were meant to be amused.

But I realised then, that like children, they had no other alternative. They were so completely ignorant and unable to help themselves, that their only defence against what seemed to them the cruel fantasies of chance and the mysterious injustice of nature, was resignation. But it was not like the resignation of the defeated, who, as Robert did, enter into a fortress, and will not even look out of the windows. It was more like a magic cloak of the soul, put on to make the wearer invisible and impregnable. It was as if they said: 'With this spread over me I may escape after all.'

So small children, unable to escape from or even to understand some danger, put on a cloak of indifference to it, and while they run about as usual, they are aware all the time of its presence. They don't suppress their fears, they allay them, as far as possible, by a secret act of indifference. Of course, if they do think to see any means of escape, they leap at it; as I did when I went off with Oweny, deliberately ruffled up my hair, spat and lounged about the place, trying Oweny's power for my spell.

I think that one of my rare but furious quarrels with Harry was due to this secret anxiety about school.

Harry was inventing a play, and even while we were bathing or rat hunting in the summer twilight, he would exclaim: 'Look here, we'll *use* that,' meaning that we would have a scene of two people wrestling under water, or a full moon.

'We could take that old mosquito net of Uncle Herbert's for the water and pretend to be swimming behind it. You and Kathy could wear belts painted like skin, and we'll hang you up on ropes painted green so that nobody can see through the net, yes, and you could fight with fish knives so that you won't cut each other.'

Our plays were full of devices which, of course, were far beyond our powers of construction. We actually attempted to hang up Kathy behind the green net, but we found it impossible to balance her. Either she tipped forward on her nose, or fell backwards into a kneeling position. She was heroic as usual, and when Delia once found her entirely surrounded by an enormous bruise, made by the belt, with large lumps on her head, she told some lie and saved us from Delia's anger. Because Delia did not like Kathy, she was particularly fierce in defending her.

We loved properties; Harry built a whole play round an old pair of duelling pistols from the attic. My quarrel with Harry was about one of our properties; an old cavalry sabre also from the attic. Harry was to be a general and wear this sabre. But I demanded it because I had seen it first. I wanted to wave a real sabre; because it was real, the touch of its handle gave me a peculiar sensation; not merely of courage and confidence, but of victory.

Harry wore the sabre, but not before I had nearly killed him with it by a blow which might have split his skull if it had not hit the lamp-bracket. This act cost me the sabre; for Delia made me give it up, as a sign of remorse.

Children are supposed to enjoy acting as a play-preparation for life; but we enjoyed acting not for its likeness to life, but for its unlikeness to our own lives. We always chose heroic parts and magnificent uniforms. While we strutted and spouted we were making for ourselves a world of romance, of poetry, and also invoking powers over the real world.

Our plays must have been the worst ever performed. Each of us chose and composed his own part and acted it without any regard to the rest. Harry, for instance, who intended then to be a soldier, came on as a general in a paper hat, waved the sabre and made speeches to his troops; or sometimes walked about with his arms crossed and soliloquised about his wars. 'I have saved my country and my faithful soldiers trust me. They know that I would die for them. As for this war which I am now going to wage, I intend to advance direct on the enemy and attack him with all my guns. It is victory or death.'

Meanwhile Kathy as a nurse stooped over a rolled-up eider-down, comforting a wounded man. 'My poor fellow, is the pain very bad? Do not hesitate to call me whenever you feel worse. Even at night you can call and I shan't mind. Remember that it is a nurse's duty to do everything she can for her poor patients, even if she might catch some horrible disease or die of it. She mustn't mind. So call me whenever you like. However tired I am, I will get up and dress and everything and come to you. Wait, I will give you some sleeping elixir. There now, you feel better, don't you, and before you wake up again, we shall cut both your legs off.'

I, since I could not be an admiral with the sabre, became a big game hunter. I walked about in a tweed hat, a deerstalker, with Harry's rook rifle and aimed it at imaginary game. 'Ah, a tiger – see how fierce he looks. He is obviously a man-eater by his great size and peculiar markings. I shall aim two inches behind the shoulder which is the only correct place. To shoot at the skull, in tigers, is wrong because the bone is so hard that bullets glance off,' and so on, giving a long lecture on the way to shoot tigers.

There was no plot in any of these plays, and our only idea of plot was to make the general greet the sportsman as his brother and ask what sport he had had. Then I, as the sportsman, would ask the general if he had won any more battles, and the general made another long speech. Kathy did not usually receive expla-nation, but sometimes the general asked her to take particular care of his wounded, or I praised her for saving the life of my favourite tracker, wounded by a tiger.

We never quarrelled about the allocation of parts in these plays, and we always remained silent when the others were speaking, merely acting our own parts in dumb show. While I was lecturing about tigers, the general would wave his sword and cross his arms and frown as if at the crisis of a battle, and while Kathy was telling her patients that it was her duty, as a nurse, to lay down her comforts and even her life for them, I would creep across the back of the stage, and gaze under my hand, as if stalking my victim. The general of course would still be meditating or strutting about and rattling his sword. I suppose no plays gave such boredom to the audience and such delight to the performers.

Kathy especially enjoyed herself so much that she used to walk about the house and even come to meals in her nurse's cap. Unluckily, in her happiness, she tried to nurse both of us, reminding us about our medicines and washing our cuts, until one day Harry, in agony after tearing his knee open, shouted: 'I don't care what you do to it as long as you keep Kathy away.'

Kathy was so much hurt in her feelings that Harry was made to apologise, but she was not consoled. Kathy could never understand how her warm impulse of good nature towards others might cause her to be disliked.

Kathy's misfortune, I think, was that she had no private and constant source of interest within herself. She needed company and she spent her holidays, in those years, among people who did not.

Except Aunt Hersey and Frances, who liked always to be in company, especially together, all of us were capable of being much alone. All Kathy's interests began from the social end, and nearly all ours, either because we had lost our mother young, or because the Corners, as a family, left children to themselves, from the individual end. Harry often demanded to be alone, and avoided us all while he pursued his ideas. To us solitude was a natural and often pleasant state of being, but Kathy when she was alone became uneasy as if she had committed some fault.

After Harry's insults she was so miserable that she was often in tears, bursting out without warning. She refused also to take her part in the plays. But she gave way at once when we pointed out that she was being selfish; because the plays would stop without her.

The plays therefore went on, and in spite of the fearful boredom they gave to everyone. Aunt Hersey brought audiences, at least five or six people, to every performance. Everyone in the neighbourhood was pressed for this duty; and Aunt Hersey led the applause to show them where to clap.

CHAPTER 38

Aunt Hersey was in extraordinary spirits because Robert had suddenly become successful and happy. He had been promoted to play rugger for the house fifteen, and all at once, it seemed, he was a popular person. He was able to look down on the little gang of fellow-fags who had persecuted him, and what was still more interesting to Harry and myself, they looked up to him and even kowtowed to him.

Robert's letters home, as read to us by the proud and delighted Aunt Hersey that winter, were like battle pieces. They were full of sentences like 'Fighting them off till the whistle – smashing through the line – that right wing was the real danger, but we knocked him about so much in the first tackles that he lost his nerve and funked.' He wrote: 'The real danger in Brumfitts (Robert's house) is that it is used to being cock of everything, and so it tends to get slack. It only lost the rugger pot last year simply by slackness; the chaps broke their training and one of the threes used to smoke in his study. Jigger, who's captain this year, says that we didn't deserve to win that year, and he wishes we hadn't, because it's a bad thing when a house eaten up with rottenness and slackness as Brumfitts was then gets away with it. It's bad for everybody, and simply leads to a general letting slide.'

In another letter, he wrote: 'Jigger has thrown Williams out of the team. He was heavy and pretty tough, but we all know he's a perfect rotter – smoking, drinking and everything. He doesn't really care a damn for the house and he's a thoroughly bad influence.'

These letters, which delighted Aunt Hersey, seemed to trouble Delia. She used to say: 'What have they done to Robbie now?'

'My dear Deely, aren't you glad that the boy's so happy at last?'

'Of course I am, but his letters are so unexpected.'

'Robbie was always inclined to be a little strict in his ideas – I don't think it's a bad thing at all. It's quite time someone in the family did take stricter views.'

'Yes, but he's so fighty all at once – he sounds absolutely ferocious. And he's so intolerant.'

'He's very young still.'

'It's not like Robbie – they're doing things to him.'

'He's only growing up.'

'But people grow up in different ways.'

Aunt Hersey answered only that it was better for Robert to think of nothing but football than to be miserable.

But Delia continued to be anxious. She was near enough to childhood to feel how easily children can be altered, not merely by such a powerful influence as a school, but by very small accidents, and old enough to see that the change might be for the worse. She was losing the optimism which in us was still expecting nothing but advantage in growing up, in experience.

Delia alone did not praise our plays. She said that we ought to take more trouble with them. But she provided music for the opening of each performance, and would strike up if one of us could not find anything to say. She was no longer our companion, but she was more sympathetic to our follies.

It was the servants who gave us most encouragement. They came to the first performance, and giggled from beginning to end. It startled us very much that the dignified Mrs Fee and the sensible Jessy should giggle, but soon we realised that they could not help it. They had never seen a play before. When we went into the kitchen afterwards we found Mrs Fee still very red and even, I felt, a little ashamed.

'Why did you laugh at her play, Mrs Fee?' I asked. 'Didn't you like it?'

'It was beautiful. Oh, you're the clever wains. But don't call it a play, my lamb, plays are bad things.'

'But it was a play, Mrs Fee.'

'No, my dear. A play has all kinds of wickedness in it, but you spoke grand words. And Miss Katherine, it was lovely to hear her, the angel.'

Jessy, too, was astonished. She asked me where we had learnt to do such things and if we had got our speeches out of a book. We answered her no, but she answered coolly: 'You'll have picked them up at that English school. Ah! a hundred guineas doesn't go for nothing. Why should they?'

Jessy often made such remarks. She had a great opinion of the value of education. But she never expressed any envy in her tone, only the fact. After that we used to be always in the kitchen ranting and lecturing. We became conceited and took advice from nobody. I imagine our plays became worse and worse.

CHAPTER 39

Even during these plays I spent much time with Oweny, who was supposed to be carting turf and building up the winter stacks in the stack-yard. I would go to help on the stack, but often, if old Roe were not watching us, we would slip away among the trees or up the creek. Our favourite hiding-place was an old mill on Dunamara upper creek. It was a huge four-storied building with several yards, surrounded by a couple of acres of rough ground, overgrown by nettles and scrub. The mill leat turning aside from the river, ran under a wing of building through a dark archway; then formed a pool from which it escaped soon by a fall over the open sluices. The great rusty wheel was hidden behind another archway opening from the pool.

Oweny and I would prowl through the buildings by day, as if hunting for something. Indeed I would pick up any old nail or fragment of wood, and carry them away with me as if I had found treasures. But Oweny would say: 'Ah, what's the good of it?'

We would throw chips into the leat to watch them sail under the arch. Oweny would spend an hour at the top of the high wing which overlooked the stream flowing between walls below, and when the chip came under the arch, he would call out in his high, musical voice: 'She's here'

My excuse was to see how fast the stream ran, and I used to count one, two, three till Oweny called, and then shout: 'Eight that time, Oweny – eight seconds. It's getting quicker.'

But this was only an excuse. My pleasure was watching the chips float out from the sunlight into the dark arch, and Oweny's, I suppose, was to be occupied without profit.

The charm of Oweny's company arose a great deal from his lack of ambition. He did not look forward or back; he gave value to the real life as it occurred, though without the intensity of Pinto or my father. For them the moment was to be seized.

Both had the sense of being whirled forward through life. But Oweny was indifferent to time and dawdled through life as through an evening spectacle.

In spring he was quick to find nests building and then we would lie under the bush to see the birds arrive.

I was not allowed to rob nests. My father had made me understand that it was cruel to steal eggs. But I delighted to know where one was in order to enjoy the preoccupation of the birds. It gave me the keenest pleasure to see a small bird fly in and out of a bush, if I knew that he was carrying food to a nest, and I would creep as near as I could to hear the couple twittering together. This seemed to amuse Oweny also, in his own way. He, too, would lie under a thorny bush half a morning, and when, at some new outburst of cheeps, I would say: 'There they are again,' he would answer: 'Aye, that could be another worm he's brought in.'

This interest in birds did not prevent my shooting with my airgun at everything that flew; or, if I could get hold of it, with Harry's rook rifle. Harry had been given this rifle for his last birthday, and we often went hunting with it. Harry would go in the middle with the rifle, Oweny, Kathy and myself would act as flankers, seeking to trail the game. Although Harry did nearly all the shooting, we were never tired of the sport. I never saw Oweny excited except when Harry was aiming at a bird and if, which happened rarely, he shot one, he would even laugh, the only time I ever heard him laugh. Yet he, like Harry and like us, seemed to feel quite differently about a bird after it had been shot. When we held the warm body in our hands we felt like murderers, and Harry's air of surprise and triumph would pass into another kind of surprise.

Oweny, grinning sideways at the company, would say at last: 'Ah, it never knew what hit it,' and Harry, half consoled, would say: 'It would probably have died quite soon anyway. Millions of birds die in the winter.'

At night we went rat-hunting along the stream. Whenever the moon was bright enough to see, as we hoped, a rat in the water, we would clamber up the steep path from Dunamara yard, through an entanglement of briars, and creep under a broken gate into the mill.

Oweny never came with us at night. The country people avoided the mill in the dark, and though Harry and I stoutly denied the existence of ghosts, we would not go alone at night through the yards.

We were more frightened of the yards than the buildings themselves. I often ventured alone through the nearest high building, from which one could hear through a glassless window or loophole door, high up in the wall, the rustle of the stream below under the arches and detect the dead arm of the pool, not by its surface, but by the reflection of the stars, languidly rocking up and down or elongating themselves first in one axis and then in the other. But even upon a journey to this view which attracted me so much, I went with a feeling of terror which often made me stop and wonder at my own rashness. I think I went only once through the yards alone, and then out of bravado, at top speed. The rows of empty black doors and windows, four stories high, were too much for me. Our feeling was that each hid a secret watcher.

This was the sense of our imagination, that we were being watched and that when we went from one yard to another, the watchers silently followed us, passing to the windows of the next yard, and crowding down after us to peer through the doorway that we had just passed. We never spoke of these creatures of ours, but we referred to them obliquely, as when Kathy would jump and cling to Harry and say, 'I thought I saw a face,' or Harry would assure the party that there was nobody there.

'Nobody ever comes here, you know – that noise is just bats or owls or the floors creaking.'

I would agree heartily and add my favourite argument, that no one would want to come there – there was nothing for anybody to do there.

But my imagination still created for me grey faceless shapes, like little rags of cloud, trooping from window to window or crowding together behind us in the yard, and staring after us out of their no faces, with eyes like bats.

They were faceless because my will was so resolute not to believe in ghosts. They had eyes because, in spite of my will, I felt watched, and the eyes were large and prominent because since I was watched in the dark, the watchers must have bats' eyes.

In spite of these terrors and though there was a direct path to the millpool through the buildings, we used nearly always to go by the yards. Partly this was bravado, because we were ashamed to be frightened, partly it was the attraction of the enterprise. Children are said to enjoy terror as a whet to their nerves. I don't believe fright ever attracted any of us. What sent me up the ladder at the Maylins', and down the mainstay of a brigantine one day and through the yards at the old mill, was the challenge of an enterprise.

We did not believe in ghosts, but we were frightened of them; and I at least, as a child, was frightened of the dark. Also, I was nervous of heights. Therefore every dark cave or haunted wood, and every high building or mast, seemed to say to me: 'I dare you,' and I was ashamed not to dare.

I used to climb the shrouds of a turf-carrying brigantine at Cran bay and sit in the iron cradle which held the mainyard, and I can still remember the terror of my passage when I had to swing myself from the shrouds to the cradle, and the delicious sense of mixed triumph and security with which, hooked on by armpits and legs, I sat down into the iron semi-circle and looked over the little port, the stone pier, with its miniature lighthouse, and my cousins bathing or running about below.

But the mainstay, a thick iron rope starting at the truck just over my head, seemed to say, every time I accomplished this feat: 'I dare you,' until it spoilt my enjoyment of the cradle. So one day I set out to slide down it. Unluckily my body was small and light, the rope thick and made of thick strands, so that it felt like a corkscrew. As soon as I began to slide the rope tried to turn me round and throw me off.

At every yard I had to stop and regain my balance. Finally I came over the forecastle; – I can still smell and feel the hot reek rising from its chimney to me on the rope. The scuttle was open, and I saw straight down past the rope to its floor. This extra ten foot drop, for some reason, threw me into a panic and I stuck on the rope, holding on for life. Meanwhile I had been seen, a crowd gathered on the quay; my grandfather was fetched; and the crew came up the shrouds to give advice. This advice, however, was merely to go on down the rope and to keep a loose grip. Finally, having collected my courage, collect is the word to describe the gradual process, I slid on, and by fits and starts reached the forecastle head.

I felt both foolish and confused when I stood among the family, and was reproached for giving so much distress by a piece of mischief. My confusion was due to the fact that though I felt guilty, I also felt like the victim of circumstances. I did not realise then that I could have blamed the stay for challenging me; and my own nervousness of heights for accepting the challenge.

So I was challenged by the windows of the old mill. I kept very close to Harry and Kathy while we went through the first archway. We advanced like soldiers moving through enemy country, among ambuscades. Harry, now and then, as he walked between us carrying a loaded rifle, would often turn right round in a slow circle to look behind and make sure that we were not followed. He continued at the same time to keep with us by stepping first sideways, and then backwards, coming round at last into the line, when at once we closed in on him from each side. We kept so close to him that he sometimes complained of our tripping him up.

'Don't press on my shooting arm, Kathy – suppose I had to shoot quickly. I shouldn't be able to get the gun up in time.'

Beyond the yards there was an old wooden bridge across the top of the sluice, where the leat ran down in a short waterfall. Here we would wait, side by side, leaning on the old rotten top bar of the bridge, looking across the millpool and waiting for a rat.

The walls behind the bridge were low and windowless; we felt safe there and we felt, too, like adventurers who had passed through dangers to reach an important and honourable goal. We therefore made much of the rat-hunting, and Harry would say: 'It's important to kill the rats – they eat up every year millions of pounds' worth of stuff. Besides, they carry plague and all kinds of disease'; and both Kathy and I would warmly support him.

'People *pay* rat-catchers to kill them.'

All of us knew that the rats were water-rats and perfectly harmless, but we did not say so as there would have been no good motive for our exciting journey through the old mill; or for standing on the bridge, under the moon, close together and gazing at the deep green-black shadows of the bank, the water smoother and brighter than mercury; and hearing the ringing sound of the waterfall below our feet. We felt it, too, for it shook the bridge, not violently, but with a steady vibration; like the cause of its own note. It was as though we were part of the sound, not a sleepy sound like that of the sea, whose waves could still be heard as if from another world, of a wide and low expanse and flat distance, but an invigorating noise with power in it, which filled the tall sky-space above our heads. The leat was no longer turning a wheel, but we felt that it had turned wheels, and its song was full of energy. Although we stood close together on the bridge and often permitted Kathy to take our arms, even to put her arms round us on each side, so that our bodies were sentimental, our talk was full of purpose. We discussed what we should do in the world and Harry pondered schemes for new boats, flying-ships and weapons, or new governments. Harry had suddenly begun to invent these schemes; he would suggest, for instance, a new kind of state in which money would be abolished and everyone could exchange goods. 'We could go and catch some fish and take them to Macneil's and buy a double-barrel gun.' He invented a government of the world by means of a flying-ship armed with twelve-inch guns. 'If anyone started a war against the government, the ship would go and blow them up.' Another of his plans was to conquer the world by freezing all the air over a given spot with fans suspended from balloons. The fans were to blow upon a fine spray of water dropped from the balloons and collected from the clouds. 'Because you couldn't have balloons big enough to carry the water tanks.'

Harry was always particular about details, and worked out the carrying power of balloons and the weight of his steam fans. He also argued that even if the air did not freeze, it could be made so cold that whole nations would surrender rather than perish.

Harry had a passionate belief in all his schemes, when he first thought of them, and would not listen to criticism. They seemed to him perfectly feasible. All that was needed was the money, ten thousand pounds for a flying-ship or the balloon-freezer. To Kathy and me they also seemed feasible and yet, for some reason, we doubted if they would work. Something, we thought, was bound to go wrong.

We agreed upon this between ourselves, but we did not tell Harry, who would have asked: 'All right, *what* – tell me *what* wouldn't work.' To that we had no answer.

The truth was, I suppose, that we were much more childish than Harry, and more distrustful of the world and our own powers. Harry had begun to form ideas of government, the world and so on; very simple ideas, but coherent and rational; whereas Kathy and I were still like savages, who understand so little of the forces surrounding them that they cannot even imagine a means of controlling them.

I listened to Harry with deep admiration and yet with a sense of guilt and helplessness; as if it were some defect in myself which would cause all these splendid plans to come to nothing; my ignorance, my lack of enterprise.

At other times Harry invented merely new stage devices or plays. I can't remember that he ever shot a rat, and I remember only once hearing one dive into the black shadows under the bank. Harry was then too startled to shoot, and all three of us watched a little silver arrow head pass across a segment of the pool, from the wide shadow of one bank into the narrow bar of the other. This was the bow wave of the rat. Its wake rumpling the surface of the water without the least injury to its fascinating smoothness, as the pull of a needle wrinkles silk, extended gradually over the whole space and continued for so long that after what seemed the silence of ten minutes, Kathy said: 'You can still see where it went.'

We looked again in silence at the water and I seemed to feel in it the track of the warm body through its cold transparency.

'I wonder where its home is?' Kathy said. Kathy was always wondering where creatures had their homes and what their homes were like. We affected to despise this sympathetic curiosity and received her wonderings in silence. Yet between ourselves we debated the same question. We liked to think of foxes and badgers in their earths, rabbits in their burrows; and tits in their hanging bowers; of wild creatures, hunted by the world, safe in some hole or private fortress. Open nests did not excite this feeling; we did not think of them as homes; because they had no roofs, they were not enclosed and private. To us, small creatures were like other children. We hunted them and abused them; we had no special affection for them; but we entered into their feelings much more readily than those of grown-ups. I never heard Kathy say of any grown-up: 'I wonder where he's at home.'

Our play-acting, although we thought it a spontaneous inspiration, was actually part of a dramatic revival which had affected the whole neighbourhood. This was due, in the first place, to Pinto, who had revived, or, at least, put new energy into a local dramatic society. He had reorganised it, collected subscriptions and given already some dramatic readings. He was now attempting to get up a play for the winter. But his members wanted a modern comedy; and he was determined on some classic, Sheridan or Shakespeare.

Aunt Hersey was one of Pinto's keenest supporters; much to her brother's irritation, she even joined the dramatic club committee and entertained it at Dunamara. On those days we children suddenly met a crowd of people who, even if we had known them before, appeared to us in an entirely new aspect. They talked nothing but plays, or argued during a whole tea-time about the merits of actors and actresses, which play gave the best opportunities to the hero or heroine.

Sometimes one of them would jump up from table and show how Alexander or Tree did such and such a speech. There was one little man in pince-nez, very fair, with a face like a goose, who was always waiting for an opportunity to spout long speeches from Shakespeare. He was very lively and intelligent; an enthusiast, and we delighted to see him, quite unembarrassed, waving his arms in Aunt Hersey's drawing-room, or, as Macbeth in the last scene, posing with one foot on a hassock and his hand across his eyes, gazing at Dunsinane wood as it approached through the picture of great-great-grandmother Grattan over the fireplace.

This little man was a Dunvil grocer's clerk, whom we had seen before only behind the counter; or sometimes at the regatta. A friend of his, who came from Derry, used to sing operatic airs from Verdi to Delia's accompaniment. This man, who was in charge of Pinto's new-founded orchestra, persuaded Aunt Hersey to take care of all its music.

In a few weeks at the end of the summer the quality of Dunamara life was changed, and, what was still more unexpected, Aunt Hersey changed the whole routine of years and even her character. She no longer spent all day wandering about with an anxious expression, because there was no mutton to be had until the major killed a sheep, or because Kathy had a roaring cold, or because Delia was unkind to Frances, or for any of a hundred reasons. She passed most of the morning writing or answering letters about the club, which she carefully filed, rushed off to Derry by the mail to order a script, or a song, or stuff for a dress, and came back in the afternoon to a committee, or a reading, or a practice. Often she brought back two or three new subscribers, sometimes complete strangers, who would at once take charge of the drawing-room, push the furniture about, draw the curtains, light candles, and set down Delia at the piano to play accompaniments while they acted some scene from the *Geisha* or *Patience*.

Meanwhile Aunt Hersey's household ran itself; and so far from worrying about it, she would call out to Delia: 'Do go and tell Jessy to tell Mrs Fee that I've no time to see her this morning – she'd better do what she can – there's a darling.'

Our Uncle Herbert, of course, disliked this change very much. He was especially bitter against Freeman, who used to invade the house at all hours, often in a very bad temper. He would come in often with Rose Maylin, who, as secretary to the club, went everywhere with him, and shout for Aunt Hersey.

She would come as if to a master, and he would demand if she had written to so-and-so or ordered something or other.

'But you didn't tell me.'

'You knew it was wanted – have I to do everything myself?'

Aunt Hersey, with a look of consternation, would apologise, and promise to write at once. Then she would ask Freeman to luncheon or tea, and he would say gloomily that he had no time. But he would stay, after all, and complain for an hour of the badness of his actors, saying he would throw up the club.

All this infuriated Uncle Herbert, and I suppose it would have enraged any man who had set in a critical form. To him Freeman was an affected, useless person, who exerted a mysterious fascination over silly women and stage-struck young men. But his attitude could no longer do harm, because Freeman was now a popular member of society. Partly on account of the Maylins who introduced him everywhere and partly on his own merits, he had more invitations than he could accept. He used to complain of them in our hearing and say that he had no time for anything; his life was being wasted on amusing a lot of silly old women.

To us it seemed natural that Pinto should be received everywhere, even though he was argumentative, and talked of the local gentry, to their faces, as vegetables. To Uncle Herbert it seemed extraordinary. But Annish was then a very remote place where people were at once good-natured and bored. Almost any stranger, however odd, was received once he had been accepted. It used to be said that the last home of the eighteenth century was the west and north-west of Ireland. If so, both the rigid wall of caste which shut out Freeman on his first arrival, and the boundless urbanity with which, afterwards, he was accepted and allowed to say and do exactly what he liked, were traditional. Old Maylin bore with his guest because he had seen his parents bear with similar.

CHAPTER 41

The mill stream running over the sluice through its channel of rough stone made a regular pattern at each side like a fan; and in the middle where there was a post with runners for the sluice gates, a shape like the beginning of a four-in-hand cravat. Lower down the two side fans crossed over the middle stream so as to complete the tie. Two other fans sprang out here from two stone posts, set in the walls, and completed the pattern.

In daytime, when I wandered through the mill and the stream with my airgun, I was apt to get no further than the bridge. I would even lie down and put my eye to the cracks between the boards in order to catch the water flying underneath. What fascinated me was the swift movement of the water and the regularity of the pattern. The water flying over the smooth stone top of the fall was as bright as a melting icicle; and so clear that the smallest blade of water-grass stirring within it could be seen as sharply defined as a specimen in ice; it was disturbed only by the creasing of the water as it darted forwards, as if dragged by the weight of the fall. Then suddenly this bright sheet broke into spurts of foam against the bridge posts, and flying still more quickly, drew out, for ever new and for ever the same, the complicated fan pattern.

The edges of the different fan-shaped squirts of water were frilled with round work which reminded me of the crochet on Aunt Hersey's best tea-cloths; but every form was perpetually active, jumping up and down, dancing on the glossy stream between the fans like a living creature. Every dancer performed his own extraordinary steps, whirling up, turning round, tossing an arm or head right off into the air, and he was never actually in the line; yet the whole long row was always one line, and it had been dancing like that, day and night, for nearly a hundred years. This, too, the sense of perpetuity fascinated into my feeling while I lay on the bridge, fascinated, and watched, for an hour at a time, the gentle waving of the emerald grasses within the calm, smooth water, the leap of the foam which always seemed about to break out from the pattern and never did so; the careless variety of the dancer's invention. Kathy and Harry would look at my dancers, as I called them, but not for long. Their expressions condescended to me while they did so, as if they thought me childish. Anketel, too, now restless and easily bored, for lack of any notion of what he wanted to do, would either run off at once or say something foolish.

'It's all wollypoddle round the weddles.'

This was not, like Anketel's old speeches, a sentence that expressed some idea. It was a foolish noise. Anketel had been told of his former clever inventions, and now he imitated them. This made him unpopular, and he was accused of showing off, so that he became still more cut off and more affected. He was a nuisance to us, and he seemed to enjoy spoiling our games, as if, not being able to amuse himself, he felt spiteful against those who could. Appeals, punishments, spoiling and presents all had no effect because nothing could reach him through his self-consciousness. He was like one of Fabre's caterpillars that lost its way and wandered into a glass test tube, so that it could neither go on further nor get itself out, nor learn anything about its own unhappy situation except that it was unhappy. Anketel had become a lonely and miserable little boy.

CHAPTER 42

Delia alone seemed to feel the same kind of pleasure as I in the rapid movement of the water, the patterns, the dancers; and the loud lively music of the fall. One day she even accepted my invitation to look through the crack; and afterwards knelt beside me for a long time, smiling at my new crochet, and agreeing with me that there was no spot so delightful.

Delia and I became friends as if we had met for the first time. We had been friends three or four times before, and now I have a recollection of a friendship with Delia which must go back to the time when she was a young girl and I was five or even younger. But I am remembering our ages by calculation, because that friendship began at a party given when she was not more than thirteen. In the recollection itself, the living image of that moment, she is the same Delia that I had known since; a grown-up girl. She remained the same in all my memories because I did not take note of outward changes, but only of people, and their actions belonged to themselves rather than their characters. I was not in the least surprised by anything they might do. I would not have noticed the change in Aunt Hersey if Delia and her uncle had not remarked so often upon it; nor in Anketel, who had suddenly grown tall and awkward and plain, nor in Kathy, whose very face had changed its shape.

It was Delia who said to me one day, at the mill, that I was changing, and everyone was changing; that Robert had changed into another person whom she did not know.

It surprised me to know that I was changing, but I did not pursue the subject. Though I did not notice real changes I was accustomed to the idea that the whole world was changing all the time. I was growing up and I saw in front of me a row of new lives, public school, university, a career, like doorways leading through some place, each room larger and more magnificent than the last. All round me my cousins of all ages were growing up, going to school, getting married; disappearing to the far corners of the world or suddenly appearing before me in uniform wth large moustaches and stories of some war. I lived in the idea, in the very sense of change, of life flying like the water in the mill leat and throwing up its little dancers, always new, always different, but never going far out of the pattern.

I did not think this; I thought nothing; and it was at least a year before I began to form primitive conceptions of the world; but I felt it because I remembered that now when I was friends with Delia, I expected her to get married soon and was extremely jealous of a young man, who was then pursuing her. We called him Bootle. I can recollect nothing of him but his great height, his large black moustache and his extreme sadness. He always looked as if he had just had bad news.

Delia herself was sad. She had given up her music. Someone in London had told her that she would never play well, that her hands were too small. She had been so humbled that she asked Freeman for advice and he told her that she might learn to play accurately, but that he did not care for her touch. 'You can fire it off already, but it's only an imitation of the real thing.'

Everybody was furious with Pinto for this judgment, and even Aunt Hersey reproached him. But he was not in the least disturbed. He answered that he had told the truth; Delia's playing was not real playing at all. There was nothing in it. She had nothing to say in music.

To our surprise Delia said that Pinto was quite right; and from that time she would never study the piano. But she was unhappy in a manner no one would have expected. She became dreamy and idle; and I fancy it was because she had nothing better to do, that she would come and sit with me on the bridge, listening to the mill fall, or allow herself to be dragged through the briars to see my favourite ant's nest.

Delia, for my sake, even tolerated Oweny, though before she had always called him an idle rascal. She watched us one day playing the chip game; Oweny sending down the chips and me shooting at them with the airgun. At last she said: 'Doesn't Oweny ever get a shot?'

'Oh, I wouldn't want to shoot,' Oweny said. 'What's the good of shooting at chips?'

'Oweny's too old,' I explained, feeling a charge of selfishness. 'He's eighteen – he's grown up.'

'I suppose you'll be getting married soon, Oweny.'

Oweny grinned at us and said: 'No, I'll never be married. Who'd marry me? It's not so easy to get a wife.'

'You ought to have a wife to look after you.'

'Ah, I can look after myself better.' Oweny said, looking more serious than usual. 'It's better you should.'

'So long as you know how,' Delia said.

CHAPTER 43

Harry wrote another play for that winter, what he called a real play. He worked at it often during the term and took advice from some of the older boys, who patronised him rather as a dictator's court takes up an author.

There was actually a dictatorship for that year in our private school. Three boys held a reign of terror. But Harry, because of his special position, did not suffer; and though I was publicly and solemnly kicked several times, I had also received a nickname, Whiskey, which I took to be a mark of honour; so that the kicks did not make me feel like an outcast.

School was not what I had expected, either for good or evil. I was left at the term's end in such perplexity that when Aunt Frances Corner asked me how I liked it, I could not discover my own feelings, or rather, like other children in the same position, I had such a mass of impressions that I could not describe them. A sense of crowded life, of friendship, of interesting lessons, of a pleasure especially hard for a child to define, that of enlarging knowledge, for instance, my first dim notions of general principles, was mixed with my dislike of the tyranny, which I did not know to be a passing phase, in a school which had been, and would be again, entirely happy. I had delighted in glory, lasting I think five minutes, on the football field; but the favourite of one moment, as I had found, was the victim of the next, and his disaster always came when he least expected it. That, of course, is the humour of tyrants who see and know their power, where alone it can be seen, in a change of countenance, and who cannot see it then if their cruelties are expected. The boy who suffered most was one who never betrayed his feelings; a clever boy with an old mind and an old sad face. But I was always taken by surprise, and in my happiest moments, so that I must have shown each time as gratifying a change of face as a bridegroom at a marriage feast who is suddenly taken out to be hanged. I remember indeed seeing not only the chief executioner Y, a cheerful boy, with a strong sense of humour, but the dictator himself, A, cold and dignified, smiling down at me as I was brought out for punishment.

Even after two terms of this, and till the very eve of our rebellion which, led by one bold and organising spirit, broke the tyranny in half an hour, most of us never did expect to be the next victim. Our spirits, when not in the actual presence of the tyrant or any of his agents, were gay, and my recollection is not of terrified slavery, but of the lively twittering of a flock of children who, like sparrows, were silent only when the hawk dived, and a moment later, were hopping and chirping again, quite forgetful of the late comrade, now blubbering in the boothole; and of those three or four who, under continuous and designed misery, probably suffered damage for life. I felt the tyranny only when it was near, or when it fell upon me; and my dislike of its irresponsibility expressed itself to me not as an idea but as a vision of A, with his handsome, arrogant face, as he strutted among us, turning in his toes; and the smiling, freckled face of the giant Y, his bodyguard, lounging after him. I did not even hate, in this visionary form, A's cruelty or Y's brutality; the picture of arrogance and lounging strength, lazily confident and proud of its power, merely gave me a sense of uneasiness and uncertainty. It was as though they introduced a subject on which I had no information, and could not form judgment.

So I did not know what to say to Aunt Frances. I felt and probably looked foolish and murmured something conventional about footer being rather fun.

CHAPTER 44

The three Corner aunts took us to Ireland with them. Harry at once asked them to criticise his play; he wanted them to admire. But instead of saying as Aunt Hersey would have said, that it was a wonderful play, they quietly browsed over it and made unexpected remarks to each other about it.

'I like this bit,' said Aunt Frances, and she read out a speech by the queen. 'She reminds me of Miss Daly that kept the sweet shop in Dunvil.'

'But Miss Daly was Royalty – she was descended from the kings of Annish,' and then they would all talk about Miss Daly for a while and tell stories of her dignity and her pungent sayings. Aunt Fran would then read out another bit of the play and say: 'If you have a sea battle, Harry, we must get you a Bengal fire – it's the finest thing in the world for a ship blowing up after a battle.'

Then Aunt Rose would say: 'Do you remember poor Andy?' and they would talk of the loss of the *Victoria*, a battleship, sunk five years before at manœuvres, when a midshipman cousin had been drowned.

The aunt's talk was all about people, which can be either the most interesting or the dullest in the world. Theirs was the most interesting because it was full of their own observation and character.

Different people had different effects on our feelings, and our pleasure in them did not depend so much on their amusing tricks, as on their characters. Their effect, of both grown-ups and children, on us children, was personal, and it was exerted like an influence. We felt people much more than we noticed their separate words or actions; though of course our feeling arose from a total experience which extended often from babyhood.

My feeling of my old great-aunt Mary Corner is as sharp and clear, if I choose, as if she were here in the room with me; the complex sense of a love which demanded nothing, not even thanks or remembrance; of that pride of family which, turning full circle, became a humility and simplicity far deeper than any religious virtue, for it did not even perceive itself as virtue. But I remember my feeling of people about whom I remember nothing else, neither their voices nor their looks; of an old fisherman, for instance, who used to come to my grandmother's kitchen at Castle Corner, and about whose great boots I hovered at four or five, attracted by the sense of his strength and courage and desperation. I suppose, he had performed some brave and dangerous act, but all that remains to me now is his boots and his spirit.

As small children, before we had conscious judgment of people, I think we lived almost entirely in these feelings. Our changes of mood, inexplicable to grown-ups, were due often to the entry of some new person into the room, or even into the house. The sound of a voice in the hall would change my mood, making me suddenly bored with my occupation. The peculiar step of Uncle James Foley on the gravel, one wet day, when I had been calmly engaged in laying out our joint stock of soldiers in a battle, each regiment deployed on one piece of paper, for convenience of movement, caused me to jerk a paper, throw over a whole squadron of lifeguards and give a loud, imbecile laugh. I was not going to see Uncle James, but his presence, even in the rooms below, made me perverse. With Oweny, at the same time, I could be happy all day long, or with Darcy Foy, the Castle Corner coachman and dogman, or with my father or Aunt Frances Corner. But my happiness with each of these was quite different in kind. With Oweny it was reckless and devil-may-care, with Darcy, important and serious, as if I were enjoying a distinction; with my father, tense and expectant as if we were on a military expedition together. With Aunt Frances it was peaceful and carefree.

This arose from the character which belonged in some degree to all my Corner relations, a certain detachment from the world. Family influence, stronger than any precept or sermon, is both subtle and complicated. All the Corners, for instance, set great value on hospitality and on courage, as root virtues; but they were also very clannish and very suspicious of popular heroism. Their carelessness of small worries gave them always a gentle dignity. It pervaded their whole nature, their walk, their voices, their careless dress, their looks. But it went with a total lack of ambition and produced a general indifference to engagements and punctuality. At the same time, it made them, for me, the most delightful companions in the world.

CHAPTER 45

Thus, while the energetic Harry was walking about the decks exploring the ship or inventing some speech for his play, I loved to sit with the aunts behind a lifeboat. They sat there nearly all day, smoking cigarettes and chatting. Behind the boats there were no rails, and a notice forbade passengers to go there. But the three aunts for all their lack of self-assertion regarded ordinary rules as made for the general public and not for Corners. They always sat behind the boats, with me wedged between Frances and Offa. There was nothing between us and the precipice of the ship's side but the gunwale raised about two inches above the deck. Against this flat broad strip of wood the three young women rested their heels, their backs against the lifeboat. It seemed to me that each roll of the steamer would shoot us all into the Atlantic, which looked from this height even colder and more dangerous than from the Castle boat beyond the Heads.

It was January, and the wind kept up in the iron rigging that dismal chord of wails and howls which is heard only on a steamer making a winter voyage in the north Atlantic. The clouds were whirled along like ragged ice on a river of freezing air, at once dark and extremely clear; and every now and then a squall of rain was dashed against the ship, making a noise like small shot on the iron ventilators, and rattling like kettle-drums on the tight boat-covers. Everything about us was streaming with wet except the patch of deck on which I sat under the overhanging brow of the boat's side with Aunt Frances holding me firmly by the hand in order that some deeper roll should not throw me overboard.

The wailing of the ropes, the staggering movement of the ship under the blow of a heavy sea, the streaming wet, the feel of being cut off from the respectable world of passengers who sat in saloons or at least obeyed the notices and kept themselves behind the rails, the very tweed cape of Aunt Fran standing up above her ears, and her lovely serious face, turned towards the sea, all gave me such intense delight than I was glad to know we were already six hours behind time and I wished the voyage to go on for ever. But the sea itself was the most fascinating object from which my eyes turned only to glance hastily at one of the aunts to check some remark by her expression or at the black shrouds overhead to know why they had changed their key, in some change of course or shift of wind. Meanwhile the aunts' chat went on over my head, part of my pleasure, even when I was not conscious of hearing it. But much of it I did listen to, because of its curious reflections on grown-up life. 'Do you know,' Aunt Fran would say, 'that when the old reverend Mac came and asked Dolman for his daughter, she was only fifteen and it was all fixed up. But just when the two old men were going to sign the settlement, they heard a queer noise in the hall and went out, and there was the girl with her skirts round her waist, sliding down the balusters. So her father was afraid the match would be no go and he asked her what she was thinking of. She hadn't done a thing like that for years. So she said, no, she hadn't, but she had thought she would like to do it once again before she was married because she might never have another chance in her life.'

'The poor wee thing,' said Rose.

'Nor in the next life, I suppose,' said Offa.

'Ah, there'll be no stairs there – you wouldn't need them with wings.'

'And where will the angels sit between the dances?'

'There'll be no dances – how could anyone dance on the sky?'

'Like June midges, I suppose – going up and down in a cloud of themselves.'

The Corner aunts, unlike Aunt Hersey, used no emphasis whatever. Thus the effect of their remarks was delayed. It came to my ears all at once like a little explosion.

'The midges certainly enjoy themselves more than those fellows the other night in the polka – did you ever see such a hand of faces?' Rose asked with reminiscent scorn.

'Oh, they were only boys, poor dears – afraid for their lives and their brace buttons,' Offa would murmur.

'Did you ever write to young so-and-so, Offa?' Rose asked. Rose was a little more businesslike than the others.

'I think so, but I don't know if I posted it.'

'He's breaking his heart for you.'

'No, I think it's too soft – you couldn't break butter.'

On the lee side, the sea appeared like a mere confusion of peaks like a relief map of the Alps, except that they were all in continual violent movement. But when, on a change of course, we took the wind on our left cheeks, the Atlantic rollers showed themselves beneath. The broken peaks which had been the horizon, suddenly took line; a bar of darkness, as blue black as the upper hollow of the night sky, appeared before them, and they themselves became suddenly paler; grey green like winter fields high up on a mountain. Then all at once these waves which a moment before had been great mountains, became mere jags and spikes on a vast range of Himalayas extending from one side of the earth to the other and shutting out the whole Atlantic. It became the horizon. It was like the whole top of the world moving towards us, not fast, but with an indescribable power and massive dignity.

Our ship would now lean over towards the immense valley below this monster and the wind overhead, catching the shrouds at a different angle, would change its note. The noise of the raindrops, too, on the boat cover would suddenly die away, so that there seemed to be a space of silence. In fact there must have been noise enough to deafen any room full of people. But I could hear one of my aunts, much more clearly, as if in a silence, while she told how she had lost a bet on some race by failing to use a tip, or perhaps Aunt Rose chaffing Aunt Frances. The aunts always had a private joke at each other's expense; that year, about Aunt Frances who, as a beauty, had been presented to the old Prince of Wales. But he had said: 'I hear, Miss Corner, that you smoke,' and reproached her severely for this crime against her beauty. Aunt Rose wrote satirical rhymes, in the family magazine, on this incident, which always puzzled me. I wondered that the aunts took it so lightly, and why Aunt Frances continued to smoke. My ideas about royal authority became confused, especially as the family feeling was very loyal.

Each part of the aunt's talk carried with it a whole group of feelings and undercurrents, which formed at once part of the complex experience in which I lived, waiting for each roller in turn to smash our iron sides and sink us.

All that was happening, the weight and size of the grand powers at work, the feel of thousands of iron tons beneath me driven forward by the engines which shook in my body like a pulse, and the enormous force of the wave, the touch of Aunt Frances' ulster on my cheek, the wailing of the stays, the fringe of raindrops each with a spot of green sky upon it, shaken from the boat side above me, the very shining of the wet planks and the hiss of the water below against the plates, seemed to be part of me, and their grandeur, charm, minute finish and beauty, even the dismal chant of the rigging which seemed like the very complaint of loneliness, all separate nerves in my feeling.

The crash of the wave, which made the whole ship tremble, dispersed this complex pleasure and replaced it by a single triumph. I would shout: 'That was a big one, wasn't it?' and it seemed to me that I personally had won an important victory. My aunts would complain only that the spray was now being thrown over the side and that Captain Willy or Jimmy or Sammy, whichever was their friend in command, always had a wet ship and made it difficult for them to find a quiet spot for a cigarette and a chat.

They also complained that the change of course had brought them from the lee to the weather side. One or other would say now and then: 'Really, we ought to move out of the wind – I'm getting quite wet.'

'Who was it said that, Fran? – it was up at Lough Hinn when the boat sank.' And they would remember another story.

Then another wave would break over us and one would say mildly: 'Does he mean to take the whole sea with him in my lap?'

'It's one way to have a dry passage.'

'I'll have to remind him that a ship's bottom has no legs.'

'Do you remember, Fran, that little man who fell in love with you one day at Shell Port when we borrowed his matches to light our fire?'

The changing play of talk kept my mind perpetually amused; the big ulsters wedging me in from both sides, kept me warm. Aunt Fran's hand assured me that I could safely enjoy the delight of sitting where no other passenger dared to sit, and watching the sea not through rails, like a lion in a cage; but in that majesty which belonged only to its dangerous roaring freedom.

Although Harry did not spend so much time as I sitting behind the boats, he too had enjoyed the rollers, for he said to me once, as, wet and cold, we went down to some meal: 'I'm going to use this for the play – we'll have a storm in the second act, and Kathy will have to make the noises. The only thing is, will Aunt Hersey let us saw the floor to get a trap-door for the sailors to go down. Perhaps we'd better not ask. We'll saw it first.'

Although we were stage-struck, we never asked how real plays were performed. We did not even read plays. Yet usually both Harry and I, like other children, were very anxious to know how things ought to be done. I can only suppose that having seen the school plays, in which we both acted, and some pantomimes, we thought we had mastered the subject; we were certainly quite sure that our play was as good as Shakespeare; or better.

We set up our stage in the coach-house. Harry had long wanted this building for our theatre, but Uncle Herbert had forbidden its use. Now, as it seemed to us, by a direct stroke of providence, but really because he had quarrelled with his sister about the dramatic club, about Freeman, about what he called this idiotic craze which made the house unfit to live in, he had gone to Nice for the winter. We were free to do what we liked with Aunt Hersey's property.

The coach-house, which was a long low building, occupied now only by the old carriage, a cart, and an outside car, had been a stable. It was built into the hill, and the old hay-house, at the upper end, was raised about five foot. This had struck us as a ready-made stage. We nailed our wings, made of brown paper, to the beams; hung our curtain, which was the school-room tablecloth, on a washing rope, and put down a row of candles, in guards cut out of tin, for footlights.

Our play was a drama in which Harry was a king, a prime minister and a general, myself an admiral, and Kathy, first of all a nurse, and finally the general's wife. Anketel was the king's page and afterwards Kathy's son. All of us, of course, were also messengers, soldiers and sailors; each of us had three or four changes of costume in every act. The plot was so complicated that I can't remember anything about it except that Harry as the king was waging wars against three or four enemies, including the Germans, and Arab slave raiders, and that he was frequently wounded and several times nearly killed. I was also wounded, but only once, and not badly. Kathy, as nurse, tended us both; as the queen she begged us to protect the mothers and children from the slave raiders, and she also shifted scenery, fired off cap pistols, beat drums and sometimes waved a sword with one bare arm projected from the wings, as part of the army or navy.

Most of this plot was carried on by messengers who came in and announced to the king, general or admiral that a battle had been lost or that one of his dearest friends had died a hero's death. Then he or I would make a long speech about the glory of dying for freedom.

These speeches seemed to us the finest things we had ever heard. Even Harry was astonished by them and could hardly believe that he had written them. Kathy and I having put together a few words like 'To die gloriously for honour is better than to live a hundred years and dry up like an old tree,' speeches full of echoes from the Golden Treasury or the Prayer Book, walked about all day murmuring them to ourselves with indescribable delight. For it seemed to us that we were the creators not of words but of the sentiments themselves, and that such sentiments, just like those in the Prayer Book or in the great poets, would have an equal effect. Our whole idea was to create an effect. We talked all day of how we should look, what we should wear, and we were convinced that our audience would be astounded by our play. We knew that Pinto's play, as we called it, was to be repeated, by invitation, at some great house, I think Baronscourt, and we all expected a similar invitation from the Duke of Abercorn. We did not say to each other: 'When the duke sends for our play—' we had already learnt the affected humility of school speech and used it among ourselves; but we used to say: 'If we have to do the play anywhere else, we must get some more candles and a better curtain without the stains on it.'

Meanwhile rehearsals were a wild confusion. Each of us gave instructions almost the whole time, speeches were forgotten; the admiral had to speak without his trousers because he had had no time to change; and the scenery fell into the pit. After hours of shouting, arguing, sometimes violent quarrels, and furious work in the dark hay-house, amidst clouds of old hay dust, which made us sneeze, and covered our perspiring faces with a thick grey dirt, we would stop only because we were exhausted; gradually making our rests longer, being a little later for our cues, not troubling to change our clothes, or uttering our final speeches without getting up from some box on which we had fallen after the last battle, until the performance came to an end by itself. Then, completely happy, we went to find something to eat in the kitchen, and to tell Mrs Fee as a secret, how we were going to astonish the family with our play.

We had no doubt of our success; the hopeless bewilderment of the rehearsals, when everything went wrong, and when, on account of Harry's frequent alterations to the piece, we never knew our cues or our parts, did not give us the least anxiety. We did not even say like real actors: 'All will come right on the night,' we lived in a dream of glory which no facts could touch.

CHAPTER 47

The Annish Dramatic Club did actually perform a Shakespeare play that winter, the *Midsummer Night's Dream*, and kept Aunt Hersey busy with rehearsals for it. But when she asked us to go to the play, at the Maylins', we refused, to her astonishment, saying that we were too busy. Since our play was supposed to be a secret, Aunt Hersey said nothing more.

It was Robert who asked us if we didn't think that we could learn something from Shakespeare. This question surprised us. Harry answered after a time that of course Shakespeare's plays were very good, everyone knew that.

'But you think yours is just as good,' Robert said, smiling. Robert had become good-natured again, but immensely old. He hardly noticed us except to laugh at us. He was still hollow-eyed, stooping; and he still lounged about all day with his hands in his pockets. But now he seemed more like a wrestler than a street lounger. I suppose that he was imitating, or repeating, the crouch of a scrum-half, in which he had made his new glory and his new career. Many scrum-halves acquire the same habit of walk. The only difference was that Robert adapted it from his former dejected slouch.

I can understand now that Robert that winter felt like a man who has achieved greatness by a powerful effort of will. There is no position more honourable and honoured than that of a scrum-half in a rugby team; especially when that team, lighter and weaker than all its opponents, is fighting for its life. Six years later I was in a similar position to Robert, though I never distinguished myself as he did. I was a light forward in a light team, trying to defend the glories won for the house by a series of powerful and heavy teams. I lived for a couple of winters in the atmosphere of Sparta before Thermopylae; except that we fought our desperate battles every week. We felt like a band of heroes, and so we were regarded. The feeling was not of happiness, but sobriety, responsibility. We were grave and responsible. I believe I was a little less idle during those winters, only because even as the humblest member, the least of forwards, among a team of heroes, I breathed the air of greatness.

For there was true greatness in our leaders; I mean those simple fundamental qualities which are the elements of all greatness: courage, independence of will, devotion to a cause larger than one's own; a contempt of mean ambition. Of course, these elements were mixed with others which were childish, like a love of swearing, for its own sake, or of making a noise. They used to romp in the changing-room like small children. But the greatness was there all the time, in however simple a form; just as in a small child, some simple idea of the world, some confident faith remains beneath its chatter to produce all at once a remark of profounder value than anything heard from its elders in the drawing-room.

It seemed to me, of course, that these leaders were the greatest men in the world. The air about them was charged with their personal magnetism, electrifying my own particles; about the elder N., afterwards killed on the Somme, with his pale face and broken boxer's nose, a lively humorous courage like that of a terrier, boundless good humour, and an intelligence both sharp and quick; about his younger brother, killed at Ypres, a fanatical grim courage, like that of a devotee, a pondering mind in which humour was lost in a sense of the urgency of moral and political problems; a dreamy love of poetry, which forgot work in the midst of some contemplation of beauty: the sun on the blind; or the motes in a sunbeam. There was Max, with a glass eye of which he told no one, and in which he played, risking a blow that would have driven it into his brain. About him there was the charm of reckless sincerity, a moral courage which had, when he was a fag, stood up to the heaviest pressure; a mind effervescent with wit and imagination; feelings as quick as a flash, and a tongue which answered your thought before you had put it into speech. Neither am I deceived by hero-worship in thinking that these had true greatness. There is plenty of that at every school, among boys between fifteen and eighteen; simply because many of them, up to that time, have been taught only large and fundamental ideas. Of course, this simplicity is often lost very soon afterwards in a confusion of detail; or what looks like the contradiction of experience. A boy who believes at school in some abstract scheme of social justice, may find out later on that actual social reorganisation is difficult and complex, and produces very unexpected results. Then he may lose his grasp of the simple large fact, that injustice is a deadly wrong, in a mass of superficial issues. He becomes, on that point, little-minded. When a boy leaves school the small but often clear stream of his life runs into the larger stream of national life, and begins to take colour from it. If that stream is muddy, as powerful streams often are, especially when they are changing course, he, too, may become cloudy. His ideas lose all their clarity and certainty. But this does not mean that they were trivial before.

Robert, too, had something of greatness in his achievement, and he had made his own success. Some of the fifteen watching a junior game, had noticed his play and given him a trial among the seniors. He had seized his chance and played with such desperate courage that, though he knew nothing of the game, they had thought it worth while to teach him. In a few weeks he had become scrum-half to the fifteen. He had raised himself from the most miserable position to the most glorious. But as I say, at home, we children noticed only that though he was only more good-natured, he was further off from us than before. I think he was also removed from Delia. Like the Spartans he kept aloof from girls, and Delia was still too young to understand that this good-humoured indifference to her was only another phase of his growing.

They even quarrelled. When Robert smiled at us, Delia flew to our defence: 'How superior of you, Robbie – I think it's a splendid play.'

'Yes, rather.'

'Everything is yes, rather. What you mean is that you are too grand to admire anybody but yourself.'

'Just as you like.'

'I don't like.'

'Poor old Deely, it's a shame about the music.'

'I'm not worrying about *that*.'

'What are you worrying about, then?'

'Oh, go away do, and leave us to our childish amusements.'

Delia, I think, wept privately over Robert's indifference; but we profited by her kindness. She gave us, especially me, the affection which he would not take, and spent hours cutting and sewing a curtain for our play, or making dresses for us.

CHAPTER 48

During the last week of preparation for our play, which had not even a name till the day of performance, we were so completely absorbed in its exciting atmosphere that we could scarcely eat. The rest of the world lost all reality for us, and we saw their forms or heard their voices as through special organs adjusted to keep in touch with their trifling and preposterous affairs. I believe older actors and actresses sometimes have the same feeling about contemporaries. If so, I can understand it, for I, too, have lived in a play and found it more real than life; more full of grand events and noble feelings, all adequately expressed, even than history.

As I said, we refused to go to Pinto's play, because we wanted to rehearse our own. We heard of the success of his play, without interest; and I don't remember that we even cared to know that he himself had refused to attend the performance.

He thought it too bad. The only news that moved us at all was that he could not come to our play, because he had left the Maylins and gone back to England.

I gathered long afterwards that Pinto's temper, as the date of performance approached, had got worse and worse; that he turned Rose Maylin out of her part; swore at old Maylin; and quarrelled so violently with the committee that none of them, except Aunt Hersey, dared go near him. Finally he had said that people were more stupid, more philistine and worse actors than he had ever imagined, and he could not bear their company any longer. So he had gone off one morning and old Maylin had afterwards paid about a hundred pounds' worth of expected debts, not on account of Pinto himself, who went away as shabby and seedy and penniless as he had arrived, but on account of his club.

Our own play was one of those failures which make a sensation by their badness. But though we had done nothing to avoid disaster, though we had not even fixed our cues or written down all our parts, it was not till two minutes before the curtain that Harry, slowly waving his sword, the sabre, and repeating his first speech softly to himself with a look of confident power which would have sat well upon Napoleon or Marlborough, was suddenly affected by a doubt. He stopped, listened to the noise of the audience chattering together, and suddenly his face took an anxious and wondering expression. He seemed all at once surprised and even confused. His eyebrows rose and his eyes opened widely. He turned to me and Kathy and said: 'I say, there's simply hundreds of people.'

'Hundreds,' we agreed. We were perfectly happy because we felt no responsibility; and besides, we were sure of Harry's success.

In fact, Aunt Hersey had gathered nearly thirty guests who were now sitting on kitchen chairs, forms and boxes, even on the seats of the car, propped up as a dress circle, and the top of the carriage, which was the gallery. Even our uncle, Major James Foley of Tulla, had come down from his mountain to see our play.

'Look here,' Harry said, 'we ought to have a prompter – we'll have each to prompt the others.'

'But we don't know all the parts,' I said.

'No, but we can make them up – we'll *have* to,' Harry said, looking more and more alarmed.

Then Delia rang the bell and Jessy, carefully coached, pulled the curtain. The play began by revealing the three of us having a conference in the middle of the stage. From that moment, I remember only the acutest misery I had ever suffered, the three of us falling over each other on the stage, sweating, fighting in the dark corner behind an old Japanese screen which we used for a dressing-room. I found myself, for instance, in an admiral's hat, football shorts and one boot, being pushed on the stage by Delia or Harry, and hearing one or both of them repeating words which I faintly recognised as my part, but which suggested nothing to me, not even the appropriate use of my only three gestures. While Delia was saying: 'Your Majesty, I lay the swords of your enemies at your feet,' I would feebly wave my sword in the air; and when she was saying: 'But still a fearful danger threatens – a cable has been received that the foe has gathered a million men on the Himalayas for the conquest of India,' I would put my paper telescope to my eye as if to watch the cable flying through the air.

I never knew when my part was finished, and while I was still waiting, hopefully, sword in air or telescope to eye, for somebody to repeat my next speech, Delia's strong arm would come out from the wing, catch me by the back of the shorts and drag me off the stage.

In the second act, Kathy and I, fighting in the corner for a pair of blue trousers which we each claimed, knocked the screen down and revealed ourselves to the audience on all fours, snarling at each other like dogs. All of us, even Harry, were several times in tears of exasperation; the furious sobs which in small boys express rage and nervous irritation beyond bearing. Without Delia we would have broken down altogether. She not only spoke at least half the play, kept one or other of us, partly dressed, always on the stage, blew our noses and wiped our faces; but worked the scenery, relit the candles when they went out, played the piano in the intervals, and when the curtain, catching in the footlights, flared up, put it out with the water mixed with sheep-wash ochre which was to have provided the blood for the last great battle scene.

This fire left a large hole in the curtain, and afterwards the footlights guttered down, until in the third act they began to go out altogether. We had forgotten to buy more candles, so that Harry had to cut out the last two acts, and finish the third in a hurry by bringing on Kathy as a messenger to give the rest of the plot in a single speech. Kathy, however, had completely forgotten the plot so that Delia, in the wings, made the speech, Harry muttered it to Kathy, and Kathy, making all the time at Harry those distressed faces which mean: 'Do speak up, I can't hear,' gave it out in little spurts.

There was great applause, and Frances came to congratulate us. But we had lost heart. We were not only ashamed and disappointed; we had suffered a shock. Deeper than the sense of failure, there was the feeling that we had misunderstood the situation; that plays were not so easy as they seemed. With this went, as always, the feeling that life, too, was not so easy as it seemed. Like most children when they fail in a grown-up enterprise, we were subdued and secretly frightened; we wanted to get away by ourselves, preferably out of the grown-up world and back into our own refuges, the schoolroom or the kitchen.

Kathy and I shrank away from the crowd which wanted to praise and reassure us. I remember that we held hands as we stood in a dark corner behind the door, waiting to escape. It was rare for us to show any sentiment in those days, after we had both gone to school; but that night, feeling suddenly our inadequacy, we reverted to an earlier simplicity.

Harry was caught by a circle of admiring grown-ups who blocked the door. I remember his pale, surprised face as he stood, in the cardboard fireman's helmet which had served for the warrior king in his last triumph, insisting that the play had failed. He kept on saying: 'No, it was all wrong – we didn't take enough trouble – it was simply rotten.' We could see that his obstinacy, his determined misery in face of so much kindness, offended a great many of our guests. Aunt Hersey was annoyed with him and said several times: 'My dear boy, if we tell you it was good, you oughtn't to insist that it was bad.'

Aunt Hersey's whole education in good breeding made consideration of others the first of virtues, beyond truth, beyond any standards of perfection. Even Delia reproached Harry, while he stood there, obviously on the edge of tears, and said again and again in a loud, angry voice: 'It was bad, I tell you – it was *rotten* and you *know* it was rotten.'

But though I wished Harry would give way a little in order to let us all escape from the hateful place and the embarrassing situation, I felt that he was right and all the grown-ups wrong. I never admired him so much. Though I could not put words to it, my sense was that he was sticking to truth and something bigger than truth, to a serious point of view; while they were all playing a kind of game, condescending to us in our folly.

At last, Frances, with her quick sympathy, realised Harry's misery, and called from outside the door that it was beginning to rain. It was perfectly fine, but the grown-ups scuttled across the yard, and Harry slipped away with Frances to her room. Kathy and I then went to the kitchen where the maids, of course, praised us to the skies. But though we enjoyed these praises, we imitated Harry at the same time and insisted that the play had been bad. In this way, as our spirits quickly rose again, we were able to get a double pleasure. Unlike Harry, we had no integrity and we could enjoy undeserved praise and the self-respect of refusing it, at the same time.

CHAPTER 49

Harry did not quickly recover from this disaster. For days afterwards he went about with his shoulders even higher than usual and an impatient, surprised expression. He was, I think, always inclined to be severe upon himself for any failure due to carelessness or optimism. He was proud and did not allow himself the indulgence he gave to others. But some of his angry dejection may have been due to Robert who depressed us all. He came into our room on the very evening of the play and asked us why we weren't in bed and what Kathy was doing in our room.

'We couldn't sleep,' Kathy said. 'We're so awfully sick about the play.'

'Well, what did you expect?' Robert said in his careless, laughing tone. 'How could you expect to write a play worth listening to? I don't suppose any of you will ever be able to write even a passable play.'

We heard this in silence. Robert went on in the same cheerful tone: 'Why, really clever men write rotten plays, rotten everything. Nearly all the books that come out are rotten. It's only once in a hundred years that anyone does write anything worth reading.'

I don't know why Robert, having achieved his own success, always tried to make us feel that we had great difficulties in front of us, and could never hope to succeed. He was neither spiteful nor conceited. He was not trying to make himself out the one exceptional person. He was expressing his new idea of life, an idea very strongly grasped, of its danger and difficulty, and his cheerfulness was like the pitying smile with which a nurse pulls back a baby from the fire. But I daresay that Robert, like Philip, had another unconscious motive in his attitude towards younger children; he expressed his own latent bitterness against the insecurity and injustice of things, by making us feel insecure. All over the world children suffer their chief discouragements from other children; and this can't be helped. Children live in their own world from which all grown-ups are excluded by the nature of the case. Even if they understood what is going on in that world they could not enter it as a child who alone carries the special authority of one child for another.

Kathy, after he left us, said in a disgusted voice: 'How silly we were – we really were silly.'

She spoke in a manner which expressed to us a real conviction. It was not the tone in which we had been reproaching ourselves before. We felt agreement with her and we were so much depressed that even Robert noticed it and chaffed us. Harry did not attempt any more plays. I don't think he ever wrote anything again. His mind took a practical and critical turn. But of course this may have been its natural direction.

CHAPTER 50

Cousin Philip passed his examinations; in the next summer we saw him a gentleman cadet; a perfect dandy with a pale brown moustache like two partridge feathers, which made his nose seem longer than ever, and wonderful suits of check. He had always exercised a power over us because of his tricks at our expense, his good looks, his neatness of hand. He had something of my father's dexterity and the same scorn of clumsy fingers and careless work. Also there was something else in Philip which gave him power over us, that quality, hard to describe, of seeming to know a great deal about us which he couldn't be bothered to tell. He would smile at us in a way which seemed to mean: 'I know all about you, you little fools – I know how your silly minds work and how perplexed you are about all sorts of things. Perhaps I shall tell you some day and perhaps I shan't.'

It seemed to mean this because he did now and then make an exact guess at our thoughts and also he would sometimes give us a piece of information. It was Philip who told me what are called the facts of life, in the crudest manner and words. I imagine he was amusing himself, to see how I would take it. But the words were to me merely words, and I was delighted to have the information.

When we heard that Philip was going to Dunamara that summer, on leave, we were almost as much excited as if by the promise of a visit from my father. We had both been charmed by his extraordinary kindness at Christmas when he had dragged us round the ice two or three times and told us that the only way to learn to skate was to try the difficult things first. Both Harry and I had then made jumps and nearly killed ourselves; to his calm amusement.

But though we went out in Roffey's boat, the only members of the family to meet him at the steamer, he ignored us from the beginning. He thought only of Delia and Frances; his first and only question to us when we saw him was, 'How are the girls?' and before going to Dunamara, he called at the shipyard and hired a new boat. His plan was to take the girls sailing, and he promised to win them the dinghy race at Dunvil regatta.

To us this scheme of Philip's, so carefully formed and deliberately carried out, seemed at the time as reasonable as anything else that grown-ups did. It was unexpected, but no more so than many of their actions. We were therefore surprised to hear Aunt Hersey urging Delia to be kind to the poor boy, and telling her: 'You mustn't say he's too silly – he's only a boy, after all, and it's the first time he's had any money to spend. You ought to be flattered that he wants to spend it on you.'

But Delia had bitterly hated Philip after his second trick upon Robert. She blamed him now, probably without justice, for Robert's coolness, and if she did not still hate him, it was only because she did not allow herself, that summer, any strong feelings. Delia during the winter had begun to study for some women's college, I think Holloway. At Easter we had found her, on our one short visit to Dunamara, deep in books and already quite changed. She had been gentle and affectionate to us, as during our play; but now she was gentle in a special way, a little absent-mindedly. She had embraced us, but with the air of a mother-superior who gives way, for one moment, to a natural weakness.

In summer we found her a finished scholar. She was dressed in badly-hung tweed skirts, severe blouses and men's collars. She would even screw up her eyes when she looked at us, as if she were a little short-sighted. Her eyesight was as sharp as a bird's, but she had somehow the feeling that scholars and wise people ought to be a little blind and confused in ordinary vulgar daylight.

I don't mean that there was any pretence in Delia's effort to acquire wisdom. She worked very hard indeed, and gave herself no indulgence. But she felt, I think, that wisdom had its outer as well as its inner form and she wished to be extremely and completely wise. A staff officer, after all, may wear red tabs without being accused of childish display.

So Delia, when she screwed up her beautiful eyes at Philip and said in her new absent-minded, gentle tone: 'It's awfully good of you, Cousin Philip, but I really haven't time. I have to do all the Industrial Revolution before Tuesday, or Miss Macgill will slaughter me, and I'm afraid I'll deserve it,' was not pretending or practising a part. She was being a part.

In the same way, because it seemed to her unscholarly to hate anybody, she really had ceased to hate Philip, and would be quite pleasant to him when they met at meals. She would ask mildly and dreamily: 'Where did you go today, Phil?'

'Right across to Sandy Point.'

'Yes, that must have been lovely. Shell Port is always so nice.'

'Sandy Point we went to.'

'Of course, yes, Sandy Point is always so nice, isn't it? I wish I could have come, but I hadn't a moment.'

But Frances willingly sailed with Philip and he fell deeply in love with her.

We wondered that a man like Philip, who appeared to us the most attractive young man we had ever known, should fall in love with the mild, uninteresting Frances. She seemed to us now almost silly. She was very fat, her face was almost round, and she was excessively lazy and always laughing. She was still very affectionate to all of us, especially Anketel the unpopular and neglected, but her caresses bored us. Why, we asked, did Philip like her so much that he could sit a whole afternoon on the beach holding her parasol and talking with her in soft tones about life, and ambition and happiness and love.

In fact, though we did not know it then, Frances was seven months pregnant and this had increased her love of flirtation and also charmed Philip. He was, I suppose, the kind of man who tends to fall in love with every pregnant woman. Such men have a kind of adoration for a woman in child; a religious impulse which is, probably, the exaggeration of a sympathy and respect natural to humanity.

Philip worshipped Frances. He liked to sit or kneel before her, leaning against her skirt, and gaze up at her; he would have looked absurd if it had not been for his earnestness. Even we could feel there was nothing laughable in such intense serious feeling.

All this made a great scandal. It was said that the couple had been out all night together on the lough, and it was known that Frances treated her husband with public contempt.

We ourselves heard Frances speak of Mackee with contempt. 'He's determined to be a nobody all his life – he won't even go on the council. And they say Mr Mackinney is going into parliament – think of it – that fat stupid grocer.' When she spoke so, her eyes, which seemed to us too bright, as if always moist, like her lips and even her fair plump neck, her upper lip with its fine down and her little, round, prominent forehead, expressed an anger surprising in the placid Frances.

So far as everyone knew, she had been etremely happy with her lawyer, who was her devoted slave. But now it seemed that she was disappointed in him, in his hair, his figure, his voice, above all, in his character. He was too retiring, too unenterprising. You could see behind Frances' vague complaints a sudden ambition for every kind of glory in her husband. She wanted someone as handsome and dashing as Burnaby and as distinguished as the Prime Minister.

Dingbat himself was in despair that he could not hide, that desperate wretchedness which only falls upon a young married man who has reason to be jealous. We knew his misery and despised it. We were accustomed to see the man at Dunamara, for he came at all hours, either to seek Frances, or to obtain comfort and help from her mother. He would wander after Aunt Hersey from room to room, with his old look of humility now mixed with despair, while she, with a piece of music in her hand or trailing a length of cheap gaudy cloth which was going to be a stage dress, or carrying a copy of some play in one hand, a note from Pinto in the other, and a pencil in her mouth, would turn suddenly, and finding him at her skirt fringe, would gaze at him down her beautiful nose with the most polite impatience. She would take out the pencil and say in a lively, encouraging voice: 'Yes, Sidney, did you want me? But wait, just *one* minute, while I mark off these cues and then I'll be all yours.'

But she never found time to hear Dingbat's grief or to warn Frances. She was far too busy with committees. The club had undertaken to give a Shakespeare festival that winter, and was already arranging parts and designing scenery.

Freeman at this time was still aloof. He had come back from England and was staying, to everyone's amazement, up in the mountains, at the Tulla, with my uncle James Foley. But though he came to see Aunt Hersey every day, he would have nothing to do with the club. In fact, there would probably have been no reconciliation and no Shakespeare at all if my father had not turned up one day unexpectedly at Dunamara.

We were painting the scow when suddenly my father stood beside us, and taking the brush out of my hand, showed me how to run a clean band of colour along the rubbing strake. As usual we were fascinated by the dexterity and lightness of his touch; and perhaps, too, we enjoyed his own pleasure in it. He loved to use his hands on some delicate work, requiring the utmost neatness and precision; like the building of a model slide valve engine; or the fitting of a model boat deck, mahogany shaved till it was almost transparent.

He had got off the mail car on its way to our grandmother's, to spend the afternoon with us, prepared to take us for a sail. But the painting amused us much better.

We were dodging round his legs, like moths round a candle, when I saw Harry's face change. He was looking towards the house, and when I turned, I saw Pinto strolling slowly along the lawn, smoking a cigarette.

He was dressed in his usual dingy suit, grey or dirty black, and wore a dirty collar. His hair hung over his eyes, which were red and swollen, and his face, except his nose, was a yellow colour. I was used to Pinto's appearance, but now, because of Harry's expression, I noticed his shabbiness and I remembered that even at Dunamara he was often a little drunk.

This did not offend us any more than his shabbiness. We were accustomed to drunkenness everywhere, in London, Scotland, Annish. As a very small child, I had seen the village gutters filled with dead drunks on a Saturday night; and in that summer we had all laughed over the stairs while Aunt Hersey skilfully conducted one of her guests, a magistrate and churchwarden, to the door, so drunk that he ran into the chairs and reeled against the walls.

But we never saw Freeman really drunk, only gay, and we did not think of this as drunkenness, but as 'having taken drink.' I think, as children, we liked our grown-up friends to have drink taken, except those few whom drink made morose. Pinto, gay, was good company. We liked especially his lawless stories, which, I suppose, appealed to our childish experience and hatred of subjection. Perhaps he enjoyed telling them for the same reason. He told us one night how he had climbed out of the window of some lodgings when he could not pay his bill. But he got out of the wrong window and fell through the greenhouse. The landlady rushed out. 'But I knew how to manage her. I apologised at once; I said: 'It's entirely my fault, Mrs Smith. Charge it to me – put it in the bill.' Of course when I got out of the window again, the greenhouse was no longer in a position to give the alarm; so I was able to make a fresh start with clean sheets. The first week was always the best.'

Pinto would not come sailing with us. This was not because Philip did not ask him. Philip detested Pinto, whom he called 'That dirty little scrounger,' but to please Frances, he several times asked him to picnics. Pinto always refused saying that he was bored with the water. 'I can see enough of it from here, and I've done enough sailing on it. I can imagine myself sailing without getting wet and without having to row two miles home every time the wind drops.'

Pinto had changed in these years. He was not only shabbier and lazier. Probably he was growing more discouraged.

I read now about the men of the nineties, their bohemianism and disillusionment, and their figures seem romantic. In Pinto, as I realised long afterwards, I knew one of those men, or at least one of the provincials who were affected by the same movement of the time spirit; but he did not seem romantic to us. He was either a shabby, depressed little man in a bad suit, or a lively and amusing companion; or sometimes, when he was dealing with plays or poetry or music, masterful and positive, as little romantic as any of the local magistrates, laying down the law.

CHAPTER 51

Harry and I had long ceased to boast of Pinto as a discovery and possession of our own, and lately he had taken so little notice of us that we seldom thought of him at all, unless he was amusing us. But we had always a particular concern for him as if he both deserved and needed special kindness. We felt the same about one of our old nurses who had spoilt us, but who had been sacked for drunkenness. I'm not sure that Pinto's attraction for women was not partly due to the same cause: that he excited in them, as in children, a protective instinct.

Harry and I were therefore alarmed to see the meeting between Pinto and our father, and our alarm teaches me something about both men. We must have felt a strong incompatibility between the sportsman and man of the world, who had not one slovenly fibre in his whole body, and Pinto. But to our surprise it was my father, who, putting down his brush, advanced right across the lawn, using a slow and deliberate step and carrying his head noticeably high, thrown far back. It was a progress at once ceremonious and, because so easily performed, without stiffness, welcoming. It made the guest important enough to merit every dignity. Then, having come near, my father spoke Pinto's name and took his hand, with a peculiar sideways bend which I had never seen him use before except when complimenting a beautiful woman, and, with a smile full of deference, began to congratulate him on his great work in Annish, which Annish had badly needed. He said that he had never regretted anything so much as missing his last production, and looked forward with the keenest anticipation to his next. He also thanked him for all that he had done for 'my poor boys – I'm afraid it was a waste of time from your point of view, but I can assure you that for them it was the best time they ever had.'

To this Pinto answered with a stare and the gloomy reply: 'If you mean the dramatic club, I've chucked it. It won't be my production you'll see.'

We were equally astonished by my father's compliments and by Pinto's surliness. We could not know that in my father's special politeness, we were seeing a last fragment of the eighteenth century; perhaps the very bend and smile with which a gentleman of the grand tour saluted an artist, any painter, or actor or singer or ballerina; and in Pinto, the first symptoms of the early twentieth, with its suspicious reaction from anything like a grand manner. Not that my father was eighteenth century. In idea, he belonged to his own time. But from his father and through him from his great-grandfather, as I knew from a great-aunt, born in 1810, he had certain courtesies which belonged to the great age of polite forms and social ease. We had seen him use them to ladies. But apparently they were due also, with some slight modifications, to artists.

CHAPTER 52

My father, in spite of Pinto's gloomy look and rather surly tone, continued to be charming to him. I daresay he was quite prepared for a different manner in an artist and accepted it as normal. He turned the subject upon plays, as one that Pinto might be expected to enjoy, and even quoted Shakespeare, 'All the world's a stage.' Pinto then began to thaw out and asked him if he had acted himself.

'I can act myself only too well, but I don't think I could act anybody else.'

'Then you ought to take to it and you'll be an actor-manager in no time,' Pinto said, and he began to abuse actor-managers. From this, of course, he passed quickly to his own ideas about the stage, about art and about philistines, and vegetables. In the upshot he talked to my father for the rest of the afternoon, and when Aunt Hersey, delighted to see her adored Pinto in such extraordinary spirits, began to talk about the difficulties in the committee, without his support, he suddenly agreed to attend the next meeting. 'After all, we might be able to do something with one of the comedies.' He was still there when we went up to bed, talking about what might be done with *Much Ado About Nothing* or the *Tempest*.

The eighteenth century had overcome the twentieth, and I think my father was quite aware of the fact. I noticed, as he drove away, a peculiar expression in his blue eyes, as he turned them towards Pinto. They were laughing, not at the artist, but at the man.

Aunt Hersey's delight in Pinto's reconciliation surprised and amused my father, but we found it natural. Children, accustomed to their own enthusiasms, find nothing odd, but everything that is reasonable, in the conduct of a grown-up who shows an excited pleasure. The smiles with which we heard Aunt Hersey crying out to Delia: '*Isn't* it splendid – Mr Freeman is going to produce for us after all,' were not condescending; they said only: 'See, Aunt Hersey, too, is capable of a rational excitement.'

But we noticed only the detail of her pleasure; we did not notice that Aunt Hersey, like Delia and Philip and Frances and Dingbat, was caught up into a new phase of life. What was for us the daily succession of events was for them critical and exceptional. Philip in his new profession, suddenly with money to spend, carrying out his long-cherished plan to entertain the girls and now in love; Frances, pregnant, full of new ambitions, a new sense of power, a new dissatisfaction; Mackee, lost in a new kind of life to which he had no clue, must well have felt a sense of crisis. But children cannot distinguish crises, even in history, from ordinary life; all they notice of family troubles or great wars is a change of scene or of friends.

The end of Frances' flirtation was not the one usual to such affairs: the birth of the baby and the immediate dropping of Philip. The baby was born, unexpectedly, at the end of that month, and at once the whole life of Blackhall was changed. Nurses appeared, baby's bottles, congratulating friends, christening presents. Frances was once more caught up in events, to which she yielded with obvious joy. She seemed to welcome them as a guiding fate, for which she had waited. But she was making small decisions all day along, and since she was now a mother, they were important to everybody and gave her dignity even in Delia's eyes. Yet Frances, when she was not nursing or bathing the baby or deciding what it should wear, was just as ready to play with us or to flirt with Philip. She never dropped a friend; she insisted that Philip should be a godfather, and he spent the greater part of every day at Blackhall. In the end Dingbat was forced by circumstances to do the wise thing. He accepted Philip as a friend, and made quite as much of him as Frances. I daresay the gossips laughed, but for serious men like

Mackee, with strong feelings, gossip does not matter much more than the chirping of sparrows on a telegraph wire.

CHAPTER 53

Meanwhile, before the arrival of Frances' baby, we were entirely happy. For the couple using us, I suppose, as chaperones, took us with them almost every day to some new cave or beach, where we clambered, bathed, fished and made water-works.

The summer was hot, and while Philip held a sunshade over his Madonna's head, and gazed upon her with awe and respectful adoration, we dived from the rocks deep into the green water, as clear green as a swimming bath, and turned over, to see the others above us, struggling clumsily like primitive birds, through a firmament like melted glass; fiery and viscous. The heat filled us with a restless energy, so that there was something rebellious in our noisy games. We ran about stark naked and shouted at each other from a distance, forbidden words, which made Philip frown at us, and Frances, as impudent as ourselves, laugh. We broke the windows in the bathing huts and stole the coastguard's boat. We took this boat, heavy and stout, to visit Shell Port cave. It was on this occasion that Philip nearly drowned us. He had been deprived of Frances from midday by some engagement of hers, and he had spent all the afternoon walking slowly about the beach at Dunamara, winding among the rocks, with his hands in his pockets and his straw hat over his eyes. But when we arrived with the boat he volunteered to sail us to Shell Port Cove.

It was after tea. We arrived late and the tide was already rising. Shell Port cave, as I said, opened from deep water, and the only ledge by which it could be entered was covered except at low tide. It was not six inches above water when we reached it.

My recollection was that my father had entered easily. The gap between the rock walls seemed very wide to Harry and myself with our short legs, but as usual we did not care to say that we had thought better of the enterprise. We jumped from the boat on to the end of the ledge, a kind of bracket about a yard wide, and set off before we had time to lose our bravado. But the cave was now almost in darkness; the waves rushing at the rocks below made a noise, which, though it was not loud, had an overwhelming power over the senses. It seemed to change the air itself so that it pressed more heavily on our ears and beat, not loudly but persistently, on our whole body, pushing us downwards. Also it gave us both the feeling that the tide was rushing upwards at a rate of several feet a minute. As soon as Harry could see into the central chamber, he turned and said to me in a quick, angry tone: 'There it is, now we'd better go back before the tide catches us.'

'I can't really see the cave,' I said. For I wanted to boast to Delia and Kathy that I had reached the cave.

'Yes, you can – that's it – don't you hear the tide? It's simply rushing up.'

At once I felt panic. In spite of my long knowledge of the tides about Shell Port, it seemed to me that the tide actually had changed its habits and was rising at a faster rate.

This sudden fear that the ordinary laws of nature would cease to work was quite common with me as a child. Even in the midst of some enjoyment I would be attacked suddenly by the idea that air might cease, that very minute, to be breathable; that it would refuse to bulge into my mouth; or alternatively, that my lungs would forget to breathe, my heart to beat, and my muscles to work, unless I kept them going by definite acts of will, as one moves a hand. In steering a boat, I have been frightened by the idea that perhaps, when I put the tiller down, the boat would turn the same way, and gibe. So I was quite ready to believe that the tide had changed its routine, simply to drown us. I said: 'It's up feet since we started.'

We both turned and scrambled back to the ledge as fast as we could go. But when we got there the boat had disappeared.

This had the effect, not uncommon at such moments, of turning our panic into a kind of resignation. We felt that the world had become incomprehensible, and that we were helpless among new mysterious developments. I would not have been surprised to know that Philip and the coastguard's boat had turned into air, and that everyone in the world had died, in some last judgment, except the pair of us in our prehistoric cave.

'It's sunk,' Harry said. 'I thought it bumped too hard.'

'But where's Phil, and where are the oars?'

'I don't know,' Harry said sharply, 'but they aren't here.'

'Phil could swim miles.'

'Yes, but this place is full of congers – and he might get cramp.'

We stood looking at the water which was now rising round our feet and then at the smooth rock face which bulged over our heads.

'What shall we do?' I asked.

'Swim round, but I'm going to pray first.' Harry and I, in our last term at school, had both joined a Bible society. I think almost the whole school joined, after some lecture. The result was that Harry was now inclined to be religious, and I said one extra prayer every night, with the private understanding that when I was as old as Harry, and a prefect, I also would be sincerely religious, and say all the extra prayers.

Harry took off his clothes and knelt down in the water. Seeing that I did not kneel, he said: 'It's nearly a mile round, and we'll have to go through the breakers. You'd better say *something*.'

I had remained standing only from the feeling that it would perhaps be rather cheeky for me to pray, too, and also from the idea that Harry knew the right prayer for this occasion and that I did not. My notion of religion was still completely formal.

But when Harry advised me to pray, I hastily knelt down and made an appeal to God to save my life. I made some kind of promise at the same time to do everything that He told me to do, in the future. My conception was that of slave and master. But I remember very well, not the words of this appeal, but my strong sudden feeling that it was no good, that God either did not exist or could not help. A year later, for at least three years, I became very pious, more so than Harry, and read the Bible every day. But just then I was a sceptic.

Harry and I then dived off the rock and actually managed to swim round the head, through some fairly rough water, into the entrance to Shell Port. But we were both nearly done when Philip picked us up. I, who had been half swimming, half floating on my back for the last ten minutes, was so full of water, so wearily bored with the waves which kept striking at me unexpectedly and with such persistence, that I was quite prepared to go under. I was not unhappy or frightened, but merely brought into a condition of receptiveness. I was ready to be drowned. Both of us, when Philip had at last got us into the boat, were too limp and exhausted to speak.

Philip was very angry. The boat had drifted against the rocks while he had been pulling us aboard, and was nearly swamped. When he had got away from the rocks and run on to the beach, he realised that we had left our clothes on the ledge.

'You are a pair of damned imbeciles – why couldn't you wait?'

'You didn't say you were going away.'

'I didn't say it was Monday – or that water was wet. I thought you had some sense.'

'But why did you go away?'

'Why not?'

'Evelyn was nearly drowned,' Harry said severely.

'Why not?'

'No, but really he was.'

'That would have made a lot of difference, wouldn't it?' Philip said impatiently. 'One of those earth-shaking events.'

Harry, always ready to resent any slight upon me, turned red and said angrily: 'You wouldn't say that if it was you who got drowned.'

'Oh, yes, I would,' Philip said, in that cool contemptuous voice which expresses a young soldier's scorn for civilian egotism and weakness.

Philip, and Moonlight, too, by a single glance of his eye, could make us feel less than nobody, a vulgar kind of person making a fuss about himself, that was, nothing. I murmured some kind of apology to which he answered: 'Yes, so am I sorry – why weren't you drowned – it would have saved everyone a lot of trouble. I suppose the best thing you can do now is to go up to Lizzie Doherty's and ask her to let you sit in her kitchen while I scare up some clothes for you.'

Lizzie Doherty was a fisherman's wife, who gave us hot water for picnics. We duly spent two hours in her kitchen while clothes were procured for us. Our own had sunk. Then we were sailed home, and Aunt Hersey heard the story which we had composed together, that we had taken a bet to swim round the head and won it; but lost our clothes.

It was a great success. We were heroes and enjoyed ourselves greatly. Even Delia admired us and there was no drawback to our happiness, for Philip seemed already to have forgiven us and even to have forgotten the whole affair. He was once more strolling aimlessly about in the rooms with a cigarette in his fingers and his eyebrows raised high as if wondering at his own obsession.

Aunt Hersey, who was working over some dress designs with Pinto to know how he wanted them made, still went on praising us for some time after she had plainly forgotten our existence. But suddenly she looked up and said: 'I have one bit of news for you – good news – your father is shooting Uncle Jim's mountain tomorrow, and he's asked for you both to be sent up early.'

CHAPTER 54

My delight at my father's visit was mixed with anxiety. I did not know whether I was to be asked to go with the shooters. Harry had been asked two years before, just after his tenth birthday, and I considered that since I was now ten, I ought to be asked.

I had been looking forward during the whole summer, perhaps the whole year, to my promotion into a shoot. For my great ambition, beside going into the navy, was to be a sportsman. I had always lived in a company, except at Dunamara, where sport of every kind, shooting, fishing, sailing, driving, racing, coursing, was the principal topic among the men, and the chief pleasure of life. I had heard my grandfather admired as a great sportsman, driver and shot; and I saw that my father was now admired in the same way. In fact I thought of him as the typical sportsman, and associated therefore with the title, the wit, the courage, generosity, the dash and bravura, which belonged to him. Because he was an extremely handsome man, I even imagined my ideal sportsman as handsome; although, of course, every day I saw plenty of sportsmen who were red-faced, fat, clumsy and stupid. But I suppose I did not think of my uncle, James Foley, with his spindle legs and quaking voice, or our neighbour, MacBean, with his huge belly and enormous bottle nose, as sportsmen.

My ambition, therefore, to be a sportsman was really to be like my father, whom I had seen, in a huge mob at Barnum's Circus, take by the collar an enormous six-foot hooligan surrounded by his gang, which was crushing through the women, and make him cower by mere force of eye and tongue. The man and his two or three companions stood like sheep till the crowd opened and some fainting women were taken away; then they went off in a very hang-dog manner. for me, a sportsman was a hero, a wit; a glorious being; who was also necessarily a first-class fisherman, sailor, rider, swimmer and shot.

To go to a real shoot if only as a carrier of somebody's game-bag or cartridges was, therefore, to my mind, a very important step in life; towards the glorious existence of a grown-up.

But the very keenness of my desire brought up at once a special misery which always attacked me on such occasions. I felt almost sure that I would not be asked; that something would prevent it. I imagined already, in two minutes, all sorts of accidents which might cause me to be overlooked; for instance, as I stumbled upstairs, thrust forward by Delia's hand who was commanded to put me to bed at once with a hot pig, I imagined that my father would send a message by the Major asking me, as I was now ten, to join the shooters; but that the Major would purposely not deliver it. I knew the Major disapproved of children at shoots.

This doubt quite spoilt the expectation of seeing my father, as similar doubts spoilt other meetings for me, in advance. For there was always some privilege, which had fallen to Harry, and which now seemed due to me. Yet I can't remember that I ever failed to receive my due. I believe the true roots of this recurrent fear were in my conservatism; my respect for what I imagined the proper rules of life; among which I counted this one, that boys at ten were allowed to go with shooting parties, and also, a secret fear that these rules might not apply to me personally. This went so far that, sometimes, when I had been swimming, and I could not remember the time when I was not able to swim, I have suddenly feared that the water, literally, would let me down.

This feeling, in various forms, was common among us chil-dren, and I suppose all children. Harry had fits of it, as when he thought that the tides had changed at Shell Port. All kinds of childish experiments were due to it. I used to like playing with matches, and Anketel would light all he could get hold of. He would take out a match, place it ready to strike, and then pause a moment with slightly raised eyebrows, set lips and wrinkled nose, an expression full of curiosity and desperation. At the flash, he would blink and then gaze at the flame with surprise and intense curiosity as if to say: 'What are you? – Where did you come from? How did you come?' He would let it burn almost to his fingers before throwing it away. Then again he would take out a match, closely examine it, its shaft as well as its head, carefully select a new spot on the box, and prepare for another strike. His look at that moment was very like that of a gunner I knew in the last war, in the Cameroons, when he was about to pull the lanyard and fire off his screw gun. The gun was worn, ranges were deceptive and the ammunition was old. But the gunner had more resignation in his forehead, Anketel more interest and curiosity. So he would go through the box, if no grown-up caught him. We did not interfere, for though, forgetting our own experiments, we thought his a babyish game, it was a rule among us children to let others play at anything which did not hinder another's game. Destruction of grown-up property was not a consideration, for it was as common and free to us as the blackberries or chestnuts.

CHAPTER 55

The experimental spirit, going with a lack of faith, lasted with me till I was, in the ordinary sense, grown up. I feel relics of it now; survivals like the appendix, not a new intuition. But when I was a child, words like law, nature, consistency, were given me as names for real things; not as convenient descriptions for a situation which nobody understands; and which, like beauty or goodness, is known only by a direct sensuous experience. So I had my idea of things in one pocket of the brain, and my experience in another, and every now and then, my self slipped down between the two. Not that I perceived any flaw in the ideas; I did not dream of questioning any grown-up views, much less those about matter and spirit and body and soul, which were, even in words, extremely vague and misty. I simply felt the situation itself and the queerness of its hanging together. Like Anketel, I found repetition itself a miracle. So that, of course, like Anketel, too, I was highly conservative about routine. Anketel would never eat stirabout except with a certain bone spoon, and a certain mug, given him by Mrs Fee and marked 'A present from Portrush', for the milk. As a boy, much older than Anketel, I had carried a broken wooden horse, a mere round lump of wood, to a party. I would not go without it. I was afraid of the party and wanted to take a bit of my familiar household with me, as if it could carry with it a familiar routine. If I had had, at ten, any equivalent of the horse, I would have taken it to bed with me that night; as a reassurance that some things did continue to be themselves, that there were some rules and uniformities in the world, and that therefore there was a reasonable hope that my father would take me out shooting.

But I had no horse and I hardly slept all night. At half-past five when Harry, who had not slept either, out of pure excitement, came to wake me up, he found me as wide awake as he. Robert was already dressed, and went to make sure that the horse was being put into the car which we were to take. Aunt Hersey and Delia and Kathy were to follow in the castle trap for luncheon.

The car was ready. Old Roe was never late for any sporting event. At six we reached the Major's, and found the party there already and breakfasting between the kitchen and the dining-room. My father greeted me with his usual affectionate quizzing smile, which seemed to say: 'What has been going on in *your* head lately?' and then was engaged at once by Harry in a discussion about Harry's Winchester which had misfired. Harry was to take his Winchester to shoot at any rabbits or crows which might be caught sitting. My father and he took the rifle to pieces and oiled it, both with the same expression of apprehensive gravity. Nothing was said about my going to the shoot, and I stood on the outside of the circle, which always seemed to gather about my father, whatever he was doing, in desperate anxiety. What, I thought, would happen to me if I were forgotten altogether, if I were left behind, in this huge, unfriendly house.

The Tulla was a fine house with big rooms, set on a hill; but it was surrounded so closely by trees that it was over-shadowed and gloomy within, and most of the rooms were empty. The furnished rooms, a huge dining-room, drawing-room, the hall and a parlour, were very much furnished; full of shining mahogany, new gilt frames, chintz-covered armchairs and light

Turkey rugs; but the rest was bare. Even the Major's bedroom contained nothing but an iron bed, an iron tripod washstand, such as one sees in groom's quarters, and a single chair.

The Major had bought this barrack on his retirement from the army; and furnished as much as he thought necessary. He took great care of the furniture, polished it himself, and when he entertained, two or three times a year, he received his guests in style. He gave, however, only tea-parties, always in the drawing-room; and the whole of his hospitality was old-maidish.

Aunt Hersey used to warn us, when we went to the Tulla, against making a noise, kicking the chairs with our heels, eating too much, spilling crumbs on the carpet, or staying too long.

Uncle James was the terror of us children, even of Delia, who never went near him if she could help it. But if once he knew that a person disliked him, he gave him no peace. I have heard him exclaim to Delia, in his loud quacking voice, before a large party: 'You're pale, m'dear, what's wrong with you?'

Delia blushed, her thick brows frowned, and she answered that she was quite well.

'Not a bit of it – you're pale. You're tight lacing – that's what it is. Trying to pull in your fat and give yourself a figger. Vanity – vanity. And starving yourself. I know you girls when you get to that age – anything to catch a feller's eye. What you want is buttermilk, and throw away those ridiculous engines of torture – squeezing up your innards and ruining your digestion.'

He accosted me one day in the garden and said: 'Hullo, hullo, how old are you now, Evelyn?'

'Nine, Uncle James.'

'What, what, nine – you're not nine, are you? Why aren't you at school?'

'I am at school, Uncle James.'

'No, you're not. You're here – why don't your father send you to school? Perhaps you're a fool – are you a fool – are you a fool? What sums can you do?'

'It's the holidays, Uncle James.'

'What sums can you do? Can you do long division?'

He questioned me for ten minutes on my arithmetic, with as much interest and curiosity as if he were on the track of the most important and exciting discoveries.

The Major was a thin, stooping, small man, with very thin legs and singularly long feet which he turned out like a dancing master. He always wore tight knickerbockers with box cloth fastenings round the knee, which showed off his legs to the worst advantage. His face was hollow, like a dish, his nose long and depressed at the tip over a grey, bristling moustache. His voice was like his brother Herbert's, high and thin; but its note was quite different. Uncle Herbert's was either soft and cooing like an oboe, or desperate and complaining; Major James' was always sharp and lively. He quacked like a duckling all day long, an endless stream of questions, comments, usually malicious.

He treated his servants in the same way, questioning them and cackling at them, and he offered the lowest wages for the hardest work, yet he kept them long. At this time he had one man outside, to do about three men's work, and one girl indoors, to do the whole work of the big house.

CHAPTER 56

This girl had been at the Tulla for a couple of years, and I had seen her half a dozen times. Already, by some means I could not trace, I had found out that her position in the house was unusual. The word scandal meant little to me, but it or some half-heard remark had pointed my attention at her. I had studied her attentively, trying to see her difference from others. I saw that she was beautiful, though I did not like her singularly pale skin, not freshly pale like Delia's but silvery like a bindweed flower; and I was attracted by her quick, neat movements. But her silence and something formidable in the look of her bright grey eyes and set, firm lips, made me shy of her.

She had never spoken to me, and she noticed my presence only by a side-glance which seemed to say, without rudeness, but firmly and resolutely: 'You mind your business and I'll take care of mine.' Yet I kept putting myself in her way, in the hope of striking up a friendship. As a child I always looked confidently for friendship among the maids and men in any Irish house wherever I happened to be.

The impression this girl Pegeen made upon me increased in future years, and I don't think it was due only to the stories I had heard about her, and her beauty. Beauty, in fact, is very little noticed anywhere unless well dressed and shown off. I pass lovely faces every day, in which the possessors, shabby, and often appearing overwhelmed with worry, take no stock. Children love beauty, but they do not notice it unless it is brought to their attention. I think Pegeen's attraction for me was purely magnetic. She must have had a very strong character as well as a Napoleonic independence of will. She remained with the Major for nearly twenty years, entirely cut off from the people about. I believe indeed that she never left the house and garden, and never spoke to a soul except the gardener, Ben, and the Major. He had made some provision for her in his will, but he died without signing it, and also without any money. His investments had all been completely foolish and disastrous. He had been existing on his pension, and the sale of the house barely paid his debts. One of these debts was the girl's wages. It turned out that he had never paid her any wages; and had not even fixed a wage. The executors decided to pay her at current hiring rates and actually worked them out, from fair records, for the whole eighteen years. She received six pounds for the first year, eight for the second, stood at twelve for several more, and so on. The whole sum paid was more than two hundred and fifty pounds, with which she went to America and, so we were told, bought an hotel, married well, made a fortune and brought up a family. This was quite possible, for she had gone to Tulla as a young girl. She was probably not more than thirty-five or six when she emigrated.

I have often wished that I saw more of this household. I was rarely at Tulla and I avoided the Major. Yet he, too, was an interesting man, for, in spite of his eccentric, miserly ways and his solitary life, he remained gay and lively. Even as a very old man, he used to fire off his questions and chatter; his little eyes full of a curiosity which was childish in its intensity and independence. His spirit never grew old and one felt of him always as of some young, energetic spirit: 'He's capable of anything.'

It was not goodness of heart that kept the Major's soul alive in the vault of Tulla; nor any love of beauty, nor sport, nor any disinterested hobby, like amateur research or gardening; nor even love of his Peg, for they say he kept her under military discipline. It seems to have been purely curiosity; a boundless interest in the affairs of the world, as mirrored in three or four neighbouring families.

I imagine, too, that the Major found a perpetual source of interest in the girl Peg, for although I never saw him even speak to her, I'm told that they were much together, and that, at least in his later years, he spent all his evenings in the kitchen, firing his questions at the girl or discussing local affairs with her and her own reactions to them. I wish I could have heard these talks, not for the Major's comments, but for the girl's. I feel that they would have been worth hearing from a mind so cool, independent and far-sighted. Unless, of course, she planned nothing, and had merely drifted into a situation which required her to behave like one who controls fate and builds for herself a triumphant success out of the most unpromising stuff.

If so, my childish senses were deceived, because I felt a strong attraction for her. Though she would not make friends with me I was, at the Tulla, always conscious of her presence and inclined to hover about her skirts.

CHAPTER 57

So on this morning I hovered about her, not strictly noticing her, because of my preoccupation, but suffering her attraction while, in bare legs, very white and rather too fat, and in what looked like a single garment, a shabby black dress unbuttoned at the back, she blew up the turf in the kitchen fire and filled her kettles. I said that breakfast was between dining-room and kitchen. The Major had not, of course, intended his party to seek the kitchen. He had prepared a kind of breakfast, sandwiches and tea, in the dining-room, where it was laid at one end of the large dining-room table. The shutters were still closed, and a lamp had been lighted, an oil-lamp with a yellow globe. This single lamp with its evening light in that huge room made the little pile of sandwiches seem yet more dismal. My father, seeing them, said at once: 'We only want a body, James, for a wake. Where's your whisky?'

'Whisky, whisky – before shooting the Slieve Bawn? You'll never get up to it at all if you begin on whisky.'

But the party of guns, led by my father, had demanded something more substantial and at once crowded the larder and kitchen where they were now making themselves toast, buttering soda bread, cutting into a tongue and a ham and waiting for the girl to fry them bacon and sausages. The Major, horrified to see his larder laid waste by this invasion, which, I fancy, was prompted largely by my father's scorn of any meanness or inhospitality, ran among the party, quacking: 'But how do you fellers expect to shoot – you won't be able to walk – I never eat anything before shooting.'

My father and Harry were still cleaning the rifle at the big kitchen table, four or five men surrounded the table, chaffing the Major, complaining that his knives were not designed to cut meat, eating and calling out to the girl not to grizzle the bacon.

The tall dark room with its walls of dirty plaster was full of blue smoke, and all about it, as everywhere in the back parts of the Tulla, there was a sense of emptiness and damp and gloom; but here within, round the fiery island of light thrown on the stone-paved floor by the fire, there was the rich life which always clung to my father. Wherever he was, it seemed to me, one found the same atmosphere of energy, sport and vigorous purpose; above all, the sense of life being used and enjoyed.

It was this sense of a glorious kind of life, the sporting life, which so excited me in that company, and the mixed smell of Donegal homespun, unwashed sheep's wool, turf smoke, gun oil, bacon, hot soda bread and hot stove remains in my memory as the breath of a special delight. Though I was anxious, I suppose I was happy also; as I was certainly curious, watching the little lovely girl, with her calm Raphael face, slip in and out among the noisy men with kettle and fry-pans.

CHAPTER 58

Pinto now suddenly appeared in the kitchen. In an old overcoat as dressing-gown, with two days' beard on his chin, he wore even more wretched an appearance than usual. Yawning enormously, he was shuffling slowly across the room when suddenly the men noticed him. One of them sang out: 'Hullo, Freeman's up – come on, Freeman – do us the cabby with the honeymoon couple.'

This was one of Pinto's impersonations, which we children had never seen. It was only for men. But we had heard the roars of laughter with which it was received.

Even my father raised his head from Harry's rifle to join the circle round Pinto.

Pinto, however, staring through his hair with a gloomy and depressed face, said only: 'This is no time for Christian amusements – what on earth are you chaps doing in the middle of the night? I thought the house was on fire.'

But they surrounded him, laughing and shouting for the cabby, the cabby, and then suddenly the whole party moved out of the room.

I was left in extreme perplexity. Nobody had yet asked me to join the party. Also it struck me that they might not want me because Pinto was going to do the cabby for them. This additional and unexpected problem threw me so much off my balance that I must have seemed a little mad. I ran about the kitchen saying: 'But what am I to do – what am I to do?'

Does anyone realise, unless he takes the trouble to recollect, the perplexity in a child's mind before the question: 'Am I wanted, or am I not wanted. What do they expect of me now?' and the confusion produced by an attempt to solve the problem by induction. Such problems often seemed so complex and difficult to me that I really did feel mad. Extreme confusion of mind, the inability to form any clear idea, is a kind of madness. I was used to apply to Harry, or Delia, or even Kathy, who told me what to do. On this occasion it was the little girl Peg who suddenly, as I circled round her like a pickled gun-dog crying out for explanation, gave me her sidelong glance and said: 'Aren't ye with them?'

'I don't know.'

'Ah, go then – what could you be doing *here*?' with an emphasis on the last word which annihilated Tulla. She pushed me into the corridor and I followed the shooting party, to find them waiting for me on the road. Pinto had disappeared, probably to bed. My father had already noticed my absence. 'Come on,' he said. 'We're late already. Sportsmen haven't time to waste on breakfast.'

These words, however unexpected after our long delay for

breakfast, and full of misunderstanding, filled me with the highest possible pleasure. To be included among sportsmen was something I hadn't expected. The sequel was also unexpected. Having driven another two miles to the mountain, and got down from the cars, the party was sorting out the dogs and discussing the best direction for a first move when I fainted. That is, I found myself all at once lying on my father's arm, and against his knee, with a circle of red faces staring down at me.

Enquiry then brought out the fact, surprising to myself as well as the rest, that I had eaten nothing since tea-time on the day before. I had forgotten.

'But weren't you hungry just now at the Tulla?'

'I forget.'

My father hastened to put out a more sensible explanation. 'He was thinking out a new poem.'

I silently protested, because I thought that real sportsmen did not write poetry, but I could not insist that I really had forgotten; that for the last eighteen hours life had been too interesting and too anxious for meals.

But while I still lay, feeling not foolish but merely confused, one of the men said: 'Oh, yes, that was a great poem of his you showed me about the ant.'

This was a piece I had written for the family magazine. I was astonished to hear that anyone had seen it outside the family circle.

Others took up the cue, and a rich bass voice declared that I was undoubtedly going to be a great poet, that they'd all be proud to know me, some day.

I was, I suppose, innocent for my age, but I took these remarks seriously. While I was being wrapped in a rug, given a sup of brandy and packed into the well of a car, to be carried forthwith to the luncheon rendezvous and the ladies, I was already feeling, in the midst of surprise, a sense of illumination. I was surprised that the Ant should be admired. I had written it in the nursery as I might have painted a battle or a red Indian. It had been a wet day pastime. All of us for as long as I could remember had written poems, now and then, on wet days.

But I accepted without question the judgment of grown-up critics. My conclusion and discovery was that poetry was not so difficult as people made out, and that I had got the hang of it.

The two glories were open to me: that of a sportsman and

that of a poet. It should be said that I had no idea of being a distinguished sportsman or poet. I never dreamt, for instance, of being as good a shot or rider as my father; I only wanted to be as like him as possible. I don't think that children ever do imagine special and separate glory for themselves.

I believe that Delia, with all her ambitions, and Robert, who was masterful and independent by nature, never had the idea at this time of being great and glorious, in the Napoleonic sense. I never imagined myself a real admiral. My boldest hope was captain, like a grand-uncle who had commanded the Queen's yacht and whose widow I had visited in a quadrangle of little red-bricked cottages, a kind of open convent for naval pensioners, near London. There I had looked through his telescope, handled his sword, and learnt with delight that captains wore cocked hats. I had also been strongly attracted by the cottages, because they had a porter at the great gate. It seemed to me that life could offer no greater happiness than glory in a captain's cocked hat, followed by security and peace in that old quadrangle guarded by a porter.

I made myself admiral in the play, of course, but only as a horse coper asks fifty guineas in order to make sure of fifteen. The subaltern of twenty, who dreams of being a field-marshal, is so rare that there may not be one in a hundred years. The ordinary subaltern's farthest reach of ambition is to command the regiment, or pass the staff college. But he has at the same time ten times more than any field-marshal, the ambition to be a credit to the uniform.

This was our feeling as children. We sought glory, but not our own exclusively; we wanted to be part of a glorious experience; and when now I discovered that a poetical reputation was open to me, as well as that of sportsman, I did not look forward to being a Tennyson, or even a Kipling, who was just then a family hero, much quoted by my father, but simply a grown-up poet, a member of the grown-up world which was all-glorious.

CHAPTER 59

This new idea that I had hit upon a grown-up craft, and that it was not too difficult for me, so excited me that like a real poet I hardly knew what was going on about me.

'What's wrong with you today, Evelyn? – You'll lose your head next,' Delia protested, when I dropped some spoons in the heather; and Aunt Hersey kept on smiling at me, as if I had become an amusing object.

I heard and saw and understood, but with a detachment so complete that I felt no reason to apply any meaning to myself. I was, in fact, as annoying to the grown-ups and Delia as Anketel sometimes to us, when we told him not to walk across our beach castles or water-works, and he, though we knew he had heard, would continue straight forward over walls and sluices.

'Do keep your feet off the tablecloth, Evelyn.'

'What's the matter with the boy?'

'I believe he's still drunk with that brandy they gave him.'

Possibly I was still a little drunk. But I was so excited by the sudden appearance and expansion of a private world, probably my first to be realised, that brandy could have done no more than add some sparkle to a scene already brighter than day, through which I moved in a kind of aerial diving bell. I saw everything from my own centre, but as in an alien and outer element.

When the shooters returned to luncheon I found that my faint had already become celebrated. This, I think, was due to my father, who seized upon it as an opportunity to make a little glory for me. But he had changed his plan of creation. Instead of seeking to make me admired as a poet and thinker who starves himself nearly to death, because his unwordly mind forgets supper and breakfast, he had developed a new theme; that my love of sport, my keenness, had given me no time to eat. I had martyred myself for sport. The red faced old man, MacBean, whose nose was purple, and an old magistrate called Slatter, who did not shoot but ran everywhere after my father, babbling compliments, both praised my sportsmanship.

'A grand wee fellow,' the first said. 'He'd be kilt not to miss a day after the moor fowl.'

'Takes after his da and his granda,' Slatter cried. 'Aw, they all have it – ye couldn't stop them killing something if they had to do it with Keatings,' and he told a story about my father walking two miles with a tin of insect powder to hunt fleas in a horse rug.

I didn't like this story till I saw that my father was pleased. He did not laugh, but his blue eyes sparkled and his nose looked even more like an eagle's beak; no doubt because he threw up his sharp, square chin to hide his pleasure. Then I, too, laughed, so much that I became noisy and had to be silenced by Robert.

The attraction of being confirmed as a sportsman and the delightful feeling of sitting among the men, which made me, as usual, too noisy and I dare say cheeky, inclined me strongly to join the shooters on their second walk in the afternoon. I was asked to do so, but just then it happened that Delia mentioned Oweny's name.

'Oweny was going up to the bog and I don't see why he shouldn't take the Co back with him. That will save a double trip for the car.'

I said promptly that I didn't want to go back, but this was a piece of hypocrisy. I was delighted by the notion of telling Oweny about my new glories, and much pleased when Aunt Hersey insisted that I was not fit to climb any more mountains that day.

CHAPTER 60

As soon, therefore, as Oweny's ass cart was seen half a mile away along the breast of the hill, table cloths were waved, and, in the course of half an hour, he arrived to pick me up.

The charm of Oweny's company, for me, at such a time, was that I could boast to him as much as I liked. Modesty had always been taught to us children, and at school it had been enforced by school convention, which demanded even affected modesty. For instance, I had been kicked for telling another small boy, perhaps with too much exuberance, that I had shot the winning goal. I think I had suffered for this enforced modesty more than Harry, because I needed a great deal of boasting to

encourage myself. So during the last year I had bragged outrage-
ously to anyone who would listen to me, and especially Oweny.
I began now, as soon as I had climbed into the ass cart, by
telling Oweny that everyone in Annish had been reading my
poem, and they couldn't believe I had done it; it was too good.

'That's what they'd say,' Oweny remarked, jerking his rope
reins and giving a kind of howl at the ass. 'They'd say anything
to you.'

Although I took keen pleasure in bragging to Oweny, he never
gave me any direct encouragement. My enjoyment was, I
suppose, purely expressive. I spoke out my private hopes, and
enjoyed them as if they were real, while Oweny's remarks simply
passed me by. It was his company I needed, his ear; and not his
support.

'Do you think,' I asked him, 'a man can be a poet and nothing
else?'

'Aye, it could be as good as anything else and better than
some,' with another howl.

'It's a good thing to be a poet, isn't it? But you have to be
born a poet. It's a gift.'

'Ah, there's a tinker comes to Dunvil every Easter has it. But
it's a poor tale he tells. All the real poets is dead this thousand
years. Haoooooo.'

This was almost the whole substance of a conversation which
in various forms went on for a long time. I told of the glories of
being a poet; Oweny mildly doubting if any such thing could be
found, and sometimes throwing in a complaint of the lack of
fiddlers. Oweny was a great crossroad dancer and much preferred fiddles to the accordion. Both of us were happy in our
own way, for Oweny certainly loved company even more than I
did. As I say, he had swum chips for it by the hour. Both of us,
too, loved the ass cart. I had often travelled in Oweny's ass cart,
on such a day, between the hay harvest and the corn, hot and
dry and good for carting turf. I would lie usually at full length
on the floor with my hands behind my head against the
headboard, and Oweny would kneel beside me, sitting on his
heels. So that my remarks were aimed at the backward quarter
of the sky, and Oweny's were dropped on me from above. There
were long intervals between them for reflection and for quiet
enjoyment, while Oweny would look round at the landscape,
sometimes waving his whip at some distant figure on a turf

cutting, too far off and too much like the bog in colouring for me to distinguish, and I would look at the sky, thickened with heat, in which the clouds themselves, yellow and opaque, seemed over-cooked like the white of an egg too long in the pan.

Nothing travels more slowly than an ass cart, and it cannot be hurried; so that the ass traveller, like an invalid or a prisoner, is committed to a special kind of existence, when, if he is impatient, moments are hours of torture, but if he sort his pleasure to its means, hours acquire a value they never had before, and cannot be too long.

It is hard for anyone to grow tired of lying in a summer meadow, even though he does not move at all, or barely feels, if the stars appear early, the slow roll of the planet under him; but in an ass cart there is plenty of movement and noise. Its jogs are sudden because of its narrow axle; and its rattle quick. It has also a peculiar swaying motion from side to side because of the movement of the ass, carefully picking its way among holes, and shifting the weight from one foot to another. These movements can give the sense of travel, to add to the other pleasures of lying under the sky, with infinite time at disposal; provided that it is accepted as an additional pleasure and not demanded as a necessary foundation of the whole. It was pleasant to think, now and then, we are moving; whereas it would have been maddening to expect a destination. I had long learnt not to expect it, and so, far from impatience, I felt a keen, lazy pleasure in the slowness of our motion, because as I thought, it will last a long time. Ass cart travelling is pure life in the present.

After returning to the place from which Oweny had been called, nearly an hour before, we stopped, and I saw Anketel, crouching in the heather behind a rock and looking gravely up at me. Oweny grinned at me slyly, while the child scrambled into the cart and squatted down beside me. Oweny's grins confessed their plot to take a day out together, while the family was on the moor.

But I was not greatly surprised to see Anketel even so far from home; for, in the last few weeks, he had become devoted to Oweny. This friendship began accidentally one day when the child fell and cut himself on the upper road and was put on Oweny's cart to be driven home. Anketel had known and ignored Oweny for years, but when he reached the house he was heard chattering to him about the ass; how old was it, how strong was it; and from that day he had spent most of his time with Oweny. He had changed also from a bored, peevish, affected child, a nuisance to everybody, into a friendly and sensible little boy. When he did come among us, he came, not as a parasite to get what he could and spoil the rest, to worry us, but as a free and independent person, full of private interests and usually bursting with a *story. This was always about Oweny, Oweny's relations, Oweny's latest job, or the ass, but we needed not to listen to it, and Anketel did not require us to do so. He sang it like a thrush out of his superfluity of news.

The friendship was so much approved that I don't think, even if Anketel had been detected on the ass cart four miles from home, that anyone would have protested. But Oweny loved a plot.

Now there was a new strain in our talk, for Anketel began to talk of Oweny's relations, Patsy and Willy, and Willy's Pat, and Joe's Willy, and Biddy, who was going to be married to a boyo with one foot and one eye, and he rising sixty, 'but he has a pension from the army and a board floor in the room.'

'Aye, it's a wee turn of luck for all of us, but Biddy was always the lucky one,' Oweny would say. 'For he's hearty, too, and his brother is seventy-one, has seven children under ten.'

'Biddy won't be going to Scotland this year.'

'No more potato-lifting for Biddy. Ah, she's lepping lucky. Haaoooo – hup.'

'And, Evelyn, do you know, Patsy's leg's better and he's back to school.'

Anketel's voice was as eager and excited as if he had told me of some new present to himself. All human sympathies had come upon him at once, as if with accumulated richness, through his passion for Oweny and anything to do with Oweny.

Anketel, I think, was the only one of us children who was struck by Oweny's poverty. He asked several times why Oweny was so poor, why he had lost his teeth, and so on. These questions gave me uneasiness. Some natural sense of justice stirred in me. But the answers of my aunt that Oweny was not fit for better work because he could not read or write, satisfied me. I could understand that limitation, and I did not ask why Oweny suffered from it. I, like most children, accepted the world as I found it. It was very gradually that I came to have any doubts at all about the excellence of its arrangements. Even

Anketel's curiosity and sympathy probably had no general idea behind them. They were prompted by interest in Oweny and not by the sense of difference, enormous in those days, between our lot and that of the poor boys.

Anketel's sympathies were deep, but they did not reach far. He took not the smallest interest in the troubles of his own family, and had not even visited Kathy, in bed with a quinsy. Yet he seemed so completely changed in nature, as if he had grown a new mind and a new heart. He kept nothing of the old Anketel, but his secretive ways, his habit of disappearing when he was wanted, his pernickety appetite, and a smile, charming as it was rare; 'one to the new moon,' as Delia said.

Even his looks were changed for he had insisted on having his hair clipped like Oweny's younger brother. He thus appeared no longer charming to ladies, but a bullet-headed little boy with small pink round ears projecting at each side like the blind handles of a pipkin, large blue eyes, a long nose, and a long, pale face, usually dirty and full of a subdued excitement as if the pipkin were simmering, as it always did, with thoughts of Oweny.

CHAPTER 61

We reached the bog about three o'clock where the turf, already dried, had been gathered into loose heaps beside the cut, and began to build up the load. The talk of Patsy, Willy and Joe, of poetry and its dignity continued as before; no one felt any difficulty in passing from one subject to another, for our minds were as disconnected as Oweny's was flexible. The talk and the work were both leisurely, not at the pace of a task to be finished and concluded; but of an occupation for spare time, over which to linger was a pleasure. Anyone of us would stop, with a turf in the hand, to set forth our argument, of which the clincher was the tossing of the turf into the cart.

It was a hot afternoon, and the buzz of flies mixed with the rich smells of turf and heather like the effervescence of some heady drink. We grew more lazy and more talkative every moment. Often we were all three talking together, Anketel would sing: 'We'll cut the turf, we'll foot the turf, we'll dry the turf, we'll stack the turf, we'll *burn* the turf'; I would explain to Oweny that I had already hundreds of poems in my head, and Oweny, tossing broken ends into the hollow middle of the load, would mourn the want of fiddlers. There were no new ones and the old ones were dying.

At whatever time I started with Oweny to the hill bog for turf, I never came home till dusk. All our operations were conducted with this limit in mind, so that, if we had a full six hours for four miles drive back, it took six hours. We would stop by the way for a bathe in a stream, or to chase a rabbit, or merely to use time, wandering away from the cart and leaving the poor ass to make its own way. We knew that it would stop at once, but none of us cared if the sun was still above the hill-tops behind us.

CHAPTER 62

Although it was true, as I told Oweny, that I had thought of new subjects for a poem, such as the Mouse, the Fly, the Tit, the Microbe, the result of talking so much about what I was going to do, as usual, disinclined me for doing it. I seemed to have had all the pleasure of it already and nothing remained but the hard trouble. I deferred it for several days, and it was only the concurrence of a wet afternoon and solitude that brought me to the necessary effort of will. I chose then to write about the Microbe, which seemed to me a subject so much better than the Ant, as it was smaller and bound, therefore, to be more successful. I had written the Ant in half an hour, and I did not expect the Microbe to take longer. To my surprise, it cost me several days of worry and repeated efforts, and I was still dissatisfied with it when I sent it to Aunt Rose, who was, for that month, editing the family magazine. But I thought: 'Since I am a poet and the Ant was good, this must be pretty good, too.' I was astonished when my aunt sent it back to me and asked for a battle drawing instead. She wrote me a kind letter and explained that there was no objection to the Microbe, as a poem, except that it was a repetition of the Ant.

I compared the two poems, and felt very indignant. I could not see any likeness. The Ant was in three eight-line verses; the Microbe in eight four-line verses. But when I complained to Harry, he began to point out similarities, and gradually I perceived that the two poems were very much alike; in fact, almost the same. For instance, I had described the Ant's legs as 'small as hairs but full of joints'. Which seems a miracle by God.

In the Microbe I had written:

> Their wondrous legs are like a bee's,
> Finer than hairs with several knees.

In the first poem I had wondered how the Ant:

> In body made so small and tight
> Has got insides and lungs complete.

In the Microbe I wrote:

> Unseen by man because so thin
> His heart is like the smallest pin.

At first I could not believe my eyes. It seemed as if someone had played a trick on me. It can be seen that I had no notion of what a poem was, less perhaps than at five or six when I chanted nursery rhymes for their pleasant noise. After a year at school I thought of a poem as a subject treated in verse, with rhymes. I don't suppose that this was anybody's fault. The school, except for that one reign of terror, was very good. The masters were excellent. My idea of a poem had come into my mind like dry rot into a beam, because no one had known of its presence and removed it from the wood. But the result was again that my feelings about things had become separated from my idea of them; my childish pleasure in musical sounds and telling phrases and my natural delight in the world, in its colours, sounds and friendships, had no more connection with my notions of them than the contents of a trunk with the label on the outside.

Since I thought that the Ant was a poem, I also felt a secret fear that it was the only poem I had in me, and that the Ant, if I tried to write any more poems, would go on reappearing, even without my knowing it. It was not till the Shakespeare festival that I found courage again to write.

CHAPTER 63

The Shakespeare festival, which in the end came down to one play, the *Tempest*, was given not at Christmas, but in April, just after Easter. It was designed for the open air, but luckily someone reminded Pinto that Annish, at Easter, was often very wet.

Therefore, as for the former play, the Maylins' ballroom was used. When we saw this room, at the beginning of the Easter holidays, it looked as if it had just been bombarded. A great piece of the parquet had been pulled up at the stage end and two large holes cut through the boards into the cellar. Window-frames had been taken out to give side entrances and temporary sheds built in the garden for cover. Other windows were blocked up by scaffolding to carry seats. Boards were screwed to the ceiling to carry pulleys, limelights and curtain fittings.

The stage was being erected on fish-boxes partly filled with gravel. On one side of the barricade of fish-boxes Robert, Harry, Kathy and I, under direction of the Maylins' old carpenter, Macillhinny, screwed planks and hammered nails. At the other side Pinto carried on rehearsals, often shouting furiously at us: 'Not so much row there, damn it all.'

Robert was contriving the ship in two parts: a stern which was to be drawn through one hole by a gardener's boy, while he pulled down the mast through another. Stern and mast, of course, had to rock and sink together. To manage this, since the floor beams prevented the holes from being joined together, the top of the stern, which was made of cardboard tacked to a clothes-horse, was joined to the mast by two struts and a ring. The plan was that when the stern had sunk down as far as the struts, it would be out of sight behind the row of cardboard waves. The mast could then be pulled down further, through the ring, till it was out of sight.

We were all delighted with this contrivance, but it did not work well. The struts twisted, the stern collapsed, the mast fell over or stuck in the ring; Robert and Macillhinny toiled at it all day; Harry and I, quickly bored, amused ourselves by hammering competitions, trying to drive in a nail with a single blow; or pure mischief, like drawing faces on the back of the flats.

We were enjoying an unusual freedom because Aunt Hersey and Delia were now both at Pinto's rehearsal and we could hear him ordering them about like slaves. 'Mrs Candish – where's Mrs Candish? – oh, there you are – where's Ariel's wings? – not ready yet – but they must be ready – we need them now.' Aunt Hersey would apologise humbly and sit down to work. Delia, too, who was call boy, attended all rehearsals, and when some artist failed to appear Pinto would blame her. 'But what are you for? – it's your job, isn't it? – never mind if she's got a cold, bring her in a stretcher if you like.'

We were astonished to see how humbly Delia accepted his angry abuse, often unjust, and how patiently she worked for him. But Pinto during those weeks obtained an extraordinary power over all his people. He ordered them about, laid hands on them and pushed or pulled them into place and insulted them before the whole company; and they bore it like children. We saw old Colonel J., one of the proudest and touchiest men in the county, who was taking the part of Stephano, ordered off the stage because he didn't know his part; and the old man, red and half laughing, kept on explaining to us, that is, to a little group of children and three or four lady musicians, that he had known it perfectly well that morning. 'But when Mr Freeman jumps on me like that, I don't know where I am.' The big red-faced man might have been one of us, a child of ten or eleven, in his disappointment and his explanations; even in the shape of his round eyes and relaxed uncertain lips.

None of these people would have borne Pinto's bullying in the ordinary dramatic club, getting up some drawing-room farce. They stood it only because they felt that he was in earnest about something important, and for the same reason they worked very hard at their parts.

All this was a surprising and new experience for Harry and myself. We moved in a world of new values, where the despised Pinto was a dictator, where powerful and rich people, having been publicly abused by him, humbly apologised for their shortcomings; where our dignified aunt painted her face and dressed up in tinsel stars; where meals were any time and consisted of anything, tea for luncheon, and whisky and sausages for tea; and where, above all, we did what we liked.

We were soon bored with the stage carpentering. We explored the Maylins' cellar; stalked birds in their woods with Harry's gun, or stayed at Dunamara and read for whole days by the fire, till we were dazed with heat and blind with print.

It was spring, a time which intoxicates children by a physical excitement, and the weather was unusually good. Yet I was bored, so that Delia said of me one day, probably when I was making a nuisance of myself: 'He doesn't know what to do with himself,' a phrase of real truth.

Delia herself was busy all day, but with an unhappy preoccupied air. She had failed in her examinations and no longer toiled at mathematics and history; she had even changed her style of dressing, as if she felt that she had lost the right to look like a learned person. She didn't complain against her local teachers who had promised her a brilliant success; but I heard her say one day to Aunt Hersey and Pinto: 'How does one find out *anything* about oneself – anything true, I mean.'

I don't remember what answer she received, if any, but the question must have asked something that I too wanted to know, or it would not have stuck in my brain. Delia, now more than ever, took her mother's place in the house. She ordered the meals, commanded the maids, wrote the letters, and mothered us children, even putting us to bed and hearing our prayers. She returns to my mind as a new and separate Delia, anxious, preoccupied; always hurrying through the hall with papers, with some property wanted by the actors, with trays and tea-cups, with one of our bathing slips picked up on the beach or wet towels to be dried. She was always calling through the rooms: 'Mother, your tea,' or 'Pinto (she always called him Pinto), you've forgotten your medicine again. You really are *hopeless*.'

'Evelyn, Evelyn,' she would cry, and I, bored and idle, playing with the blind cord in the schoolroom, would deliberately not answer. I did not want anyone to interfere with my boredom. Then she would wearily climb the stairs, and finding me, say: 'My dear child, fancy stuffing here on this lovely day – out you go.'

'But I've nothing to do.'

'Then you can go to Dunvil on the mail car and bring me back two bottles of J.J. They drank the whole tantalus last night, and I don't know what Pinto will say if he finds it empty.'

Harry was not bored. He, too, read the same kind of books, but he got the most unexpected ideas from them. He would say suddenly: 'Listen to this,' and read a description of ice-floes or a seal hunt in a tone of excitement. He would say: 'Can't you see these chaps going for the seals and the floe shaking, and the seals looking at them and wondering what they were, taking them for a new kind of animal? It's queer when you think of it – they don't even run away. Of course men were a new kind of animal – it was animal against animal – the battle of life. But what a shock for the seals – something they never imagined.'

He suddenly began to use a quantity of new phrases, like 'battle of life,' 'it's queer when you think of it,' 'something you wouldn't expect.' He would read out a description, even of a sunset or a landscape, which I skipped, and exclaim: 'That's pretty good,' or 'pretty terrific.'

Harry and I, reading from the same shelf, were getting an entirely different experience from the same books. Delia noticed this when she complained that I was always demanding new books to read and then skipped them. Harry had made a sudden leap ahead of me.

He was beginning to take charge of himself, while I, still floating along the stream of feeling, was at the mercy of events. Some event, some accident, for instance, had lately run me aground on a mudbank, so that for the first time in my recollection I felt monotony and boredom.

CHAPTER 64

From that boredom, that mudbank, I was floated off again into current life by the play.

Harry and I had watched rehearsals of the play until we were so bored that I, at least, would not have gone to the performance if Delia had not begged me to do so. Pinto, I knew, was not going to the performance, he had quarrelled once more with the committee and resigned his presidency. I pointed this out to Delia when she warned me to go and dress because the horse was putting into the car.

'Pinto isn't going himself.'

'That's nothing to do with what you do. And you know you'll love it.'

'No, I shall hate it. I've seen it already a hundred times.'

'You'll love it, Evelyn – it's just what you want, and Harry's almost ready.'

'Harry doesn't mind if I don't go.'

'But I do, so no nonsense – come along and I'll dress you. I suppose you can't tie your own tie yet?'

'Of course I can.'

But I hesitated to resist. Delia, as I knew by her voice, her pallor, her darkening eyes and something vigorous and threatening in her movements, was in a most resolute and ferocious mood. She thrust me upstairs.

'I don't need dressing.'

'I'll see you do it, my lad,' and she did in fact hand my coat and knickers and tie my tie. But already her presence and her firmness had removed my sulkiness, for I knew that in a conflict she would win. She was capable of boxing my ears. Therefore I gave way.

'It's only to please you. I shall loathe it.'

'Of course you will, but you are pleasing me, and it's time you did something for somebody. Go on now,' and she disappeared with the same preoccupied face.

But when I stood below on the front step with Harry, pushing my fingers down my Eton collar, and admiring my patent shoes, suddenly Delia came up behind us. The vigorous swish of her skirts made us turn and we saw her with a peculiar smile on her lips. Delia was apt to laugh at us when we were in our best clothes; derision which always made us a little stiff and dignified. For I, at least, felt an injustice in being laughed at for a propriety imposed upon me. But as we drew ourselves up, she put her arms round our necks and gave us each a warm and strong kiss.

'Goodbye, my dears.'

We were surprised by this outburst of sentiment in Delia and stared at her. Harry answered in a polite, rather cool voice: 'Goodbye.'

The car came along the gravel and we climbed up. Jessy came out to pack us in the rugs. Delia had disappeared. Only just as we were moving off, we heard her voice calling from a window: 'Goodbye, darlings,' with a note both laughing at us and at the same time so affectionate and mournful that both of us turned our heads, again surprised. But the horse was already digging his hooves into the rise of the avenue, a sound which meant to us both that we were going on an expedition. As his head went down, ours craned forward to see if the gates were open; and we never saw Delia again. The very thought of her, my wonder at her sudden fit of tenderness, though its impression was permanent, had passed, on the surface, from my mind.

I was already enjoying the drive, the feel of my party suit, and the sense that after all I was going to have a delightful evening. For even if the play should bore me, I would have supper among the grown-ups, I would stay up till midnight and drive home, with luck, in the outside car, under the stars. I was full of expectation and, by that fact, alive in all my senses, ready to receive new impressions.

The play, of course, from the first lift of the curtain, carried me off my feet. Harry and I had watched the first scene rehearsed a dozen times; the mast and stern of a ship rocking, among the sound of waves, that is, pebbles dashed against a board by Macillhinny with a shovel, while the boatmen and sailors talked in front of the stage. But we had seen it in fragments, without the lighting. Now when the curtain went up we saw the mast and the balustrade of the stern behind it, rocking against green sky in the background, while the whole stage was dark, and the figures, lit by a yellow beam of light from the side, showed only to the waist. This hid the fact that the stage itself was not moving with the mast. But not only the scene startled us, the words of the players, which we had heard several times before, now seemed to have quite a new force of meaning. From the rising of the curtain I was completely astonished and I did not recover from that surprise throughout the performance, or for a long time afterwards. My sensations were so new that I had no kind of comparison for them; they were experiences of a new kind.

So that, although, during rehearsals I had laughed at the first scene and especially at Antonio cursing the boatswain, until my elders had frowned, I now listened to the same words in awestruck silence.

Hang, cur, hang, you whoreson, insolent noisemaker.

I felt the impact of them like a real insult, they gave me a shock of delight and anxiety. I looked anxiously at the boatswain to see how he would take them, and when I saw that he did not answer at all but simply went on shouting orders to the crew, I felt deep admiration and a sense of discovery. That's the right way to behave, I felt; I thrilled to the wise boatswain, brave and independent.

The poetry played upon me directly as warmth and cold, mist and rain; carrying both feeling and idea. I never could separate the idea of little Jack Horner, who sat in a corner, from the rhymes or the picture. The whole thing, the rhymes, the vision of the shy little boy in the corner, the thumb going into the pie and the last mysterious remark, were all one piece of my experience. It left me wondering how Jack pulled out a plum with his thumb, and why he said he was a good boy, but the story was ineffaceable from the first time I heard it. It made at once a deep and permanent impression on my mind, which retained nothing of the multiplication table nor any of the moral precepts fired at it by my nurses and grown-ups.

Children are born poets and singers. They sing to themselves in the cradle and delight in the simplest rhymes. They feel them by a direct experience just as they feel everything in life directly, without analysis or reason.

I can't remember a single sermon heard in my childhood, and the face of only one clergyman, the huge red-bearded Canon P., who loved my mother, and after she died came to see me at my English school. But I don't remember his words; I remember his beard, his presence, and above all, the musical sound of his deep voice with its rich accent. In my memory that voice and its north-west vowels rolling down on my head, as I stood, a small boy in a cricket shirt, under a tree on Mount Ephraim in Tunbridge Wells, is the very reality of compassion; not merely the sound of it. As far as I know, I did not see the Canon again, and I had not seen him before since he christened me. I imagine that both Harry and I were undemonstrative, for startled by the sudden appearance of this Irish giant in the lane at a time when we were deep in the feeling of school, we said little; and I can remember the sense afterwards that the Canon had been disappointed in our response. His blue eyes look down on me still, and his weather-beaten red face, with puzzled inquiry. I daresay he went away supposing that his journey had been a failure. In fact, he had left such a deep mark on my spirit, or whatever you choose to call the living character of a human creature, that his voice and look remained there for ever, and with them, the experience of compassionate love; a true intuition of goodness in its own spirit. He taught us something new about the world;

he opened suddenly a way for the sense of my imagination. But I don't remember a word he said, only the vibration of his voice and his affection, his meaning carried directly to my feelings.

So bits of the church service remained with me because they were poetry. They gave the feeling of beauty and wisdom joined together in one unity of experience. But no prayer or poem had so powerful an effect as my first great Shakespeare play. When I heard the cry: 'All lost, to prayers, to prayers,' and the line: 'What, must our mouths be cold,' I felt death as if I had never heard of it before.

CHAPTER 65

The performance can't have been good. The Pinto scenery and lighting, I suppose, was pioneer work such as only amateurs would have accepted and only rich, good-natured people like the Maylins would have sponsored; it was far too ambitious for the narrow stage. The ship came to pieces so that the stern rocked one way and the mast another. When it began to sink the mast disappeared but the stern slipped off its rocker and stuck sideways. We could hear the gardener's boy swearing at it and invoking the saints during the end of the scene. Caliban from fright forgot every word of his part so that we heard it twice over; once by the prompter, and then, a line behind, like the psalms at church, by himself. The footlights went out in the second scene, which was finished in the dark. The curtain stuck after this scene, and old Macillhinny came in with a ladder to repair it.

He was a famous character, well known to my early childhood, for his son had been gamekeeper to my great-uncle Tristram, and he had made me my first popgun out of a hazel branch. His appearance therefore added a new element of pleasure to my enjoyment, and though I felt too solemn to laugh at the jokes which he exchanged with the audience, and Prospero, handing up his tools, I daresay I was grinning when Harry exclaimed furiously: 'Dash it all – why can't Prospero go away? He's ruining the whole thing.' I, too, then felt irritated by Prospero and the old man's interruption.

But I was not sure why Harry was so angry; my own annoyance was vague and uncertain and as usual I distrusted it. My enjoyment was on a different level from Harry's, who had already a sharp, critical feeling; and, even at his first play, resented bad acting and bad management with a bitterness almost equal to Pinto's.

Harry must have had a far keener delight and sharper ideas from that play than I had, with whom the whole experience from Ariel's speeches to old Macillhinny on the ladder telling the audience that he felt like a fairy himself, was happiness so intense that it left a permanent memory, but a mixed confused memory of lovely words, which made me feel strange as if my brain were being stretched; of the popgun; of bright colours; of painted faces and in the middle of them, eyes strangely white at the corners; of the music which always startled me and constricted my heart and made the tears rise in my eyes.

It was still for me something like a pantomime. I can remember just as vividly Dan Leno and Herbert Campbell playing ping-pong with fry-pans and onions in an enormous brown kitchen. The bigness of that kitchen impressed me so much that I see it even before I see little Leno hopping about below the vast ceiling. So that my memory of Leno's comic antics and Herbert's astounding figure while he stooped towards the table like a short slip is mixed with a feeling of serious interest and even awe such as a child would feel on entering a strangely decorated cathedral. Even my laughter at Leno was mixed with awe, with the sense of living in the presence of greatness, and historical events.

So that when I laughed at Macillhinny, I felt wonder, too; as if I had never noticed that aspect of him before, and I gazed at Prospero, whom I knew very well as the dawdling, good-natured son of a rich Derry merchant, B., with unwinking reverence, even while he was joking with Macillhinny and handing him a tack hammer.

But for Harry, young B. having undertaken Prospero, was bound to keep up the illusion so long as he wore the dress, and when he did not do so, he was a traitor, a heretic. That was Pinto's feeling and I daresay Harry had caught it from him. For Pinto, of course, the rehearsal and production of any serious play was like a religious act, and that was why, I suppose, he had such an extraordinary hold over his amateur performers. People without strong opinions and definite standards are always liable to fall under the sway of one who has both, especially if he sets them above his own advantage. They can't help feeling, even while they laugh at his earnestness, that he has some private source of inspiration which entitles him to a certain respect; that to go against him may be slightly wicked. I don't mean that if Pinto had preached a new religion, or a new social order, he would have had any success in Annish, for on those points, the local squires had strong ideas of their own. But in dramatic art they were still open to a new experience, and new ideas.

CHAPTER 66

The play lasted much longer than anyone expected and afterwards Harry and I, by dodging between the yards and the front drive, managed to miss the carriage which went away without us. This was our plan for we had always meant to go by the last Dunvil car, as near midnight as possible. Yet this plan was carried out as if by automatism, for we were still under the spell of the play. As we wandered about among the Maylins' outlandish conifers, which looked in the moonlight like toy trees out of some gigantic Noah's Ark, Harry was still muttering about the ship and saying: 'It was such dashed back luck on Pinto,' and I was feeling the kind of turmoil which follows upon my great experience and discovery. I don't think I could remember a line of the play, except perhaps –

> Full fathom five thy father lies
> Of his bones are corals made.

and 'Must our mouths be cold', but thousands of musical phrases, of half-understood images, had fallen upon my senses enriching them as if by three or four years of ordinary seasonal falls, flower, harvest, leaf and snow, so that I felt dizzy with the weight of experience. It was the poetry, I thought: 'I didn't know poetry was like that,' and then at once it seemed to me that it was not the poetry, but the people, the brave boatswain, the wise Prospero. 'But it was not the people – it was the way they felt,' and it seemed to me that I felt like them; that this was the way real people felt. Words like beauty, death, love, took living form and sang in my head like angels.

'Hullo, hullo, hullo, what's this – what are you doing here – where's your aunty – where's that old flea-box of hers – missed it – trust you – a proper pair of Corners – now, I suppose you expect me to go a mile out of my way. Have you peed? Well, go and do it. I'm not stopping the car to let you down on the way, and the mare catch cold.' To the Major all children had the same characteristics as the smallest babies.

His car was waiting. Perhaps subconsciously we had put ourselves in his way to catch it, for it was almost the last. In three minutes we were swaying through the lanes, with the boat-like motion of a jaunting car over the waves of a country road. The Major was quacking to his driver, long Ben. 'Did they give you anything to drink – porter – was it any good – how much did you get? Did you meet that fella from Cran that's lost his wife? – they say it's the second one he's poisoned.' Then he would ask us how we would like Pinto for an uncle, a question we were now used to. Everyone asked it, but I doubt if anyone believed that Aunt Hersey would marry Pinto. They expressed in their assurance to us, that she meant to, a spite against her for showing so much liking for the man and such unconventional warmth in his cause.

'Uncle Freeman,' he would cackle – 'very free,' suddenly turning on his elbow to shout at us across the well of the car: 'Wonderful chap for stories, though,' and then to Ben: 'Did Mr Freeman ever pay you that half-crown for the time he spoilt your Sunday coat?'

'No, and he didn't, sir,' in a depressed voice.

The Major quacked a laugh, and said: 'You'd better ask Mrs Candish for it, or Miss Delia – but he's a wonderful fella, Ben – you've held a bit of a genius in your arms. Though it might be the wrong bit.'

Then, after chattering to Ben for ten minutes, asking him all the gossip fresh from the Maylins' kitchen, he would twist himself round again: 'He'll cheer you up down there in the sea fog, but lock up your tantalus.'

We heard him, but we did not listen to him. Harry was reflecting on the play. He muttered to me once: 'That chap

Prospero ought to be kicked,' and again: 'It was just dashed
bad luck about the ship – You'd think somebody wanted to
spoil it.'

I gave him some answer, but I could not take any interest in
the ship. I was enjoying myself too much not only in the ideas
and feelings produced by the play, but in the midnight drive.
Because it had been stolen, I felt that we had ourselves contrived
it and I was making full use of it. I looked with a fond eye at the
round-backed hill fields, so wet with spring dew that they
seemed to be covered with frost, and when we heeled round a
corner, I took to myself, with equal affection, the lough, dented
with millions of little semicircular waves, like the blows of a
silver-smith's hammer. The sky was pale, water grey all round
the horizon, smoke-grey overhead and full of stars as pale and
clear as its own reflection in the dewdrops on the brakes and my
shoe toes and the footboard of the car. The cool breeze off the
sea, the small sound of waves pervading the whole of this vast
grey space, the smell of the new budded hedges which brushed
against my toes, made one feeling with the echoes of the play, in
a sort of calm ecstasy.

'There you are now,' the Major said, as we pulled up at
Dunamara road gates. 'You can walk the rest of it – you won't
be eaten alive between this and the last pos.'

Our last pos was one of the Major's jokes directed against all
children approaching bedtime. 'Time for the last pos,' he would
say. His long woebegone driver Ben swung himself out of his
bucket seat into the cushion, still warm from Harry, to balance
the car, and drove away. Harry and I descended the steep curly
drive in silence. Our separate trains of idea were uninterrupted.
We had not even said goodnight to the Major.

We found the house lighted in every window and a great noise
of talk coming from them. A car and a carriage stood before the
door and there was a Corner party in the hall, two of my aunts
and a distant cousin. They stopped and looked at us, then
started talking again. I saw Harry enter their conversation and I
heard the word Delia repeated, but I had no idea what was
being said until Kathy came to us in the upper passage and told
us that Delia and Pinto had run off together. 'They went by the
Glasgow boat, and Grandy wants Aunty to go with him by
Larne and get there first and stop them – but Aunty says, no, let
them be happy while they can.'

Kathy was wearing an extraordinary kind of bandage round her neck, of linen and red flannel, as big as a horse-collar. I temember this and her hoarse voice far more clearly than the long account she gave me of Delia's sudden departure; Aunt Hersey's astonishment when she came back and Jessy gave her the news and a letter.

'Grandy says that she ought to be stopped for her own good – before she ruins herself, but Aunt Hersey says that no one could stop Delia doing what she really wanted to do and that perhaps Pinto is the very man for her.'

Neither Kathy nor I recognised in this speech the magnanimity of our aunt, who certainly might have thought herself badly treated. But perhaps on account of Pinto's own influence, Aunt Hersey took a most unconventional view of the affair, and because it was wise and simple, it was also dignified. She never once, in my hearing, made any complaint of Pinto or Delia. On the contrary, she would not allow anyone to criticise them and remained their best and warmest friend.

It was said at once, of course, that Delia and Pinto had been planning this elopement for weeks, and that Pinto was in debt all round, both in England and Ireland. But Aunt Hersey always maintained that they had acted upon a sudden impulse, on that very day, and I believe now that she was right. Otherwise I can't imagine why they went off with almost no money, and without steamer tickets, so that Delia's first act, in Glasgow, was to wire to Frances for a loan to take her luggage out of pawn to the company.

CHAPTER 67

Kathy must have had one of her sore throats, which had prevented her from going to the play. Shivering in her flannel nightdress she followed Harry and me into our room, croaking still about the elopement, which seemed to excite her in an extraordinary degree.

'Of course, Pinto is *nice*, but he's so ugly and old. I don't know how Deely could *marry* him. But then Aunty says that he was a genius and Deely thought someone ought to take care of him. Is he a genius, Harry? Robert says he's only a minor poet. What is a minor poet?'

Harry, like me, was still in some private reflection, and answered: 'If Deely catches you out of bed with that throat she'll smack you.'

'But, Har-ree, Deely isn't here.'

'I know, I mean Aunty.'

'Aunty never smacks anybody.'

'Oh, do go away – I want to go to sleep.'

'But don't you understand – it's a terrible thing – everyone is fearfully worried – they think poor Deely has spoilt her whole life. She's got no money and she can't be happy, can she? I wonder why she did it, or didn't she think. She couldn't be in love with him, could she?'

Kathy's excitement did not touch us, but we did not drive her away. For some time now it had been the idea to tolerate Kathy. It seemed to us childish and unworthy of our position as schoolboys, who had gone out into the world, to shout at her, or ostentatiously exclude her from our conferences. Between our fits of affection when one or other of us fell in love with her for a day or two, we allowed her to go with us everywhere and talk at length, and even to sit on our beds. Yet she was further from us than before, because her interests were taking a feminine turn, and just when we were beginning to form crude general ideas, or rather the feelings which are the substance of such ideas, she was absorbed in personal relations. She would talk for an hour about Frances and Mackee, or Jessy and her latest suitor, some farmer from the hills, forty years old, with six cows, and this talk was the more exasperating to us because it was all a kind of question. Kathy seemed to be asking us all the time how Jessy could think of marrying an ugly, twisted man of forty, whom she did not pretend to love and why Mackee loved Frances, although she treated him so badly. All these questions meant, I think: 'How do women really conduct their lives?'

Kathy was growing taller and plainer. Her face and neck had suddenly elongated themselves, like Anketel's, but with a worse effect. Even at eleven, I think she knew this. A girl must be very young or insensitive not to see her own looks in everyone's eyes. Kathy was an anxious little girl who had found life already difficult, and could not understand why it should be harder for herself than the others.

But we took less and less interest in her questioning talk. Especially Harry was withdrawn so much into abstract reflections that he was getting a bad name for absent-mindedness: for losing his things and never being in time for a meal.

Yet at the same time Harry's very abstraction enabled him to bear with Kathy, and even while she sat on his bed, frowning anxiously and asking over and over again, in her frog's voice, how Deely *could* be happy, and what a genius was, he was able to murmur something, now and then, without interrupting his ideas.

'I thought you were fond of Deely and you don't care what happens to her.'

'Of course I care.'

'Neither of you care one little bit – you don't even listen.'

'Deely's all right – she wanted to go, didn't she?'

'I don't believe you care for anybody.'

'Umm.'

After a pause, Kathy said: 'May I get into your bed, Harry? – I'm freezing. I won't breathe any of my bugs on you.'

'All right.'

'You don't really want me, do you?'

'Do you want to get in or don't you? Do get it straight.'

'But what do *you* want?'

'Oh, lord, I want you to please yourself.'

'But it doesn't please myself if you don't like it,' Kathy croaked, in a tearful voice, which was interrupted by a tremendous sneeze.

'Oh, lord, if only you wouldn't argue I'd be delighted. That's all I want for you to do what you dashed well like.'

Kathy sighed, got slowly into bed and said at last in a timid voice: 'It really is nicer, isn't it? Warmer for you, too.'

'Yes, all right. Much nicer. Don't go to sleep or Deely'll catch you.'

'But, Harry —'

'I know, all right, go to sleep.'

There was a pause, and then Kathy sighed and murmured: 'Of course, he'll be happy with Deely because she'll look after him – she's quite a good housekeeper. So they'd both be happy, wouldn't they?'

Harry made no answer. In silence we both pursued our own notions, not about people, but something that seemed larger and greater, the motives and ideas, which, as we had felt in the play, moved them and drove them.

CHAPTER 68

Not only words for feelings, like beauty, love, hate, had taken life and meaning for me; but also concrete substances like mountain, sea, thunder, star, boat, began to have new significances. Of his bones are coral made; it was a chord of strings, a sextet, each singing quietly in the ear of my soul; not only with music but souls of their own. A tune of lonely spirits, the sober and upright bone with his bass voice and rather austere character at one end, and the glimmering sea treasure, living jewel, rolling its merman's song at the other, in perpetual little curling waves of sound, which fell for ever on the bright sea floor, made of itself the voice of creation.

As a small child, like other small children, I had thought of my toys as living creatures, and shown warm sympathy with various rag dolls and several wooden horses. Anketel used to knock one of his treasures on the ground, and then look at it as if to say: 'How do you like that?'

He especially would examine small objects, even stones or shells, with intense, absorbed curiosity. But this interest in me was chiefly wonder at outside forms, pattern or colour, and my sympathy with dolls and wooden horses was an extension of my own self. I assumed that everything was me in some form or other. But now I was wondering at difference and the mysterious character of things. When I looked at the cliffs and clouds, plenty of which I was bringing into my new epics, I was trying to realise their private selves: as a savage touches some strange object, seeking to know, through his fingers, its unique and separate quality. So an African chief, a great religious head in his own country, asked to handle my signet ring, because he had never seen gold, and dandling it in his palm, he looked not at the ring, but into the air, with half-closed eyes, like one waiting for an illumination from heaven. When nothing reached him, he murmured softly like one muttering a prayer: 'Da nauyi,' meaning, heavy. The prayer was not successful. He handed back the ring with a puzzled and doubtful glance, saying only: 'Abin mamaki,' a thing of wonder, that is to say, another prayer for enlightenment, but so common in Africa, that it has ceased to have any force. It is used every day by thousands, in face of motors, planes, condenser engines, railway tickets, stainless knives: but it invokes no enlightenment. It expresses only the sense of man's apartness from things, which is also the acknowledgment of his community with everything.

CHAPTER 69

On the next day while Aunt Hersey was meeting the barbed condolences of all the most malicious gossips in the county, from her brother James upwards, not merely with dignity, but with frankness and good humour, Harry and I and Anketel pursued our independent life in our underworld. Anketel disappeared early to meet Oweny with whom he had an engagement to sell a sackful of chickens in Dunvil market. Harry began to construct a model theatre, on a plan of his own, of which the foundation was an old lobster pot, and I slipped away to the attic to write epics.

I don't think we were heartless, and we were not completely cut off from the world's affairs. We had been very fond of Delia, and always were fond of her. But we were full of new discoveries. We looked forward. Yesterday seemed a long way off, and Delia herself a figure of the past. Harry, in the morning, broke several times into the drawing-room to ask Aunt Hersey for copper wire, and to complain that there was no keyhole saw in the house: I broke into her bedroom, after luncheon, and insisted on reading her the first part of a long poem about a magician who was wrecked on an island where he tamed a wild man to do his will. His name, I think, was Osferro, and he had a familiar spirit called Lario.

Aunt Hersey, lying in the darkened room, was supposed to have a headache. I imagine that she was suffering the extremest misery, after Delia's loss, and after half a dozen family visits during the morning, and was collecting her courage for a great many more in the afternoon. There was no telephone then. The first thing one heard of a visitor was the grind of car or carriage wheels on the loose sea gravel of the drive.

But she did not turn me out of the room, listened to my very bad verses for at least half an hour, and then kissed me, and congratulated me so warmly and affectionately, that I promised to write her another poem, longer and still more exciting, before tea-time.

These poems were full of phrases like the lonely mountain, the babbling stream, the azure sky, the threatening cloud, the frowning cliff, the soaring eagle which now sprang up in my mind with such depth of meaning, such intense force, that I could hardly bear to wait before I wrote them into a poem.

I felt their deep meaning with such new excitement that they seemed to me new discoveries: so highly original that they must astonish all my readers.

Luckily for my poor aunt, in the middle of that afternoon and before I had finished my next instalment for her, my father arrived.

CHAPTER 70

We believed, of course, that he had come only to see us. In fact, as I realise now, he had come to defend and support Aunt Hersey. In all family crisis he was the man whom everyone called in. Although he had so little time, they demanded days from him, and although he was a poor man, they knew always that they could borrow his money.

He came now to ascertain and pay Pinto's debts, to obtain legal proof of the couple's marriage, and to make a settlement by which Delia's money, hers absolutely on her twenty-first birthday, could be tied up in trust for her, in exchange for the immediate payment of the debts. All this was duly arranged in the next four weeks, and I believe my father afterwards went to Paris, where the couple was living, and reported that both were very happy: that Pinto had met an American lady who might produce a play for him: and that Delia had become a regular French housekeeper, visiting the markets every morning at the earliest hour.

'Delia will make a success of him,' he told everybody. 'That was all he wanted – a first-class wife with her backbone well to the front. Indeed, you could always see Delia's in her eye.' My father loved to use such bulls especially in the presence of someone who took them seriously and looked at him as if to say: 'How very typical.'

My father stayed a week at Dunamara, routing the gossips, stirring up the lawyers. He must have been very busy, but to my memory it seems that this one of his visits, like all the others, was solely for Harry's and my benefit, and that it was spent entirely with us, and in the open air, wet or fine. For my father's visits were less to a house than the neighbouring fields, hills, streams and oceans. He could not be said to stay anywhere. Even to breakfast he did not arrive like other people from bed, but from the Atlantic, fresh from killing a six-foot conger eel with a tiller: or from the wood, where he had discovered some rare, beautiful bird, to be protected. Like other impassioned sportsmen, he loved animals of all kinds, even while he hunted them, and indeed when little past fifty, while most of his contemporaries, becoming rheumatic or lazy, began to take to the more killing sports, and would not go out except to shoot driven birds from a comfortable butt, he gave up shooting and even fishing. The trout in his garden stream became pets, and he would creep across the lawn to admire a water-rat, and to feel with it like a neighbour while it combed out its whiskers in the doorway of its hole.

So now at Dunamara he helped old Roe to put a kind of wire collar round a tree to protect some woodpecker from the cats: and strictly forbade us to tell anyone that there was a badger earth under the high bank behind the kitchen. But at the same time, since he was with Harry and me, he began to teach us a dozen arts, knotting, net-making, rifle shooting, stalking and, above all, diving.

Every morning, and often in the evening as well, he would teach us to dive from Dunvil pier. I think he had suddenly taken a fancy to perfect his diving, but we did not know that. We knew only the zest of his company and example.

It was a fine spring, but the mornings were chilly and the water cold. To undress behind a wall of soaking fish boxes and pick one's way down the wet planks, with the salt breeze cutting through one's skin, was, for both of us children, a misery which we dreaded. But because it was misery, we began every pier bathe, especially on the colder mornings, with a triumph, in which everything acquired an heroic glory. On three sides of us stretched away the dazzling level of the water, until it was cut off by the low, flat cloud of the sea mist resting upon it. Above this cloud, miles away, the mountains of Derry on the east and of Annish on the west seemed to float in the pale blue air, as clear as pure light, in which, as if by a lens, they seemed brought so near that we could distinguish houses, trees and streams. At the same time, and while they stood thus detached upon a mist so flimsy in its beginning that it could not be detected, they never appeared more huge and weighty, or brighter with their own private colours, greens like weed in water, browns as bright as a child's eye. All about us was like a new world born that minute: its wind was the breath of a world's morning, tingling on our skins and filling our lungs with its cool excitement.

Then to descend below, on the rock steps, slippery with sea moss, into a freezing shadow, blue as salt-water ice, screwing ourselves up for our diving lesson, was another effort of will, from which we looked up at tension, to see my father, with his compact powerful figure, climb the highest box pile, to dive twenty or twenty-five feet into the harbour, at such an angle that there was barely a sound, and only one small plop of water, a little spurting mound like that after a big raindrop. It made me cry out with delight. What a triumph, what a combination of skill, courage, neatness and deliberate mastery. It seemed to me that there was no grander deed than to dive like that.

I don't mean that this is the way I thought about diving, at ten: but this is what I felt, for I can remember how lifeless, how flat, my writing seemed, or the very idea of poetry, beside the vision of my father, one moment floating through the sky, and the next darting under the green water far below.

I didn't want to write any more epics, and Harry, in spite of his obstinacy in finishing a task, would have abandoned his theatre, if my father had not helped him with it. I would see Harry, roving with his usual quick, rather swaying walk in the upper passage, his head up and his eyes down, stop suddenly at the head of the stairs, and instead of jumping as usual the five steps to the first landing, put out his hands, as we had been taught, and fix his eyes on the air at their own level. Only then would he jump. Neither of us was much good at diving. We tumbled into the water at all angles. Therefore we practised all day, from beds, piano stools, the sofa, to feel again what it was like, to keep our feet together, and to invoke the diving god, for I suppose there is a god, or part of a god, who loves diving.

My epic, as I saw it last, in an old exercise book, when I cleared the attic, stopped in the middle of a line and had drawn over it, in blue chalk pencil, little crude sketches of diving men. Yet the quality of our living experience could be translated only into the experience of poetry which people would not read. They prefer, I suppose, to live it, if they live, in any true sense of the word, real lives: and that is even easier today than it was when we were children.

SUGGESTIONS FOR FURTHER READING

Adam International Review, nos. 212–13: Joyce Cary special issue 1950. Includes 'The Novelist at work: a conversation between Joyce Cary and Lord David Cecil', on Cary's technique.

Allen, Walter, *Joyce Cary* (London: Longmans, 1953). Writers and Their Work, no. 41. Highly useful short early account and criticism.

Adams, Hazard, *Joyce Cary's trilogies: pursuit of the particular real* (Tallahassee: University Presses of Florida, 1983).

Bishop, Alan, *Gentleman rider: a life of Joyce Cary* (London: Michael Joseph, 1988). With bibliography and notes containing references to reviews, newspaper articles, interviews and broadcasts.

Bloom, Robert, *The indeterminate world: a study of the novels of Joyce Cary* (Philadelphia: University of Pennsylvania Press, 1962).

Christian, Edward, *Joyce Cary's creative imagination* (New York: Peter Lang, 1988).

Cook, Cornelia, *Joyce Cary: liberal principles* (London: Vision Press, 1981).

Echeruo, Michael, *Joyce Cary and the novel of Africa* (London: Longman, 1973).

Echeruo, Michael, *Joyce Cary and the dimensions of order* (London: Macmillan, 1979).

Fisher, Barbara, *The House as a symbol: Joyce Cary and 'The Turkish House'* (Amsterdam: Rodopi, 1986).

Fisher, Barbara, *Joyce Cary: the writer and his theme* (Gerrards Cross: Colin Smythe, 1980).

Fisher, Barbara (ed.), *Joyce Cary remembered: in letters and interviews by his family and others* (Gerrards Cross: Colin Smythe, 1988).

Foster, Malcolm, *Joyce Cary: a biography* (London: Michael Joseph, 1969).

Gardner, Helen, 'The Novels of Joyce Cary'. *Essays and Studies'*, new series, vol. XXVIII, pp. 76–93. (London: John Murray, 1975).

Hoffmann, Charles G., *Joyce Cary: the comedy of freedom* (Pittsburgh University Press, 1964).

Hall, Dennis, *Joyce Cary: a reappraisal* (London: Macmillan, 1983).

Mahood, M. M., *Joyce Cary's Africa* (London: Methuen, 1964).

Modern Fiction Studies. Joyce Cary Special Issue, Autumn, 1963.

Raskin, Jonah, *The Mythology of imperialism: Rudyard Kipling, Joseph Conrad, E. M. Forster, D. H. Lawrence and Joyce Cary* (New York: Dell, 1971).

Starkie, Enid, 'Joyce Cary, a portrait' (Tredegar Memorial Lecture, Royal Society of Literature). *Essays by Divers Hands*, new series, vol. XXXII, pp. 125–44 (Oxford University Press, 1963).

Wright, Andrew, *Joyce Cary: a preface to his novels* (London: Chatto and Windus, 1958).

CLASSIC NOVELS
IN EVERYMAN

A SELECTION

The Way of All Flesh
SAMUEL BUTLER
A savagely funny odyssey from joyless duty to unbridled liberalism £4.99

Born in Exile
GEORGE GISSING
A rationalist's progress towards love and compromise in class-ridden Victorian England £4.99

David Copperfield
CHARLES DICKENS
One of Dickens's best-loved novels, brimming with humour £3.99

The Last Chronicle of Barset
ANTHONY TROLLOPE
Trollope's magnificent conclusion to his Barsetshire novels £4.99

He Knew He Was Right
ANTHONY TROLLOPE
Sexual jealousy, money and women's rights within marriage – a novel ahead of its time £6.99

Tess of the D'Urbervilles
THOMAS HARDY
The powerful, poetic classic of wronged innocence £3.99

Tom Jones
HENRY FIELDING
The wayward adventures of one of literatures most likeable heroes £5.99

Wuthering Heights and Poems
EMILY BRONTË
A powerful work of genius – one of the great masterpieces of literature £3.50

The Master of Ballantrae and Weir of Hermiston
R. L. STEVENSON
Together in one volume, two great novels of high adventure and family conflict £4.99

£5.99

CLASSIC FICTION
IN EVERYMAN

A SELECTION

Frankenstein
MARY SHELLEY
A masterpiece of Gothic terror in its
original 1818 version **£3.99**

Dracula
BRAM STOKER
One of the best known horror stories
in the world **£3.99**

The Diary of A Nobody
GEORGE AND WEEDON
GROSSMITH
A hilarious account of suburban life
in Edwardian London **£4.99**

Some Experiences
and Further Experiences
of an Irish R. M.
SOMERVILLE AND ROSS
Gems of comic exuberance and
improvisation **£4.50**

Three Men in a Boat
JEROME K. JEROME
English humour at its best **£2.99**

Twenty Thousand Leagues
under the Sea
JULES VERNE
Scientific fact combines with
fantasy in this prophetic tale of
underwater adventure **£4.99**

The Best of Father Brown
G. K. CHESTERTON
An irresistible selection of crime
stories – unique to Everyman **£4.99**

The Collected Raffles
E. W. HORNUNG
Dashing exploits from the most glam-
orous figure in crime fiction **£4.99**

£5.99

AVAILABILITY
All books are available from your local bookshop or direct from
**Littlehampton Book Services Cash Sales, 14 Eldon Way, Lineside Estate,
Littlehampton, West Sussex BN17 7HE.** PRICES ARE SUBJECT TO CHANGE.

To order any of the books, please enclose a cheque (in £ sterling) made payable to
Littlehampton Book Services, or phone your order through with credit card details (Access,
Visa or Mastercard) on 0903 721596 (24 hour answering service) stating card number and
expiry date. Please add £1.25 for package and postage to the total value of your order.

In the USA, for further information and a complete catalogue call 1-800-526-2778.

SHORT STORY COLLECTIONS
IN EVERYMAN

A SELECTION

The Secret Self 1:
Short Stories by Women
'A superb collection' *Guardian* **£4.99**

Selected Short Stories
and Poems
THOMAS HARDY
The best of Hardy's Wessex in a
unique selection **£4.99**

The Best of
Sherlock Holmes
ARTHUR CONAN DOYLE
All the favourite adventures in one
volume **£4.99**

Great Tales of Detection
Nineteen Stories
Chosen by Dorothy L. Sayers **£3.99**

Short Stories
KATHERINE MANSFIELD
A selection displaying the remarkable range of Mansfield's writing
£3.99

Selected Stories
RUDYARD KIPLING
Includes stories chosen to reveal the
'other' Kipling **£4.50**

The Strange Case of
Dr Jekyll and Mr Hyde
and Other Stories
R. L. STEVENSON
An exciting selection of gripping
tales from a master of suspense **£3.99**

The Day of Silence and
Other Stories
GEORGE GISSING
Gissing's finest stories, available for
the first time in one volume **£4.99**

Selected Tales
HENRY JAMES
Stories portraying the tensions
between private life and the outside
world **£5.99**

EVERYMAN

THE SECRET SELF
Short Stories by Women

Edited by
HERMIONE LEE

£4.99

AMERICAN LITERATURE
IN EVERYMAN

A SELECTION

Selected Poems
HENRY LONGFELLOW
A new selection spanning the whole
of Longfellow's literary career **£7.99**

Typee
HERMAN MELVILLE
Melville's stirring debut, drawing
directly on his own adventures in the
South Seas **£4.99**

Billy Budd
and Other Stories
HERMAN MELVILLE
The compelling parable of innocence destroyed by a fallen world
£4.99

The Last of the Mohicans
JAMES FENIMORE COOPER
The classic tale of old America, full
of romantic adventure **£5.99**

The Scarlet Letter
NATHANIEL HAWTHORNE
The compelling tale of an
independent woman's struggle
against a crushing moral code **£3.99**

The Red Badge of Courage
STEPHEN CRANE
A vivid portrayal of a young
soldier's experience of the
American Civil War **£2.99**

Essays and Poems
RALPH WALDO EMERSON
An indispensable edition celebrating
one of the most influential
American writers **£5.99**

The Federalist
HAMILTON, MADISON AND JAY
Classics of political science, these
essays helped to found the
American Constitution **£6.99**

Leaves of Grass and
Selected Prose
WALT WHITMAN
The best of Whitman in one volume
£6.99

£5.99

AVAILABILITY
All books are available from your local bookshop or direct from
**Littlehampton Book Services Cash Sales, 14 Eldon Way, Lineside Estate,
Littlehampton, West Sussex BN17 7HE.** PRICES ARE SUBJECT TO CHANGE.

To order any of the books, please enclose a cheque (in £ sterling) made payable to
Littlehampton Book Services, or phone your order through with credit card details (Access,
Visa or Mastercard) on 0903 721596 (24 hour answering service) stating card number and
expiry date. Please add £1.25 for package and postage to the total value of your order.

In the USA, for further information and a complete catalogue call 1-800-526-2778.

POETRY
IN EVERYMAN

A SELECTION

Silver Poets of the Sixteenth Century

EDITED BY

DOUGLAS BROOKS-DAVIES
A new edition of this famous
Everyman collection **£6.99**

Complete Poems

JOHN DONNE
The father of metaphysical verse in
this highly-acclaimed edition **£6.99**

Complete English Poems, Of Education, Areopagitica

JOHN MILTON
An excellent introduction to
Milton's poetry and prose **£6.99**

Selected Poems

JOHN DRYDEN
A poet's portrait of Restoration
England **£4.99**

Selected Poems and Prose

PERCY BYSSHE SHELLEY
'The essential Shelley' in one
volume **£3.50**

Women Romantic Poets 1780-1830: An Anthology

Hidden talent from the Romantic era
rediscovered **£5.99**

Poems in Scots and English

ROBERT BURNS
The best of Scotland's greatest lyric
poet **£4.99**

Selected Poems

D. H. LAWRENCE
A new, authoritative selection
spanning the whole of Lawrence's
literary career **£4.99**

The Poems

W. B. YEATS
Ireland's greatest lyric poet
surveyed in this ground-breaking
edition **£7.99**

£5.99

DYLAN THOMAS
IN EVERYMAN

The only paperback editions of Dylan Thomas's poetry and prose

Collected Poems 1934-1953
Definitive edition of Thomas's own selection of his work **£3.99**

Collected Stories
First and only collected edition of Dylan Thomas's stories **£4.99**

The Colour of Saying
Anthology of verse spoken by Thomas, reflecting his taste in poetry **£3.95**

A Dylan Thomas Treasury
Appealing anthology of poems, stories and broadcasts **£4.99**

The Loud Hill of Wales
Selection of poems and prose full of Thomas's love of Wales **£3.99**

The Notebook Poems 1930-1934
Definitive edition of Thomas's 'preparatory poems' **£4.99**

Poems
Collection of nearly 200 poems by Dylan Thomas **£3.50**

Portrait of the Artist as a Young Dog
Dylan Thomas's classic evocation of his youth in suburban Swansea **£2.99**

Selected Poems
Representative new selection of Thomas's work **£2.99**

Under Milk Wood
One of the most enchanting works for broadcasting ever written **£2.99**

£3.99

AVAILABILITY
All books are available from your local bookshop or direct from
Littlehampton Book Services Cash Sales, 14 Eldon Way, Lineside Estate, Littlehampton, West Sussex BN17 7HE. PRICES ARE SUBJECT TO CHANGE.

To order any of the books, please enclose a cheque (in £ sterling) made payable to Littlehampton Book Services, or phone your order through with credit card details (Access, Visa or Mastercard) on 0903 721596 (24 hour answering service) stating card number and expiry date. Please add £1.25 for package and postage to the total value of your order.